FIRST

A J Morris

Authorbynature

*To F1 Drivers everywhere, both past and present
for risking your lives in the name of sport.*

FOREWORD

I first fell in love with Formula One many years ago when James Hunt was the pin up boy of every British teenager. The glamour, the speed, the danger drew me like a magnet. Nothing much has changed for me since then. The drivers may be different, the cars certainly are- but the sport still has me gripped to the television screen like glue every race weekend. The sport is more accessible now than it was then and the excellent modern televison coverage opens doors to behind the scenes activities that were previously for the eyes of a chosen few only.

The drivers have become the rock stars of sport and the fanbase that follows them is huge. For an old time petrol head fan like me it's somewhat amusing to discover that there are fans following the sport who have no interest in the car itself, or even the racing, but are there because of the look of a particular driver. But it makes the tapestry around the sport more colourful and secures its future; any sport even one as global and huge as F1 needs fans to make it viable.

First is set at the end of the V10 era when refuelling was part of the pitstop, and the qualifying format was different to that which we see now. It was an era of screaming engines; a sound that is missed on the track by many, including myself.

It is my second book set in a sporting background and I hope that those who read it will enjoy it as much as I have done writing it.

They always say, "write about something you love".

So I did.

A.J.Morris

"If you no longer go for a gap that exists, you are no

longer a racing driver."

Ayrton Senna

21/3/1960-01/05/1994

FIA World Champion
1998,1990,1991.

senna sempre

CHAPTER 1.

January was cold. The kind of deep-rooted cold that seeps into the bones and leaves layers of crisp white frost on every surface. The group of men huddled together in the garage all wore thick fleece jackets and gloves and shivered beneath their layers of clothing. The frosty Berkshire air whipped in through the open doors courtesy of a strong wind, adding to the already bitterly low temperatures in the building. In the middle of the group, one man only appeared unaffected by the conditions; partly because he was sheltered by the circle of bodies around him, more so because of the adrenalin that was coursing through his veins, making his heart pump faster by the second and helping to raise his body temperature. A grin spreading across his face he lowered himself into the cockpit. This was the moment that Declan Hyde had been waiting for, the moment he could take the new season's Matros Grand Prix car onto the track. Okay, the conditions were far from ideal, and given a choice he would have preferred to have been farther south in the sunshine of Barcelona; but even in the bleakness of a British January the moment was still exciting, an occasion a long time in the making, and as he lowered himself into the seat, he felt the usual tingle of anticipation racing up his spine.

The car's engine, which until now had been quietly grumbling like a vociferous old she-cat, burst into sudden life at his touch and quickly became a lion. All around it, men reached for their ear protectors, wincing and grimacing against the staccato yelp of the engine. Booming its way around the garage the sound reverberated off walls and had tools and coffee cups rattling on tables. Reluctantly lifting his right foot from the throttle Declan allowed the lion to go back to sleep and let the placid old she-cat back into its place. He looked up and nodded, indigo eyes glittering with excitement. The time had come to unleash the new beast and see exactly what she was made of.

Behind him, separated from the rest of the garage by a pane of glass, Gerald Matthews watched intently, a slight tremor in his cheek the only sign of his nerves. This was the result of years of hard work, and a great deal of his money, and this was what he truly believed was the best Matros to have been sent into battle. At the very start of his career, he had been a rear-of-the-grid dreamer, throwing away his hard-earned cash, and then a chance meeting had led him to Carlo Rossi. Rossi was a true Italian *Tifosi* with cars and racing in his blood; Gerald sometimes wondered if Carlo had any actual blood in his veins and wasn't fuelled by petrol itself. Eager to put his experience to use Carlo had thrown himself into his new team with vigour and his experienced touch following a spell with the mighty Ferrari, quickly paid off. He made Gerald understand that these were not just cars, they were land-bound jet fighters and the aerodynamics, the ability to hold the road at a high-speed corner, were just as important as the power of the engine itself. Between them, they had designed, scrapped, and redesigned until their car began to creep its way up the grid and make its mark. The result was the streamlined and perfectly tuned machine in front of them today. Gerald could see Carlo firing up the computer, his deep-set eyes taking in all the car's telemetry as it stood idly in the garage. All the details that affected the car's performance, its fuel consumption, the thousands of parts, and even the heat of its tyres would be relayed back to the computer and give Carlo and his team the information they needed to call the right shots in a race. Today it would simply tell him if the car worked. A frown of concentration deepening his brow he looked at Gerald and nodded.

"Let's go" He smiled, wiping his hands on the battered team coat that had seen better days and pulling the baseball cap that covered his balding head tight over his eyes.

"We are ready to test, yes?"

"Yes" Gerald's voice was weak for such a tall

man. "But, carefully, Carlo. Tell that lunatic to go easy on her."

"He is your lunatic," Carlo reminded him sagely, "Not mine."

Declan ran his hands through his sweaty hair and pushed his feet back into his trainers. His fire suit was discarded on the floor beside the bench in the driver's room. He had no time to pick up after himself. He wanted to find Gerald, quickly, and have his opinion of the car's performance. Declan was on a high; nothing gave him the same rush of euphoria as driving a Formula One car; not even sex, which he freely admitted ranked as his second favourite pastime. Eyes vivid with excitement he set off in search of his employer. Declan was Irish, or at least half of him was, and it was on this side of his pedigree that he laid all the blame for his fiery nature and affection for rather too much alcohol. These were also the genes responsible for his ability to charm the birds from the proverbial trees when he chose and to have women falling at his feet wherever he went. He blamed the English half of him for his conservative views and love of all things expensive

"So" Carlo was waiting for him outside Gerald's office. "So, does she dance as well as she sings?"

"Better" Declan beamed at him. "Few tweaks here and there but nothing too major; it's a good start."

"Friday." Carlo reminded him "Two o'clock don't be late."

"Am I ever?" Declan shook his head bemused.

"Frequently" Carlo shouted after him.

But, he thought quietly to himself as he watched Declan striding away, he can be as late as he cares to be on Friday as long as he's in pole position when we get to Australia.

Outside the fume-filled, noisy warmth of the garage the January air bit at Declan's lungs and made him cough. The afternoon was fading fast, and the air held the threat of yet another heavy frost. Hugging the battered, fur-lined, leather flying jacket tighter to his body he broke into a jog, his trainers crunching on the gravel. Once, he thought to himself, this first run of tests is over, I'm buggering off to a warmer climate. His car was parked a little way apart from the others and the sight of its shark-like appearance made him smile. The little BMW Z4 was his UK run around. He loved the way it looked and the fact that it fitted neatly through the narrow lanes leading to the North Devon fishing village that was his home for the few months he spent in this country. The village was small, dimly lit, and constantly ravaged by the wind and rain that came from the sea. It appealed to the Celt hidden deep in Declan's nature, as did the rambling County Cork farmhouse currently inhabited by his sister and her brood. The public Declan, the one that made the pages of glossy Sunday supplements and drew attention from media and fans alike, lived in a lavish Monte Carlo apartment. His own little piece of overpriced real estate in a unique town where he could find the company of other drivers, glamorous women, and filthy rich businessmen on his doorstep.

At twenty-nine Declan had the Formula One world at his feet: almost. His nine Grand Prix wins gave him senior status among the drivers and the team a position of standing in that most predatory of places, the F1 paddock. But the thing that evaded him, the thing that was beginning to eat at his soul and his sanity, was the one thing in life he really wanted- the World Championship. He wanted nothing more than to put the number one flag on Gerald's car and reward him for all his faith and efforts, and to prove to himself and all his doubters, of which he knew there were many, that he was the best. He loved the nomadic, glitzy lifestyle, the thrills, the challenges, and the fact that he stared death in the face every time he got it wrong at one hundred and eighty miles an hour. Never having been one to sit back and observe, he loved being part of the action, and was driven by the need to win; a mindset that often got him into hot water, occasionally with FIA officials, but more frequently with Gerald and Carlo. Each time Declan would shrug his broad shoulders and move on.

The team couldn't function without him.

Could it?

Turning off the M5 into the North Devonshire lanes he felt the now familiar uneasy sensation in his stomach returning. This sensation, formerly totally alien to him, had been beginning to make an appearance every time he thought about this season's new teammate. He hadn't met him yet; he was some find of Carlo's and that was what worried Declan the most. If Carlo had a new protégé on the books, Declan's position as team number one was going to be challenged, and no way was he letting that position go without a fight. Wincing as he ground the gears, his concentration wandering, he shook himself. There was enough time to worry about that when it happened. For now, there was just him and the stunning-looking midnight blue car that would soon be emblazoned with the team logo and the colourful blurbs of the team sponsors.

It was, after all *his* team, *his* car and *he* was prepared to risk everything to keep it that way.

One hour later he made his final descent into the sleepy village of Mullacombe. No one took a second glance as he drove through the high street. They were used to him here and let him get on his way, which was why he loved it. Occasionally he would catch admiring glances from the village teenagers but that was as far as it went. He spent most of his nights in the local pub, and his mornings on the quayside watching the catch with the local fishermen. Here he was just one of the locals. Parking the car in his rented garage at the end of the quay he locked it up securely and made his way back along the cobbles to the little fisherman's cottage at the very end of the street. He glanced at his watch. He smiled. Just enough time for a shower and a lazy hour on the PlayStation before dinner.

As he walked through his front door, he noticed a strange girl looking at the fishing boats. The village was so small he knew everyone; or thought he did. There were no tourists here at this time of year. He hesitated, key in hand and watched with narrowed eyes. The girl glanced over at him, colour creeping up into her cheeks and turned her attention quickly back to boats. Declan frowned. Press? Surely not. Slipping quickly inside the cottage he locked the door and despite the gloom made his way upstairs without putting the lights on. It was probably best to keep a low profile for a few hours. Twitching his bedroom curtain, he glanced out and felt himself relax. The girl had already gone.

CHAPTER 2.

Gerald Matthews watched his pretty, intellectual, and spirited daughter pouring his tea and gave her a warm smile. His journey home was mercifully quick, and he was now in the warmth of the grand new building with landscaped gardens and an ornamental lake that sat on the very edge of the thousand acres of Berkshire countryside that housed the Matros compound. A large conservatory overlooked the lake, and at this time of year, the semi-tropical heat he was surrounded by came from the large radiators hidden against the wall. A wave of tiredness washed over him.

"Kate do sit down," he said quietly. "You are making me weary."

"Not hard" Kate's wayward hair was falling into her eyes, and she pulled it back irritably. "You need to see a doctor; you look bloody awful."

"Thank you, Kate," Gerald smiled at her "Any more compliments you would like to hand out while you are at it?"

Kate blushed and then scowled.

"Don't do that" Gerald scolded. "It doesn't suit you. After we've finished testing, I'll take you on that holiday I promised you, okay? We'll charter a yacht somewhere".

"No." Kate's scowl deepened. "Because as soon as we return, you'll be straight back in that bloody factory."

"Don't you want to win? Come on Kate sit down and stop pacing."

"Yes, I do." Kate sat, perched on the edge of the cane sofa, and picked at the cushion. "But not if you're going to wear yourself out. You do too much. You pay too much for everyone else to be there twenty-four-seven and then still live in the place yourself. And as for Declan," her brow furrowed "I don't know why the hell you put up with him. I've never met such an arrogant pig of a man and believe me since we've been in this game, I've met a few!"

"He's brilliant" Gerald's voice was irritated. "The best there is. I admit he has his flaws but that's the man; if you tried to change what he is you would ruin him. He wouldn't have the same hunger, the same fire in his belly, and that is what makes him brilliant. You know that, Kate."

"Then why aren't we world champions yet?" Kate raised an eyebrow at him.

"Not his fault" Gerald shook his head. "The car wasn't good enough. But now, I think we are getting there, I really do. We'll win it this year; you mark my words."

"Well, I'll believe it when I see it "

Kate got to her feet and started pacing again, the thought of Declan always rattled her.

"Let's hope he doesn't bankrupt us first. The damage he did last year was incredible; those cars cost more than this house and everything in it and he treats them like scrap."

Gerald shrugged and drank his tea. This was such an old argument, his fiery daughter versus his flamboyant driver. Gerald had earned his money the hard way, the Bournemouth boarding house he had inherited had become three boarding houses, then a holiday park and now the holiday parks had been replaced by investments in top-class worldwide hotels. That gave him the right, he thought, to spend the money how he saw fit. In modern terms, Declan's retainer was a poor one. Formula One was a big-money sport and he was only a small fish determined to make one almighty splash in the big pond. Without Declan on board, he would not even make a ripple. He needed not only his skill, but the attention Declan's presence brought the team and the fact that his famous histrionics kept everyone, himself included, on their toes. But Kate was so like her mother. Stubborn; opinionated, and irascible, she was charming and compliant one minute an absolute nightmare the next. Living with her was like being permanently in the shadow of a ticking bomb. That he always felt was the reason she could see no good in Declan. They were simply too much alike.

It had been the endless mood swings and the

hours of arguments that had seen the end of his marriage to Janice. Why Kate had chosen to live here rather than in the lavish Majorcan apartment with her mother he had never fathomed. But then, the house that was his alimony payment to his wife would never last if it housed two of them for more than a few weeks at a time. Having Kate living here was like coping with a miniature Janice and at times it drove him to his wits end. But in one thing Kate differed; she genuinely loved her father and many of her moods were borne from her concern for him. She was right, he did feel ill; far more so than he cared to admit. He would be sixty-five at the end of this year and he was far from ready for retirement, but his body wasn't coping with the pace of his lifestyle as well as it did. That was why he hadn't consulted a doctor; he dreaded the thought of being forced into a premature life of inactivity. Shaking his head, he finished his tea and got to his feet. Retirement and doctors could wait. He had a World Championship to win first; and in a short while the next piece in the jigsaw of his ambition would be arriving. He had to get ready.

CHAPTER 3.

The young man who stood shivering at the front door of Rossi's smart, detached and very large home was not what Francine Rossi had expected. Her first thought was how good-looking he was, the second that one Declan Hyde was going to have to pull his socks up if he wanted to retain his grip on the limelight and the adoration of the fans. This young man was the embodiment of the legendary Latin lover. Tall, lean, olive-skinned with silky black hair that fell boyishly over one eye, he had a long body, incredibly slim hips and an aristocratic head that was pure Roman. He was holding out his hand, which was trembling slightly.

"Fabio." His voice was deep and soft. "Fabio Fratinelli."

"Francine" Francine was beginning to wish she had made more of an effort with her appearance. "Carlo Rossi's wife. Welcome. Please come in out of the cold."

Fabio gratefully stepped into the warm, lavishly carpeted hall and forgetting his manners gazed around him. So, this was what a life in Formula One bought you. Genuine oils on the walls, antique furniture, a carpet so deep he could feel his leather shoes sinking into it. He wanted this. Now he was being given the chance to get it. A small chubby man was hurrying down the hall towards him, his face wreathed in smiles.

"Fabio Fabio Fabio!" Carlo had to reach up to kiss the younger man's cheeks. "Welcome, welcome. You met my wife, I see, and this is our old friend Nadia."

Fabio raised his eyes and had to stop his jaw from dropping. The woman gliding out of the door opposite him was straight out of the pages of Vogue. High heels, a tightly fitting blue dress that showed every inch of all her curves, a tiny waist, and diamonds at her throat. He could not have even guessed at her age. Somewhere between thirty and fifty, who could tell? Her perfectly made-up, almond-shaped hazel eyes were widening as she took his hand.

"Nadia." Francine's voice had a warning note in it, making Nadia purse her glossy pink lips. "This is Fabio Fratinelli. Fabio is the rising star of the Formula One world."

"No no." Fabio shook his head vigorously "Please, not to call me that, please."

"Modest as well," Carlo chuckled. He had never encountered Nadia speechless in ten years of knowing her, but she appeared to be completely lost for words.

"Well, that is a rare quality in a racing driver I must say." Nadia seemed unable to tear her eyes away from Fabio's face. "Have you met our Declan yet Fabio?"

"Declan Hyde?" A wary look spread slowly across Fabio's face. "Will he be here?"

"He should be." Francine glanced at her watch. "Carlo, look after Fabio and I'll see if I can find out where he is. Gerald and Kate are on their way."

"No need" Nadia had already taken Fabio's arm. "I shall look after Fabio. Come on Fabio let us get you a drink."

"Play nice Nadia." Francine laughed.

Nadia smiled politely and led Fabio into the spacious drawing room.

"Drink?"

Fabio raised a perfectly shaped eyebrow at her.

"What does she mean, play nice?"

Nadia burst into laughter, a sound which Fabio suspected was being exaggerated for his benefit.

"Damage limitation, Declan and I have a history, Francine doesn't want me to say too much before you meet him. Create a bad impression, that sort of thing."

"Ah" Fabio smiled and took the glass of wine offered to him. "Is it a love and hate relationship?"

"Mostly hate" Nadia purred sweetly. "I don't want to talk about Declan Hyde, he'll do enough of that for himself. Now please, tell me about *you*"

In the hall, Carlo overheard the conversation and raised an eyebrow at his wife.

"I hope *your* friend doesn't do *my* driver too much damage*!*"

"Declan? I shouldn't worry" His wife patted his shoulder. "He's more than capable of doing that for himself."

Something was buzzing. It was creeping into Declan's sluggish brain and irritating him. Shifting on the couch he pulled a cushion over his head. The buzzing remained. It was somewhere on the couch with him. He could feel it as much as hear it. What the hell was it? Turning again he felt something press against his backside. Of course. His mobile. He was lying on it, and someone was trying to call him. With a sigh, he pulled it out of his pocket and blinked at the screen. Who was daring to disturb him in his sanctuary? It took a few minutes for his eyes to focus in the gloom by which time the buzzing had stopped. Shaking his head, he stared at Carlo's name on the screen. Was he going to return the call, or pretend he had been asleep, which he had been, and missed the call altogether? A small voice in his consciousness told him that he should call back as it may be important. Sighing deeply Declan hit the green button and redialled the number.

"Declan" Carlo sounded irritated. "Where are you? You are supposed to be here."

"Am I?" Declan frowned. Where was he supposed to be? Oh god, yes, dinner. He had forgotten about that. Deliberately. He wasn't in the mood for an evening escaping Nadia's painted claw. He had made the terminal mistake of having sex with her, which she felt gave her a right to claim him. He had even caught her buying a copy of Bride magazine in an airport. As if that would ever happen.

"Sorry Carlo. Forgot. You should have reminded me this morning then I needn't have come home."

"Fabio is here." Carlo did not sound impressed. "This was so you could meet, informally "

"I'll meet him at the track thank you" Declan snapped. "Or am I expected to nursemaid him?"

"Do NOT start," Carlo warned. "He's young, he's in awe of drivers like you. I just wanted him to be comfortable in the team."

"That's your department, not mine. Mine's to beat his arse every time he gets in a car."

The line went abruptly dead as he pressed the red button and cut Carlo off. Make him comfortable. What the hell was this, a nursery? Running his hands through his tousled hair Declan felt an edge of irritation creeping through him. He wouldn't go back to sleep now.

There was only one thing for it. Head down to The Harbour and drink.

As Declan made his way to The Harbour Inn Fabio, many miles away, was not entirely comfortable. When Carlo had called and invited him to dinner, he had expected it to be in the relaxed ambience that he was used to at home. Instead, he found course after course being placed in front of him at too fast a rate for his laid-back Italian digestion to cope with. He had been frowned upon when, to slow things down, he had pulled a packet of cigarettes from his pocket. He was not really a smoker; it was just an old habit that he lapsed into when his nerves got the better of him and there was no other escape. Discouraged, he had taken refuge in the Chianti and was paying the price. Staring at the cream-covered torte in front of him he felt a wave of nausea and wished, not for the first time that he was at home.

His first mistake had been his clothes. A Calvin Klein polo shirt and faded Levis' were not in keeping with his companions' shirts and ties. He hadn't had time to shave and could feel the stubble darkening his chin. Fabio liked, by nature, to be clean-shaven and felt in desperate need of a shower after the drive to the house. But by far the biggest mistake he had made was allowing Nadia to take him over. Yes, she was beautiful with her glossy brunette hair and hourglass figure, but she was much older than he was, and he could feel himself being towed onto a path he didn't wish to follow. He was due at the Matros compound at ten in the morning and it would not go down well if he turned up with a thumping hangover. Sinking into his chair he began to recede into his shell, speaking only when spoken to and feigning tiredness as the excuse for his drooping eyelids. He could feel Nadia watching him with a predatory look on her face. He knew what she wanted. The same thing most women wanted when they saw him but this time he was going to turn away. He was going home to the flat Carlo had rented for him and he was going to sleep. At this point in his life, the only thing he wanted to feel between his hands was the steering wheel of a Matros race car.

The Harbour Inn was never very busy. Even on Saturday evenings, there were plenty of seats and never a queue for the pool table. On a bleak evening in January, it resembled the Marie Celeste. Settling himself into the little nook that looked out onto the harbour mouth he watched the sea beginning to swell as the wind rose. He had been there some time, sipping his beer and staring at the sea when he had the strange feeling that someone was watching him. Looking around the bar he could only see a trio of teenage girls and a group of fishermen. One of the girls looked at him and smiled, but, seeing that her flirtatious interest was not reciprocated she turned away. Declan returned his gaze to the sea and became lost in thought, barely realising that someone had taken the seat opposite him. As he went to get a fresh drink, he was startled to see a figure sitting at the same table. Taking in the sleek black bobbed hair, the heavy fringe and the very tall and slim figure that supported it he realised it was the girl he had seen from his window earlier.

"Hi." She smiled at him from beneath thick black lashes. "You're Declan Hyde, aren't you?"

"What if I am?" Declan scowled and turned away. He was well used to the groupies that followed him on the circuit and had made use of them on several occasions, but none of them had ever disturbed his sanctuary in Mullacombe.

"Would you sign this?" She offered him a black-and-white image of a Matros. "It's for my brother. His name is Simon."

"Oh." Slightly disarmed Declan took the offered photo and pen and signed it.

"Thank you." The girl got to her feet. God, she was tall, with legs that went on forever. She smelled of something, some perfume, he didn't know the name, but he liked it.

"Going already?" He smiled. "I was just about to offer you a drink."

The girl blushed and sat back down.

"Okay." Her voice had a sing-song lilt to it. "Thank you. Could I have a cola please?"

"No." Declan laughed. "Rule number one Declan Hyde does not buy soft drinks."

"In that case." She lifted her eyes again and he noticed they were a very intense brown with green flecks. "I'll have a white wine."

Standing at the bar Declan watched his new companion with interest. He was mildly intrigued as to what she was doing here, but that wasn't the first thing on his mind. He cast his mind back and wondered when the last time was that he had had sex. He almost laughed out loud when he couldn't remember. Nadia possibly, but that was before Christmas. He was slipping. What would people think if they knew that the legendary, womanising, Declan Hyde was really a loner playing on his PlayStation in his tiny cottage?

He'd better put that right and he seemed to have found just the right person to do it with.

By ten he knew that her name was Lucy Duggan, that she was twenty; a fact that shocked him slightly but that was quickly pushed to one side, that she was a first-year student of journalism at the University of Wales. Because Declan was Declan, he didn't find it odd that she was here in this little remote fishing village and never asked why; he just went on watching her long dark eyelashes thinking that she was extremely good-looking. As the night wore on, she became more and more drunk, and he found her more and more attractive.

"So." He sat back in his chair and fixed his eyes on hers. "Would you like to come back to my cottage for a nightcap?"

Lucy blushed, a trait he found rather sweet and equally alluring.

"Yes." She said quietly. "That would be nice."

"Aren't you afraid?" He smiled. "I could be a dangerous man, an axe murderer."

"But you're not." She smiled. "Anyway, I can handle axe murderers and racing drivers."

"Can you now?" Declan got a little unsteadily, to his feet. "In that case come with me, I have a bottle of red you can help me finish."

It was all very pleasant; sitting here with this leggy, lovely girl sprawled across his sofa. He really didn't want to lose the casual atmosphere, but if he didn't test the water soon, he would be in danger of losing control. Getting out of his chair he crossed the Chinese rug to sit beside her. Her eyes were slightly unfocused, and her lipstick had smudged at the edges of her mouth. Leaning forward he kissed her, very softly on the lips. Her response took him by surprise: far from the reserved, tentative reaction he had expected he found himself with his arms full of a passionate, writhing young woman. Her fingers tugged at his short, thick hair and her back arched as she pressed against him. He was taken aback, but only for a few seconds. Letting her carry on kissing him he lowered her slowly back onto the cushions and began to take over, sliding his hands around her tiny waist, letting his fingers curl upwards to cup her firm, neat bust. She moaned softly and pressed herself into his palm. Encouraged he ran his hand downwards, over her stomach and undid the zip of her jeans.

He was delighted to meet little resistance; in fact, instead of the reluctance he had expected what he got was the opposite. She wriggled in his hands and let him begin to lower her jeans down over her narrow hips.

Then his mobile rang again. He ignored it at first, too engrossed in the girl in his arms. Then it kept ringing again, and again and again. Irritated, he reached for it and looked at the screen. Kate Matthews. He paused for a second and then pressed the button to take the call.

"Miss Matthews" His tone was brisk. "To what do I owe the honour of a call at this hour?"

"Where the fuck are you?" Kate was almost screaming. "You should be here you arse; you know you should!"

" I forgot," Declan said calmly. "I have already explained that. I'll meet the Italian boy wonder at the test track."

"And what about Dad?" Kate hissed. "Don't you think you owe it to him to turn up for once?"

"On that point, I agree." Declan's voice dropped a tone. "I'll call him in the morning and apologise."

"You'd better" Kate snapped. "Enjoy whatever little whore is entertaining you tonight."

Before Declan could reply, she had hung up. Running his hands through his hair he looked at Lucy stretched out beside him. Not a whore exactly; but she was a remarkably easy pick-up. In his mind, he pictured Kate, all gun's blazing, chestnut hair spilling around her eyes as she marched through the Matros compound. The one nut he had yet to crack. The challenging, feisty, and quick-tempered Kate Matthews. The subject of an almost childlike crush and the unwitting creator of his most private fantasies. Beside her, this girl was nothing.

"Out." He didn't even look at her. "Playtime's over. Out."

CHAPTER 4.

Gerald watched the two men facing each other and smiled to himself. Fabio, as sleek and elegant as a gazelle towered over Declan by some four inches. Declan, broader and definitely more powerful, looked almost ordinary when compared to the Italian. Perhaps that thought was a little unfair. Declan would never be ordinary. He had a pulsing self-confidence which would always make him stand out from the crowd. Behind them Carlo was tinkering with the Matros; he had decided, at the last minute, to lower the front wing of Declan's car and was making the final adjustments with a look of prepossessed affection on his face; the type normally reserved for the parents of newborn babies. Glancing up he saw Gerald watching the two men and smiled. Being initially responsible for the discovery of Fabio he felt as if he had just landed a heron beside a formerly tranquil pool of goldfish. He was very interested to see how fast the fish could swim to stay alive. Carlo liked and admired Declan, always had, but he had often felt that the man needed a kick in the right direction. In finding Fabio he had maybe kicked just a little too hard. What Declan would think when he saw him drive and how he would react he could only anticipate.

It was going to be interesting, to say the least.

The test track Gerald had constructed for his cars was a rigorous one. He held the opinion that if a car was, or any part of it was, going to stand the strain of a full race it needed severe testing. It was not only speed that counted but also reliability; there was no point in having the fastest car on the grid if it always failed to finish. He was also a firm believer in familiarity and kept no test driver on his payroll letting his drivers do all the testing themselves. As a concession for accidents, he held a reserve driver on the payroll and they also had time in the car, but it was his two drivers who Gerald wanted to feel at one with the machine he had created. Yes, it was risky, but it was a chance they had to take if they wanted to drive his cars. The car, as ever, was engineered to suit the preference of the number one driver, which was currently Declan meaning that whoever else drove the Matros needed to fine-tune the machine to suit their skills. As Gerald watched his latest acquisition making his way onto the track, he felt a thrill of nerves. Beside him, Carlo had silently appeared and was staring at the computer.

"Here we go" He rubbed his chubby but talented fingers together. "First run."

"Why isn't Declan going first?" Gerald looked back into the garage and frowned.

"He has the boy's tinkering with his wing still".

Carlo raised his eyes skyward. "Personally, I think he just wants to watch the opposition weigh in first."

"Mm." Gerald shivered as the wind blew in from the track. "Life will be easier when this session is over; it will help break the ice. I want to establish a team spirit."

"Rivalry you mean, eh?" Carlo gave a throaty chuckle. "That part will be easy. If Declan thinks the star is coming off the stage door he will drive as if the devil himself is after him."

"Exactly what I am hoping for." Gerald smiled. "If he is trying that hard to beat Fabio, then he will beat others on his way."

Their conversation was abruptly interrupted as the Matros roared around the bend, twitching a little, and then powered across the timing line to a burst of applause from Fabio's mechanics.

"Hmm." Carlo beamed. "We catch the Concorde with this car I think!"

Fabio was taking the tight bends of the track with a grin stretching his face from ear to ear. He had never driven such a powerful or responsive machine. He had to wrestle with it on the bends as it fought to go faster, and when he braked, he felt as if his body would fly out of the cockpit if he touched the pedal too hard. He imagined the g-force his body would be subjected to in a race and felt a fresh rush of adrenalin. He was fit, as well as young, and his body stood the strains of a race well and it thrilled him that he travelled at such speed, he thrived on the risk, the danger, the adrenalin. reluctantly easing off the throttle he let the Matros crawl into the garage hiccupping and complaining at being forced to travel so slowly.

Carlo gave him a thumbs-up from the back of the garage.

"Carlo was right" Gerald was waiting for him. "You drive well."

"It is the car!" Fabio spoke so quickly and was so animated that Gerald could hardly understand him. "It is the best, it is brilliant!"

"Of course, it is." Gerald was as lit up as his young driver, "That is why I want only the brilliant behind the wheel."

At the back of the garage, Declan was strapping himself into his car and watching from a distance. He could not hear the conversation but could see the smiles and congratulations. He pulled on his crash helmet and lowered the visor. Fabio's drive had been good, he admitted that, but he was young and green and, in a race, in the heat of battle he would crack. He had seen it all before. They had all come, these hot-blooded young pretenders, and he had outdriven and outstayed them all. This would be no different. He would see to that. Flicking the paddle on his steering wheel he put the car into gear and pulled out of the garage, not glancing left or right and floored the throttle as soon as he met the track.

"Oh dear." Peter Trent, Declan's race engineer,

was tall and wiry with salt and pepper hair and far-sighted grey eyes. Watching his charge drive manically into the first corner he shook his head. "That man should carry a safety warning. Like a firework, light blue touch paper then retire."

If Fabio had been catching Concorde, then Declan was overtaking the Space Shuttle: driving with all the indignance he felt at the challenge to his superiority unleashed his engine which screamed in protest as he pushed it to its absolute limits. Gerald watched on calmly, nodding with a perverse satisfaction; Declan's hackles were rising, and it showed. The Irishman drove at his best with the fires of his mental inferno lit, and Gerald Matthews was an old hand at igniting them.

Behind him, Fabio was watching with something approaching awe. He had studied Declan's driving many times when he had first been approached by Carlo, and although he respected the man's record and his talent, he felt that he took too many risks in an already risk-laden sport. Watching him drive in the flesh brought home the brilliance of his abilities. A brilliance that was marred, in Fabio's eyes, by a tendency to live a little too close to the edge of safety, sometimes even crossing beyond it. While Fabio felt that was not a good attitude to have, he also knew he was the underdog here and was willing to learn all he could from his illustrious teammate. When Declan returned to the garage, he crossed to the huddle of mechanics who were waiting to hear his verdict on his car's performance.

"Too much understeer." He heard him say. "I had to arm wrestle it all the way."

Carlo pulled a face.

"You were plenty quick enough."

"Yes. But I could have been quicker."

"My car." Fabio volunteered, "Was the best I have ever driven."

Declan looked at the younger man's face, flushed with excitement and mellowed a little.

"You drove it well. It pains me to admit it, but you did." He turned to Gerald. "Again?"

"Not you." Gerald shook his head, knowing exactly what effect his coming words would have. "Let the boys sort out that understeer tonight and I'll call you. Plenty of testing time left. Fabio can have a few more laps to settle in."

"Okay." Declan hesitated. "If that's how you want it."

"It is." Gerald's face was emotionless. "Go and relax for a few days. Don't overdo it in the gym".

"Him?" Carlo chuckled. "The gym? That's very unlikely."

Declan blushed scarlet and felt his anger beginning to rise. His aversion to the gym was a long-standing team joke but he didn't appreciate it being used in front of Fabio. Without another word, he turned on his heel and went to change, determined not to let Gerald see that he was rising to his bait. Couple of days, eh? If he shifted his supposedly untoned backside, he could get an evening charter and be in Monaco by sunset. He had been told to relax and he would, in the only way he knew how: by letting his hair down.

The Z4 moved slowly out of the compound and turned its nose towards the motorway. Its driver did not notice the small, scruffy, red hatchback parked in the lay-by. If he had, he would have seen nothing familiar in the figure behind the wheel. With a baseball cap and hooded jumper, it looked like one of the wannabe racers that often lurked outside the compound waiting for a glimpse of a real racing driver.

Even if he had stopped to look closely, he probably would not have recognised the long lashes and dark, thoughtful eyes of Lucy Duggan.

Lucy followed the Z4 for a distance and then, seeing that its driver was not heading for the coast but for London, she turned around and headed back towards South Wales. She wasn't sure why she had parked outside the compound and waited for him to leave. She could not have explained to any of her friends why she had even come here. All she knew was that she had to, somehow, generate another meeting with Declan. If she didn't then none of her plans and dreams would ever come true. Her little old car was blowing out smoke by the time she parked it in front of the house she shared with her fellow students in Cardiff. Sitting staring at the house for a second, she felt a familiar weight settle on her heart. She wanted to change this life, so badly. She enjoyed her course and loved her friends and her family dearly, but it wasn't enough. Living day to day in a meagre existence with no money, no boyfriend, no prospect of having what she really wanted. She knew plenty of boys, all of whom were more than eager to ask her out and to hopefully spend a night in her bed. But they were just that, boys. She needed and wanted more.

Letting herself into the hall; that smelled of damp and yesterday's curry, she climbed the stairs to her room on the first floor. Moving quickly through the door she turned the lock and breathed deeply. No one else came in here. This was her sanctuary. Her shrine.

She went to the wardrobe and opened the door. It was still there. She was always afraid that someone would have found it and given her away: taking it back to the Bridal shop that it had left, unpaid for, hidden in her bag. It was ivory and decorated with pearls and diamantes in the shape of flowers. She looked beautiful in it, she knew that, and one day she would wear it. Lying back on the bed she pulled off her baseball cap and looked up at the ceiling. She stretched and smiled softly.

"Hello my love," she said. "Have you missed me?"

Staring down at her, indigo blue eyes every bit

as intense as they were in real life, was a large colour poster of Declan Hyde.

CHAPTER 5.

The clock on the garage wall was ticking far more loudly than usual. It could have been a result of the silence that hung in the air, magnifying every sound. There was no rattle of computer printouts, no shouted instructions, nothing, just silence and the ticking clock. Gerald looked up at the hands ticking away and sighed. Something must have happened; even Declan had never been quite this late before. A car pulled into the compound and all eyes turned to the door, hopeful. But they were doomed to disappointment as instead of Declan's stocky frame bursting through the door with its usual energy they were greeted by the sight of Kate, eyes glittering in her pale face, a look of total satisfaction on her face.

"Late, is he?" She faced her father, an expression of triumph on her face. "As I have said before Dad, many times, he is a total waste of your money."

Gerald looked at her; she really was firing on all cylinders this morning and he knew that she didn't hate making her little speeches at all, in fact she enjoyed them.

"He'll be here," he said calmly. He was not going

to be goaded into a reaction. "Something must have happened."

"Probably a female happening," Snorted Kate." Wining and dining on your money."

"His money" This time Gerald's voice had an edge of irritation to it. "He earns it, Kate. Every penny."

"By being three hours late? By keeping everyone waiting?"

"By risking his life every time, he goes on the track. This is a high-risk sport Kate, or have you forgotten what goes on out there? Or maybe you think money is more important than a man's life?"

Kate blushed and turned away. Eyes pinned to the floor she let her hair hang around her face so that the men couldn't see her blushing. Trust her father to stick up for Declan. He always did and now he had made her look small in front of the engineers. How could she maintain any sense of authority when he did that? In truth, she seldom ventured into this male domain but had been swayed by her curiosity to cast another eye over Fabio and check out the much-acclaimed Roman God on the track with her own eyes. When she had arrived and discovered that this was scheduled to be Declan's test session she had been tempted to turn away, but her curiosity had won the day. This it seemed was her reward for taking an interest. One day she really would learn to keep her mouth shut.

Her father didn't question her unusual appearance; it seemed he had no great desire to talk to her at all. Giving the clock a mournful look, he was about to tell the team to give the day up as a bad job when a loud screech of brakes announced the arrival of his errant star driver.

"Sorry! Sorry!" Declan ran into the garage, unshaven, blonde hair tousled and threw his beloved vintage flying jacket into the corner. "I really am sorry I've had one hell of a morning."

"So has my father!" Kate was on him before Gerald could even open his mouth." Do you think he wants to stand here all morning waiting for you to get out of bed?"

"I had a puncture. " Declan didn't even look at her as he spoke." Two in fact. I am sure you appreciate that even I, with my considerable talent, can't drive a car on two wheels."

"Really." Kate glared at him. "And you didn't call because?"

Declan smirked; oh, he was going to enjoy this. Despite his well-hidden fantasies about the fiery Miss Matthews, he accepted the fact that she would be far more attractive if she could ever stop being such a bitch. As it was, putting her down was one of his life's perverse little pleasures.

"I did." He handed her his mobile. "Twice. But you don't answer your calls, Kate. Not very good considering your position."

Kate stared at the screen in her hand and saw

her number listed as the last call Declan had made. Rummaging in her handbag, she pulled out her own phone and checked her missed calls. Yes, there they were, two calls from Declan made about two hours ago. Furious with herself, she didn't answer but walked back out of the garage with her head held high. She could not let him get to her. That was the second time today that her lack of attention to detail had caught her out. She needed to pull herself together and get back on top of things. Fast.

"Declan" Gerald patted the shorter man's shoulder. "Calm down. Have a coffee."

"Nope," Declan picked up his race suit and went to change. "Contrary to your daughter's beliefs Gerald I want this team to succeed, and we've wasted enough time already."

Zipping himself into his dark blue suit Declan tried to calm his already rattled nerves. He just didn't need any more hassle this morning. He had missed his charter back from Nice last night and had managed to arrange a flight that morning. He had then suffered two punctures en route from the airport. While waiting for the breakdown truck he had checked his voicemails and had discovered at least six from the girl Lucy he had unceremoniously evicted from his cottage and several text messages. Declan was used to attention and female fans. But the strange thing about this one was he didn't remember giving her his number. To say he was spooked didn't even begin to come close. A run-in with the Ice Queen was all he needed to finish the day off. He took a deep breath and ran his hands through his hair. Breathe Hyde, put it all out of your mind and focus on the job at hand.

Pulling out of the garage on Gerald's purpose-built test circuit Declan drove slowly, weaving to and fro, letting the tyres warm up on the cold track. He took his time and waited for the signal that his car was giving the right readings before he let it loose. As he approached the white line that marked the position on the timing equipment, he flicked the paddle between his fingers, lowered his right foot and accelerated into his first real lap of the day. His car was working with him today, not against him, smooth, responsive, reacting to his every touch like a sensitive lover; it winged through the curves of the circuit like a bird and flashed over the timing line, a blur of noise and colour. He repeated the performance four more times and then lifted off the throttle, allowing the car to purr its way back into the garage.

From the back of the garage, Kate watched Declan spring out of the car and engage in animated conversation with Carlo. The driver was gesticulating, twisting his body, arms permanently in the air as he described the car's performance. Carlo and his father listened intently. There was something about the very sight of the man that shot venom into her blood and made her bitter. He was like a piece of sandpaper rubbing her skin raw until it bled. She had never detested anything in her life as much as she detested Declan and if she was honest, she had no real idea why. Apart from her deep-held belief that despite all her wealth, intelligence, and power he was too good for her. His talent, his passion, and his courage all seemed to place him on a pedestal far above her head. He undermined her confidence and made her doubt her every decision and every word. All by being himself. Her job was a creation of nepotism, not one she had earned on her own merit. His talent and bravery earned him his. In comparison, she was a well-dressed, well-educated, well-heeled non-entity.

She felt the familiar cloak of depression wrapping itself around her and shuddered. No. She was not going back to that place. Not again. Whatever she had she worked for, and hard and she should hold her head up and be proud. She turned from the garage and walked back to her office. What was it about him that irked her so much? Jealousy? No, don't be stupid. What did he have that she couldn't have, or more? She shook her head and stared blankly at her computer screen waiting for her brain to kick into gear. Again, the thought crossed into her mind unbidden, and she pushed it away. There was one thing Declan Hyde had that she didn't.

Himself.

In her flat, many miles away Lucy was painting her nails with one hand and dialling a number with the other. He never answered of course, and she was wondering how long it would be before he finally blocked her from contacting him. But just by ringing and leaving a message, she felt that she was part of his life. One day, she reasoned, he may well answer or even call her back. Looking out of the window, just listening to the Irish accent informing her that he couldn't take her call right now and would get back to her she was forced to smile. Yes, Declan I am sure you will.

But until the day that he did just sitting here daydreaming wasn't going to get her any closer to what she wanted in life, so she had better start doing something to change it. Turning on her laptop, she opened a search engine and typed in the words - Jobs in Formula One Racing.

CHAPTER 6.

Fabio laid the last, neatly folded shirt into his suitcase. Looking around the bedroom, he checked that he had left nothing behind. He seemed to have far more luggage for his return to Italy than he had brought with him, but he couldn't work out why. His only purchase had been a trinket for his mother. It would be strange; waking to the winter sunshine that he knew would be shining on the lavish Italian villa that he had always known as home. Set high in the hills above Rome he had spent his childhood there helping in the olive groves and hiding from his mother in the outbuildings. It would be good to be back with the family, but he would miss the freedom that he had so quickly grown used to in England. He liked looking after himself. Washing his own clothes, walking to the local shop for a bottle of wine, cooking, and even buying takeaways. But once he went back home, he would be the baby once more. Prized and pampered, fussed over until he felt that he would die of suffocation. Any girl that he chose to meet and bring through the doors would be subject to the scrutiny of his wonderful, loving but completely domineering mama. So far, he had failed to find one who had been deemed good enough for her little prince. Except of course for Sophia. Sophia was in fact a distant cousin on his father's side, and as was the way of things, their future matrimonial statues had been more or less decided at birth. He knew that now Sophia was twenty-one her mother would be itching to announce the engagement.

She was nice enough, Sophia. Small, shapely, as all young Italian girls were. She made exquisite pasta, rode a horse as well as any man and was a talented musician and singer. She doted on her parents and Fabio sometimes wondered if she would marry an eighty-year-old if he came with her father's blessing. Yes, she was nice enough. But there was one problem, one stumbling block that try as he might overcome. He simply didn't find her attractive, not in the physical sense. Perhaps it was a perverse rebellious streak in his nature, or perhaps he wasn't trying hard enough; whatever it was when it came to his hormones, she did nothing.

Everyone said Sophia was a beauty so why did he not see it? He knew enough to understand that sex was not the most important thing in a relationship; but it helped. Oh, yes it helped. Now the leggy, lovely blonde who he had met at the restaurant last night was different. He could never have imagined marrying her, but the sex had been amazing. He had never done it so many times in one night or in so many ways. Somewhere, he reasoned there had to be a girl who would satisfy him like that and who would also be a wonderful wife and mother to his children. He just hadn't met her yet. For now, he was in no hurry to meet anyone. Something he would have to broach with his mother once he was home. In just over a month's time, he, and the rest of the Matros team would be heading to Melbourne for the first race of the season and the only thing he could focus on was his car and his job. Looking at his watch, he saw with shock that he was late. He was joining a group of other drivers including Declan as guests on a TV show dedicated to the upcoming season. It wouldn't be aired for a few months yet, but it was being filmed tonight. He was due at the London studio in less than two hours. His thoughts would have to keep he needed to go, quickly.

Gerald, Carlo, Francine, and Kate sat in the studio with the assembled entourage of girlfriends, wives, managers, and connections of the drivers on the stage and listened to the hopes and dreams of each man as he spoke. Declan, along with the current world title holder, the Austrian Kurt Braun got the Lion's share of the attention, Kurt for his technical knowledge and skill and Declan for his wit and charm and the one liners that had the audience crying with laughter. But the camera often stole from the other drivers to Fabio, capturing his boyish charm and awkwardness. The producer loved him and although he said little when the programme was aired his face graced the screen more than any other drivers did. His long, graceful body and dark looks made him stand out.

Kate was stunned into a rare silence. Her eyes were fixed constantly on Fabio's face, and she could feel her father's amused expression as he watched her. Fabio was quite simply beautiful; there was no other word for it. At the end of the evening, there was a drinks reception in the studio's hospitality suite. Rushing to the ladies Kate applied fresh makeup and doused herself liberally in Chanel. Tousling her hair so that it curled around her face she headed back out of the cloakroom to find her father. As she found him, she spotted a tall figure behind him and felt her temperature rising.

"Ah Kate." Gerald was very tired but was trying hard not to show it. "Here you are. I was just telling Fabio how pleased we are to have him in the team"

Fabio smiled and nodded his head at her and for a moment, they stared at each other. Kate took in every line of his face and felt her heart do a little flip inside her chest.

" Hello" She smiled. "We don't get many chances to speak to each other, do we?"

"No" He was watching her face intently and she could see that he was well aware of the effect he was having on her. Smiling politely, she felt him loosen her hand in hers.

Looking down at her, Fabio averted his eyes from the pulse throbbing in her neck. However, tempting it may be, this was the one direction he must not go in. This woman was his boss's daughter, and getting involved with her, however briefly, would not be a good idea. Plus, Declan had already warned him that Kate could be a prize bitch; he didn't need any aggravation this early in his career. It was her father that he wanted to impress, not her. Dead on cue, as if he could read his thoughts, Declan arrived with a drink in each hand.

"Here we go Fabio get that down your neck. What time is your flight in the morning?" He completely ignored Kate, who was staring at him, and he chuckled to himself; he could almost feel her hackles rising as she looked at him.

"Eight" Fabio sipped his drink. "I go from here to the hotel then fly in the morning."

" Nice" Declan's drink had already gone. "I'm away myself in the morning. The Maldives."

"Isn't that a little quiet for you?" Kate couldn't resist the snipe.

"When I'm alone, yes." Declan smiled broadly. "But who says I will be?"

"Really?" Kate smirked. "Anyone we know?"

"Afraid not." Declan smiled at her broadly. "More wine Fabio?"

"No thank you" Fabio shook his head. "I drive."

Declan shrugged and weaved his way back through the crowd to the bar stopping to chat to people as he went.

"I must apologise." Gerald's voice broke into Fabio's thoughts. "Declan and Kate are always at each other's throats. They can never agree on anything. Given half a chance I think they would murder each other."

"Why?" Fabio was drinking very slowly, anxious to create the right impression.

"I have no idea." Gerald helped himself to more food. "I can't even think when it started if I am honest. Hate at first sight perhaps. I can't think why although I do admit that Declan is rather an acquired taste."

"Perhaps." Fabio nodded watching his teammate flashing greetings to people as he went. "I like him."

"Do you?" Gerald looked surprised. "I had the impression that Declan hadn't exactly gone out of his way to make you welcome."

Fabio shrugged.

"He is just being himself. He want to be number one. Always. He just want to make sure that I know it."

Gerald smiled and nodded. A wise head Fabio had on those young shoulders. But then, you always grew up fast when involved in such a dangerous sport.

"Well, I must be going. Are you ready Kate?"

Kate, who had been deep conversation with Francine, looked up with disappointment written all over her face.

"Already?"

"I'm afraid so." Gerald shrugged an apology "You can stay with Francine if she will have you. I can drive myself home and see you in the morning."

"Of course, she can stay with me." Francine beamed. "It would be my pleasure."

Kate hesitated and looked at the shadows under her fathers' eyes.

"No. Thank you." Kate lifted her empty glass of mineral water. "I'm fine. I'll take dad home. I am a little tired myself."

"Are you sure?" Francine frowned. "You know you are very welcome."

"It's good." Kate forced a smile. "Goodbye Fabio, have a good trip home See you soon."

Francine watched them walking away and took her husband's arm.

"Gerald looks ill Carlo. I am worried."

"He does." Carlo nodded his agreement. "I think that is why Kate would not let him drive home. "Still" he brightened, "She has saved me refereeing another bout between her and Declan, who, you seem to have forgotten my darling wife, you have also invited to stay for the night!"

Across the room from them, Kate was rummaging in her bag looking for the car keys. In doing so, she discovered that she had in fact left them in her jacket, which was still in the cloakroom. Telling her father to wait for her she wound her way through the crowd to collect her belongings. As she did, she bumped into a dark-haired girl who was leaving the ladies.

"Sorry." Kate only glanced up briefly. "My fault. Sorry".

"No problem" The girl said, stepping to one side, "I should be looking where I am going."

As Kate walked away, chestnut hair bouncing

on her shoulders Lucy watched her with interest. So that was the famous Kate Matthews. The notorious head bitch of the F1 paddock. Now she would make an interesting interviewee. Maybe one day. In her pocket, Lucy had a reporter's notepad filled with notes taken from the evening's activities. She had managed to get herself a freelancing job with a magazine specialising in F1 racing and was about to leave and file her copy. She still couldn't believe her luck, getting the job in the first place, but to have been given the chance to come here had been a real bonus. Her obsessions were getting her somewhere at least, if not where she really wanted to be. About to turn she saw that Kate had bumped into Declan and was having words with him. Curious and desperate to get close to him for even a few minutes she edged closer so that she could listen in.

"Going so soon?" Declan's blue eyes were sparkling.

"Yes." Kate spoke sharply. "Dad's tired."

"Yes." The sparkle left Declan's eyes for a moment. "He always looks so drained these days. Is he okay Kate?"

The tone of Declan's voice betrayed his emotions. No one who heard the words could doubt that he cared deeply for Gerald. For a second Kate looked taken aback.

"I don't know." She said honestly. "Sometimes I wonder. Anyway, I had better not keep him waiting. Have a good holiday Declan, try not to overdo it."

"Me?" Declan laughed. "Now would I!"

Lucy watched his eyes following Kate as she walked away. As he turned back towards the bar, he saw her. She saw him narrow his eyes. She could almost read his thoughts; where did he know that girl? He'd seen her before, hadn't he? A faint smile played on her lips as he crossed the room. As he reached her, she saw the recognition in his eyes.

"Hello again." She smiled at him. "You were very good tonight."

"Thank you." He smiled. "This may seem rude but how are you here?"

"New job." She raised her press badge to his face.

"Well done, Lucy" He raised his glass to her. "Quick question, how did you get my number?"

"I'm a reporter," she smiled. "It's my job to know. "

She saw the concern fleeting across his face and enjoyed, for a moment, his confusion.

"Actually, my boss gave it to me, he wants me to

write an article on you."

"Ah." Declan was standing very close to her. "No other reason for the calls then?"

Lucy looked up at him, colour filling her cheeks.

"You know there is Declan."

Declan could feel the familiar rush of excitement tingling in his veins.

"Well, Lucy, I think this new job of yours deserves a celebration. Let's get ourselves a little drink."

CHAPTER 7.

On a sun-drenched island, with azure waves lapping against white sandy beaches, Declan swung in a hammock and sipped his third cocktail of the day. The surrounding palm trees saved him from the blistering heat of the midday sun, and from this position he could cast his eye over the beach in both directions. He could hear the soothing, hypnotic rhythm of the sea in the background. Completely relaxed he dozed off in the soporific atmosphere. Ten days in the Indian Ocean had deepened his golden tan to bronze and bleached his hair near white. Running his hand over his stomach, he tensed his muscles. Not as hard as they should be, he had to admit, but not bad for the pre-season. His skin was hot under his fingertips and peering below his sunglasses, he saw his reddened skin, a by-product of his morning spent sun worshipping. Shifting in the hammock, he breathed heavily and caught the scent of cooking coming from behind the mango grove. Beyond his private chalet, yet another mouth-watering meal was being prepared.

A breeze stirred the palms, rocking his hammock and cooling his sweating body. This truly was paradise. But paradise was already beginning to lose its sparkle. He was bored. Working his way through the hotel's extensive bar list had lost its appeal, as was eating everything on the menu. He had tried all the available water sports: snorkelling, scuba diving, water skiing, and parasailing. He had cruised around the island on his hired yacht. He had spent hours in the hammock and on the sand and in and out of the water. The gentle pace of life had recharged his batteries to the max and now he had an all-consuming desire for excitement. He could take the yacht and head for open water with the throttle wide open, or hire a driver and ski behind it, but the thrill wasn't great enough for him. There was something missing, that essential element of his makeup that made him who he was and he knew in the absence of a Matros engine, exactly where to find it. Sex. The heat and his tropical surroundings had his hormones working overtime and even a speed fix would not cure him. He needed to feel the heat of a body against his own, the taste of someone's skin on his tongue, the thrill of his body inside another. Sadly, for him, his chosen companion for the week did not appear to feel the same.

Declan liked his own company, but not to the extent that he could enjoy being alone on a beach for two weeks. He still couldn't understand the impulse that had made him invite Lucy Duggan on his holiday with him. Maybe it had been the alcohol he had drunk at the studio; or afterwards at the club. All he knew was that when he had boarded the jet the morning after she was behind him. He had asked her to join him with visions of passionate nights surrounded by the smells of hot flesh and coconut oil filling his mind. How wrong he had been. Looking down the beach, he could see her weaving in and out of the waves looking for shells. Her extraordinarily tempting body was clad in a one-piece black swimsuit that did far more for his sexual appetite than a bikini ever could. It clung to her small, neat curves and emphasised the length of her shapely legs. She oozed so much sex appeal that it crucified him to look at her. Her head was covered with a floppy hat to protect her face from the sun, and he was sure she was wearing her Factor twenty sun cream. They were complete opposites. He knew that now. Lucy would no more fry herself in oil for hours than she would cut off her head. She drank little and diluted her wine with soda water; the only Coke she was interested in was brown and fizzy and came out of a bottle. She had resisted the lavish menu and shied away from anything unfamiliar. She read for hours, sat, and watched the sunset over the water every night and hated the yacht with a passion. She would snorkel with him in shallow waters but could not be convinced to attempt a dive, preferring to watch from afar afraid of the deep waters and their unseen dangers. She was intelligent, vivacious, and pretty and she bored him senseless.

She was walking towards him, turning the shells over in her hand. She looked at his reddened stomach and shook his head.

"You look like the lobster you had for last night's dinner."

"I don't" Declan looked at her bare shoulders. "You look like someone who only comes out at night."

"Pale and interesting," She replied. "Don't you care about your body?"

"Of course, I do." Not, Declan thought to himself, as much as I care about yours. "Look!"

He tightened his stomach muscles and pointed to the ripples beneath his skin. He admitted he was flabbier than he should have been, but the effect was still impressive.

"Hmm." Lucy snorted. "Roasted like a Sunday lunch and pumped full of poison morning noon and night."

"Ah well." Declan drained his cocktail. "It will get some attention when I get back. No more cocktails for me, or at least not as many."

Lucy sat in a lounger and watched him

swinging in the hammock, brilliant blue eyes reddened from too much alcohol and admitted, but only to herself, that he was a glorious sight. Although he abused his body, it was still hard and powerful and the deep brown skin was a striking contrast to his almost white hair. Strong jawed, with a short nose and high cheekbones he was the most confident man she had ever met, and it was eating away at her inside that after all her dreams and desires she couldn't give him what he wanted. In that place in her mind where she and Declan Hyde walked hand in hand through the moonlight and they declared their love for each other he was soft-handed, kind, gentle, and besotted with her. The reality was that Declan was as forceful and demanding in the bedroom as he was on the track and, quite simply, he scared her. Every time she got to the point where she felt she could let herself go she saw his eyes change, darken, become more intense and the wall came down. Where were the gentle words, the whispers in her ear that she had dreamed of? She had even tried drinking too much to relax but it didn't work, the second his touch grew firmer and his kisses harder she backed off. She could just not break through her inhibitions. That first night at his cottage her joy at finally meeting her hero had swept her away and for a while she had let herself go. But that encounter had been cut short and now, even surrounded by paradise, she could not be the girl he wanted,

She was also aware that there were things about her that irritated him and that hurt. She knew she wasn't brave, but she had tried, she really had, there were just some things that were beyond her. She was far from a prude but when he strolled naked through the cabin, completely at ease with his naked body she found herself looking away and was unable to do the same. She knew her time with him was running out fast and if she didn't give him what he wanted then she would have blown all her dreams clean out of the water. She had obsessed over this man for so many years; she had thought that all her dreams had come true when he had drunkenly offered to bring her here with him and had leapt at the chance. What, on Earth, was she doing here if she couldn't have sex with him? The painful truth was that although he still was the object of her fantasies, the real Declan had far more scars and warts than the imagined one.

Her choice was simple. Give him what he wanted and run the risk that he would walk away from her in the airport and never see her again or not do anything and leave with her pride intact. But then, if that was the case what incentive would he ever have for having a relationship with her? What man in his position would want to have as his girlfriend a person who froze at their touch? She had planned this all so carefully in her head. They would meet, he would woo her and shower her with romantic trips and flowers; have her accompany him to all the Grand Prix and then eventually he would declare his love for her and take her as his wife. The reality it seemed was going to have to take a far different course.

Her thoughts were interrupted by Declan swinging out of the hammock and standing over her."

"Come on sour puss." He grinned. " Take that scowl off your face. Let's get wet."

The water was every bit as rewarding as it was inviting. The temperature of a warm bath, it wrapped its warm welcoming arms around Declan's hot skin and washed it with gentle waves. Lying on his back, eyes closed against the glare of the sun he let the water carry him outwards. Inhaling deeply, he flipped himself backwards and underneath the water. Opening his eyes, he looked through water as clear as sheer glass and saw a shoal of fish darting before him, flashing brilliant colours as they went. There were some beautiful species here. Coming up for air he saw that the other beautiful species had swum out to join him.

"Isn't this bliss?" the proximity of her wet body was starting to affect him.

"Yes." Lucy swam around him in close circles, she could see the fish below her and they made her uneasy. Something brushed against her leg and with a squeak she shot to Declan's side.

Laughing he put his arm around her waist.

" It's okay sweetheart, the sharks are a long way out."

"That." Lucy had unconsciously put her arms around his neck and was clinging to him. "Is not funny."

"Hmm," Declan looked at her and she saw, in an instant, that the light in his eyes had darkened. "I wouldn't blame the fish if they wanted a little nibble of you. I certainly do."

She blushed and he felt herself freeze as his hand began lowering the strap of her swimsuit.

"Declan" She fought to stop him." What are you doing?"

"Just looking." He was kissing her neck, hard and her swimsuit was starting to slip down towards her waist until she was standing with the water swirling around her breasts.

Taking a deep breath Lucy tried to relax, to enjoy the sensation of his lips tracing the curves of his body, he had pulled them back into shallower water and they were standing now. Then, so quickly that she had no chance to stop him, her swimsuit was around her ankles. Panic struck as she felt his hand squeezing between her thighs and could see over his shoulder people walking along the path behind the beach.

"Stop!" She gasped. "Declan there are people on the path!"

"So" His breath was heavy in her ear. "This is a private beach. They won't come here."

"I don't care!" She pushed at him. "If I can see them, they can see us. Stop!"

He stepped away from her and looked at her standing naked in the water, her swimsuit now floating around her ankles. She saw the light fading in his eyes as he shook his head.

"Okay." He bent down and pulled her swimsuit back up to her hips, passion instantly quashed. "Fuck you then. Have it your way you boring little bitch."

Turning from her he started swimming out to sea with long, powerful strokes.

She thought of calling after him but stopped. What was the point? With tears in her eyes and a heavy heart, she covered herself up and waded slowly back to shore.

The room had long grown dark before she heard him come in. She heard him shower, then go back out again. Not a word. Nothing. It was as if she didn't exist. That had been hours ago, and she had sat since then alone in the bedroom with the doors open watching the night closing in on the island. She had long given up crying and her eyes were reddened and sore. When she had heard him, she had wanted to rush to him and apologise not only for today but for the whole week, for being such a disappointment, for leading him on to believe that she could do what he wanted, but her nerve had failed her. So, she had sat on her bed, still in her damp swimsuit, wrapped in a cotton sheet and watching the night approaching; shivering, but not with cold, but with an isolation she had never felt before.

Getting to her feet she padded, barefoot onto the veranda and sat on one of the wicker chairs. She watched the sea, dark and mysterious in its evening wear and saw the moon rising huge and orange into the sky. Voices coming down the path from the main hotel made her get to her feet. She heard a girl's voice high pitched and giggly and then a deeper voice with an Irish accent that made her catch her breath. Then she could see them. Declan and a girl with straight blonde hair; small, slim, and wearing a very short tight dress. Her stomach lurched. They were coming here. Panic overtook her. She had no idea what to do so she ran out onto the sand and along the beach until the lights were far behind her.

The strength of the sun was magnified by the glass of the door, and it shone hard on Declan's face. Wincing against both the glare and his headache, he felt a weight on his shoulder and looked in surprise at the blonde head beside him. Ah. Who was she? Where did she come from? Did it matter? Pulling himself from beneath her he got a little unsteadily to his feet. From the heat that came into the room, he guessed that it was already around midday. Pouring himself a glass of water he dropped two Alka Seltzer into a glass and walked out onto the veranda. The smell of Frangipani overwhelmed him as stood and watched some jet skis racing each other along the shore, trying to stomach the drink before he threw it all back up again. Looking to the right he peered into the spare bedroom and saw that the door was shut and the curtains open. He placed his hand on the handle and tried to open it. Locked. Confused, he walked around the front of the villa and tried the front door. Also locked. The only open door was the one out of his bedroom. Where the hell was Lucy? She could not have got out and left both doors locked, the locks didn't work that way and he had the key to the main door in his room. Going back into the bedroom he checked the bathroom and living area and found there was no sign. Going back to the veranda he scanned the beach. Then he saw her, lying in the hammock he had occupied for most of the day yesterday. She was fast asleep and still wearing the black swimsuit. A pang of guilt hit him as he realised that she must have been there most of the night.

"Lucy!" He called as he walked towards the hammock. "Lucy. Wake up, you're in the sun you'll burn."

Reaching the hammock, he leaned over and pushed at her gently.

"Come on Luce, get inside."

Her eyes opened and she looked at him. God, she looked awful. She looked completely exhausted, and he could see she had been crying for hours. Damn. A wave of remorse washed over him. Poor kid. She had not done anything wrong, not really, and he had gone off on a binge without a second thought for her. The blonde in his bedroom wavered into his memory. Shit. Had Lucy been there when they got back? Despite his behaviour Declan did, deep down, have a conscience and it rose from the depths where it had been sleeping and stabbed at him fiercely. As usual, once the beast had been roaming in his head there had been no stopping it until it was sated and damn the consequences

"Inside." He spoke softly now. "Come on. You look awful."

Like an obedient, well trained, puppy Lucy walked beside him into the villa. She went straight into the shower where she stood letting the water wash away the megrims of the night. Emerging, wrapped only in a towel she saw Declan offering her a cup of steaming coffee.

"Get that down you." He placed it in her hand. "I've called for breakfast. Look, Luce. I'm sorry. Okay? Believe me, I don't say that often but last night was out of order."

"Has she gone?" Lucy didn't lift her eyes.

"Yes." Declan sat beside her. " I shouldn't have put you through that and I should never have brought you here. So, for that as well I am sorry. I thought you were, well I thought."

"You thought I was a groupie." Lucy finished it for him. "Eager to sleep with any racing driver they could get their hands on."

"I guess." Even by his standards, Declan was beginning to feel like a bit of a shit.

"Not your fault." Lucy looked at him with bleary eyes. "I suppose that's what I wanted you to think."

"Why?" Declan shook his head, "I don't understand. Why do that if that wasn't how you wanted to be treated?"

Lucy got to her feet, her towel falling to her

feet. This time she didn't have the energy to pick it up and stood naked in front of him.

"Because" She hesitated. " I've been obsessed with you for four years."

Then the phone rang.

CHAPTER 8.

Gerald was sitting patiently in the waiting room of the private clinic when his mobile phone started vibrating. Looking at the screen he saw Kate's name flashing vigorously at him. Feeling guilty, but not so much as to stop him from doing it, he waited for the voicemail to kick in and then turned the phone off altogether. He would listen to the message later, he had more pressing things on his mind at the moment than one of his daughter's frequent rants. A rant that was probably about Declan. He had spent the morning at the health clinic undergoing a series of tests and was now waiting to speak to the doctor about the results. That was the beauty of private health care; no waiting for weeks to find out what was wrong with you. Okay, there were some more details he would still have to wait for but not as long. Which was all for the good as far as he was concerned, he didn't have time to be wondering.

Starting to feel restless he got to his feet and began to wander aimlessly in circles. The waiting room was typical of every sitting room in every private clinic in the country; calmly furnished in soothing neutral colours, potted plants to add a touch of life and magazines full of frivolous articles about cake making and the latest piece of hot gossip. Light-hearted reading to take the patient's minds off whatever may be coming their way when they walk in through the door. Even the view enhanced a sense of peace. Landscaped gardens, a quietly flowing water feature; shrubs, rockeries, and lots of evergreens so that there was always colour. There were machines in the hallway offering instant tea and coffee, and the pretty receptionist would get you anything you asked. It was a service with a purpose, that was for sure. The door handle moved, clicked and the door into the doctor's room opened. Gerald froze to the spot, unable to turn and face the nurse that he knew was standing there watching him.

"Mr Matthews? The doctor will see you now."

Gerald took a deep breath, forced a smile onto his face and turned.

"Thank you." He nodded his thanks and walked through the door.

Colin Grey had known Gerald Matthews since they attended the same boy's school many years ago. He had followed his ambitious old friend throughout the years and marvelled at his ambition, his tenacity, and now, he felt, he would start to observe his courage. Over the years Colin had danced at the man's wedding, drank champagne to celebrate the birth of his daughter and comforted him during the darkest days of his divorce. Dark days, some long forgotten; but none as dark as those that were going to lie ahead of the man sitting nervously in front of him. Colin stood up and went to the window, looking out across the lawn. He found it far easier like this; it was the coward's way out no doubt, but he did not have to look at his patients' faces as he delivered his news. Some things, be they good or bad, people needed to hear with some sort of privacy not with someone staring as their emotions chased across their faces.

"Tell me." Gerald's nerves were showing, his voice was beginning to shake.

"I'm not going to beat about the bush Gerald." Colin's voice was also quaking. "No padding, nothing. As I think you want to hear it."

He paused and took a deep breath.

"You have a tumour. Near the base of your skull. A bloody big one. I wish to God you had come to me sooner."

"Why?" Gerald's voice was barely more than a whisper.

"Because." This time Colin did turn and look at him. "It would have been far easier to treat. Drugs, radiation therapy, and then a small operation. Now what we are looking at is major surgery. Invasive dangerous surgery that has no guarantee of success. After the surgery there will still be months of drugs and treatments and," he paused.

"What?" Gerald could feel his nerves trembling through his body. "Come on, tell me."

"It might work " Colin lowered his eyes "Or."

"It might not." Gerald finished the sentence for him. "So, what you are telling me, old friend, is that I will die if I don't and will probably still die if I do."

Colin sat with a thump on the chair and put his head in his hands. After a few, shoulder-heaving breaths, he pulled open his drawer and got out a decanter of whiskey and two glasses.

"Medicinal." He said grimly. "Believe me sometimes I need it. Most days."

Gerald swallowed his drink in one mouthful and felt the heat coursing down his throat into his stomach. For a moment he thought he would bring it all back up. Without realising he had done it he found his other hand had gone to the back of his head.

"If I had come sooner, would it have helped?"

"I can't say." Colin poured another drink. "It would have been smaller. Less invasive. Now it's a minefield of blood vessels and nerves and it is so close to the spine. "

"Is it?" Gerald had to pause before he could say it. "Is it cancer?"

"That I can't yet tell." Colin was grim. "We need to do a biopsy, but frankly a biopsy is a waste of time as it just needs to come out anyway. But at least we may know before we go in what we are dealing with. If it is cancerous then we have to look at the chance that it may grow back. Or spread. The sooner the better is our only option."

"And what are the real chances of removing it?"

"Again, I can't tell."

"These things have roots I suppose?"

"Some."

"Which you may not be able to touch?"

"You, my friend, are too well informed." Colin forced a smile.

"Then in that case there is no point." Gerald straightened with a look of resolution on his face. "No operation."

"What!" Colin stared at him. "Gerald, if I don't do something the pressure on your brain will cause a massive haemorrhage. You will die!"

"And I may die anyway." Gerald smiled softly. "And go through considerable discomfort beforehand. No thanks."

"Then in that case all I can offer is radiation therapy. That may well shrink it. And we will undertake a biopsy so that we know what we are dealing with. That's a short-term solution that won't help your symptoms. Hopefully, it will shrink. God Gerald the pressure inside your head must be immense!"

"Tell me about it," Gerald said grimly. "If I keep going as I am. Take painkillers, something to help me sleep, will I get to the end of the season?"

"With radiation, you have a better chance. But

that could have side effects ,you may not be able to carry on as you are."

"Without radiation." Gerald interrupted him. "Without."

"Shall I sign your death certificate now?" Colin shouted. "Shall I? I am your doctor; I have a Hippocratic oath to fulfil. To try and make you well, and save your life!"

"And as my friend." Gerald reached across the desk and touched his arm, a gesture that brought tears to Colin's eyes. "You have to understand that if this is potentially to be my last summer, I can't spend it being sick and in hospital. I have to live with it. Give me whatever I can take, whatever you think may help. But I will not go back and forth to the hospital and spend the summer in a bed. If the drugs make me ill, I won't take them. No arguments."

"I can give you medication. Read the leaflets carefully and watch for side effects. But please Gerry, reconsider. Let me at least try and get the damn thing out."

"If I can stand on this carpet in November then I will." Gerald wiped the tears from his cheeks. "Then you can do whatever you think is right. But before that, there are a few races that I want to win."

It was much later in the day before Gerald remembered Kate's message. Dialling his voicemail he listened to her frantic voice, replayed the message, and took in its contents. His call to her was greeted with her nearly hysterical tears.

"Dad, Dad, where the hell have you been?"

"I was busy." Gerald tried to keep his voice steady. "What was so urgent that it couldn't wait until I got home."

"There was a fire." Kate sobbed. "At the factory. We got it under control, but we lost a lot of equipment."

"What's the damage?" Gerald shook his head. "The cars. They were ready to create and ship to Australia, are they okay?"

"No." Kate sobbed again. "Declan's car is gone. His seat, his steering wheel, all of it. We've lost nose cones, wings, suspension... we don't have enough in the crates to make another car."

"Then in that case my dear daughter." Gerald's matter-of-fact tone stunned Kate into silence." We have a lot of work to do."

CHAPTER 9.

At the same time, but thousands of miles away Declan was standing in the middle of the villa screaming into his phone.

"I don't care," he yelled. "Get me back to the U.K. Fast!! Just get me a flight and get me out of here today!"

Lucy was watching him, transfixed by his panic and his rage. He was almost on the point of hysteria. There had been a call, some heated words and then chaos had started. He had gathered his belongings, thrown them into his case and paced the floorboards ever since trying to get first a private jet and then a commercial flight to get him back to London. He was distraught about something, but he hadn't told her what. It occurred to her that maybe she should be packing as well. But she just sat there, almost afraid to move.

"Thank fuck for that." He snapped into his phone. "What time? Right, get a cab here for me now."

Throwing the phone into his backpack he looked around the room and seemed to see her for the first time.

"I'm going." Her confession seemed to have disappeared from his mind. "Your ticket is good for your flight home in three days. The food is paid for."

"What?" Lucy got up. "You are just going to go and leave me here? Should I come as well? It won't take me long to pack."

"No!" He snapped. "This has nothing to do with you."

"Can you at least tell me what's happened?"

"A fire." The rage suddenly went out of him, and he sat on the arm of the chair. "At the factory. My car's been destroyed. All the things that are specific to me. Seat, steering wheel, and parts we've worked on to suit the way I want the car to drive. If we can't build a new one fast, I'm out of Australia."

A car? A CAR! That was what all the screaming, cursing, and frantic panicking had been about? Lucy shook her head. She had been prepared to comfort him, be his support in his hour of need but this took her aback. More to the point, he was leaving her here. For a car.

"But they can build another one, can't they?" She went and stood by him. "You don't need to be there, do you?"

"You really have no idea, do you?" He glared at her. "Whose body sits in that car? Whose hands do you think hold that steering wheel? This is my life. I need to be on that grid. I need to race. I have to have a car!"

"But it's only a few days." Panic of her own was starting to kick in now. The fear of him going, the fear of never being alone with him again, of never having the chance to be the person she had always dreamed of being.

Declan looked at her but didn't see her. His mind was racing ahead, seeing disappointments, failures, and defeat.

"Stay with me." She said softly. "Please?"

There was the sound of tyres and an engine coming to a halt outside.

"My cab." He got to his feet. "You know where everything is."

And with that, he was gone.

Out of the door and out of her life. The daydream had become reality and then turned into a nightmare. In this case, it seemed, the fairy tale ending was as far away as it had ever been. He had come into her life, and he had gone. Deep inside she knew that there was no way that he would ever be coming back. Not through this door or any other door that may have her standing on the other side. The more she thought of it the more her stomach twisted and turned, and the tears turned from tears of despair to tears of anger. How dare he? How dare he drop her like a piece of rubbish and just walk off and leave her alone in a foreign country! Because of a car. That was how he saw her, was it? Worthless? Something turned in her brain and the tears stopped.

"Don't worry about me, Declan Hyde." She muttered.

Going to the door she stepped out into the sunshine and felt resolve wash over her.

"You have not seen the last of me yet."

CHAPTER 10.

The Matros team found themselves working around the clock to repair the damage done by the fire; all the while aware that the new parts they had created for Declan needed testing in a live environment. Unhappy at heading off into the Southern Hemisphere with his number one driver short of track time in the new car, Gerald ordered a short-term sojourn to Jerez de la Frontera in Andalucia. Deep in the heart of the Sherry-producing region of southern Spain the circuit at Jerez was a frequent destination for teams wishing to do some pre-season testing. With so little time left before the big grid lineup in Melbourne Gerald wanted to make sure his star driver was happy and iron out the risk of any first race tantrums that may appear.

After the icy, wet, and windy conditions that had swept across Berkshire through most of February, the milder climate was bliss to most of the team. To Declan, it was no comparison to the heat of a Maldives beach and now that he knew he had a car, and nightmares of not lining up in Melbourne had faded, he bemoaned his cutting short of beach hours to anyone who would listen. Grumpy and short-tempered he snatched and snarled his way through each session, irritating his loyal friends and running the risk of making fresh enemies. He complained about the track, the weather and above all the car, which he claimed was totally inadequate. The throttle was sluggish, the handling was like a blancmange and the brakes had a mind of their own. All in all, the thing was a heap of scrap and should be rebuilt. Gerald watched and smiled to himself, ignoring the poor times and the barrages of ferocious language and felt an inner sense of satisfaction. The others may take offence at Declan's behaviour, but he did not; he had known the man far too long. He recognised stage fright when he saw it. The beauty of it all was that when it mattered most, in the cut and thrust of race days, Declan was a man of steel: cold, calculating, impenetrable, the most confident man on the track. Right now, he was strung so tight he was in danger of blowing one of his own gaskets.

For Declan, this was always the time when he had to confront his biggest adversary; himself. Having to confront his ability, his human error, and face the fact that this year the brilliance may have gone. Thankfully to date it never had, but there was always that unknown element, that chance that this may well be the year when he, Declan Hyde, was simply not good enough anymore. Gerald understood all this and let the histrionics pass him by. He watched as the driver, red-faced, stormed past him and slammed his helmet down onto the table beside Carlo.

"The car is shit" He pointed at the screen in front of the Italian. "It's a pile of crap! What have these arseholes built? It couldn't pass a Mini!"

"It is exactly as the other car was." Carlo ignored the rant and held out a cup of coffee. "Exactly. Perhaps the car does not travel well, Or" He paused and raised an eyebrow.

"Perhaps I didn't?" Declan paused and then burst out laughing. Mr Jekyll was back.

The mechanics looked round and sighed inwardly. There was to be no firing today then.

"Merely a suggestion." Carlo said dryly, "Going on past performance."

"Yeah, yeah." Declan was chuckling. "February is never my best month, is it!"

"No." Gerald joined the conversation. "Thank God you improve in March."

"Thank God you are my boss." Declan grinned. "No one else would put up with me!"

"Let's watch Fabio." Declan's comment struck a chord in Gerald's heart, and he wanted to change the subject, quickly. "Perhaps his car is also, what did you so eloquently call it? A pile of crap?"

"I doubt it." Declan's quick eyes, trained to react in a split second, had spotted the timing on the computer screen. "I think the sound barrier is about to go crack."

Walking to the edge of the track the two men

studied the driver as he hurtled, foot to the floor, down the finishing straight.

"Impressive." Declan shrugged. "Why can't I do that?"

"You will." Gerald patted his shoulder. "When it counts."

They reached the garage at the same time as Fabio. He was stretching his long frame out of the tiny cockpit, eyes glowing with excitement. Declan recognised the spark of passion and knew that he and Fabio, although they may be rivals, shared the same soul. Leaving the young man to enthuse about his car he went to his driver room to shower. He had changed back into his jeans and was pulling a ripped t-shirt over his head when someone knocked on the door.

Carlo was wearing a suit.

"You cannot go like that!" His eyebrows shot upwards when he saw Declan's attire.

"Go where?" Declan's hair was still wet, sitting in spikes on top of his head.

"The dinner party at the villa. Remember?"

"Oh, that." Declan reached for his beloved flying jacket. "I thought it was a meal, nothing fancy. I left my smart stuff at the hotel."

"You still cannot go like that." Carlo pointed to the ripped t-shirt that was exposing Declan's left nipple. "There will be guests."

Declan looked down at his chest and the exposed skin. He rather liked the effect as it showed off the contours of his now muscled body.

"Why? Will it put you off your food? Or will the lovely but sexually challenged Kate disapprove?"

"Just change." Carlo recognised the mischievous grin and had a feeling they were in for a lively evening. "Please?"

"No need." Declan picked up a denim shirt off the seat and pulled it on. "I'll wear this. Unless I get very hot, which I can't see happening somehow, I'll be undercover."

Kate had paid a local restaurateur to cater for her party. She had not felt like spending hours in front of an oven so had instead spent the afternoon touring the local shops with Francine. They had ended the day sitting in the pale sunshine drinking Sangria. She had arrived back at the beautiful white hacienda with its frame of flowering shrubs and spacious blue swimming pool just in time to set the table and open the wine. She was still drying her wild hair when she heard a car pull up outside. Peering through the window, she saw Carlo with Declan, Francine, and Fabio walking across the courtyard. Declan was telling a joke, waving his arms wildly in the air as Francine burst into laughter. Behind her Fabio smiled, colour staining his cheeks. She had heard Declan's jokes before; most of them were obscene. Fabio was dressed simply, demonstrating that low-key, smart chic that only Italians seemed to be able to pull off. He wore a pale blue shirt, cream cotton trousers and Gucci shoes. The paleness of his clothes emphasised his dark skin and eyes. He was beautiful; there was no other word for it. In terms of dress sense Declan was the total opposite. He had made no effort at all. Still, there was that air about him, a natural charm that would carry him through the evening and make everyone else feel as if they too should have come wearing jeans.

Giving up on her hair, she twisted it into a bun at the back of her neck and pulled her cream Chanel blouse off the hanger. She paused. It was her favourite, but it would, with her trousers, make her look too much like the businesswoman. Tonight, for once, she wanted to look like just a woman. Delving into the bottom of one of the bags that lay on the floor, she pulled out a short cotton dress, dark blue emblazoned with large yellow flowers. She had bought in on a whim after the Sangria. She smiled to herself; this would do it. Stepping into the sexiest underwear she possessed she pulled the dress on over her head. It fitted her like a glove. Looking at her slim waist and curving hips, she pulled her hair out of the bun and shook it loose over her shoulders. Tangled and still damp from the shower it made her look wanton. She decided against jewellery and dabbed her skin with her favourite Dior perfume. Tonight, my girl, she told herself, you are out to make an impression.

Francine was the first to spot her as she came through the door and smiled to herself. With her long shapely legs on show for a change and her hair bouncing on her shoulders Kate looked like a model. She had applied only enough makeup to emphasise those glittering green eyes and cover the freckles on her cheeks. Francine knew whom this show of femininity was for; but she also knew, having studied him for so long, who would be the most impressed. She looked across the room at the men who were also watching Kate. Fabio was staring at her with a hungry look in his eyes. Good shot Kate, she thought, right on target. However, it was on Declan who her gaze lingered. She saw him take in every inch of the body in front of him and saw emotions passing swiftly across his face; before the shutters came down and blocked them out. With a smile he launched into his usual attack.

"Where is Kate this evening Gerald?" He called into the living room.

"Very funny." Gerald emerged with a whisky in his hand trying not to look too amused. "Don't start Mr Hyde, she's right here and doesn't she look lovely."

"Oh, I'm sorry Kate." Declan feigned surprise. "Didn't recognise you there. I take it this display of womanhood isn't for my benefit?"

"Funny." Kate was pouring herself a drink.

"Always the wit aren't you Declan."

Declan smiled and turned away. God, she looked good in that dress. Images flashed through his mind and he shook his head. Now was not the time.

"How about suspending hostilities for tonight?" Francine ventured.

"If you insist." Declan shrugged. "But what will I do with myself all evening?"

"It's time you got yourself a woman." Gerald took a mouthful of his drink. "Then you may stop picking on my daughter."

"Never." Declan laughed. "It's in my contract. Anyway, what do I need a woman for? I have you to take care of me, Francine to organise my laundry and Carlo to nag the pants off me. The only other thing I might need is sex, and I never seem to have a problem in that department, I can sort that one out for myself."

"How about company?" Francine was laughing.

"I like my own." Declan grinned. "Always get the right answers then."

"Which is just as well. Because you are the only one that does." Kate sneered. "What happened to the latest notch on the headboard? The one who went away with you?"

"Still there I think." Declan grinned broadly. "Not my type it seems after all."

"She had a lucky escape if you ask me." Kate shook her hair and headed for the kitchen.

"Dinner won't be long."

Francine watched Declan as his eyes followed Kate into the kitchen. She had been reading the signs for many years now and wondered how long even Declan's insensitivity could stand it. But then he always gave as good as he got. She looked away before he caught her watching. There were some things that she knew were best kept to herself.

The food was delicious. A selection of salads, bread, and freshly caught and cooked fish. Declan, despite bemoaning the lack of chips on the menu, ate notably more than everyone else. Swilling down the last mouthful of rich, creamy dessert with a mouthful of wine he groaned and pulled at his shoulders.

"Stuffed." He moaned. "Is it me or is it hot in here?"

"Not very," Carlo interjected hastily. "Just comfortable."

"Well, you will all have to excuse me." Declan pushed his chair back. "But I am cooking."

With that, he pulled the denim shirt off and draped it on the chair behind him.

"Very smart." Kate looked pointedly at the exposed nipple. "Is this a new fashion? You obviously do need a woman; to tell you how to dress."

"Feel free." Declan smiled sweetly. "When shall we shop? I had my doubts previously but tonight has assured me that you do know how to look good after all."

Kate blushed scarlet and was painfully aware of the clash between her skin and hair she began collecting dishes and hurried out of the room. Fabio, suppressing a smile, wagged a finger at Declan.

"You should not tease her, my friend. She is the daughter of our benefactor."

"Who's Ben?" Declan asked with a straight face.

Fabio paused, raised an eyebrow, and then erupted with laughter. Fortunately, Gerald had missed the conversation as he was engrossed in a discussion about engines with Carlo. Wine had freed Fabio's normally reserved spirit and Declan found himself liking him far better now. Maybe at last he had a teammate that he could also class as a mate. Someone to share a joint with, a joke, a few beers. Brothers in arms instead of rivals. Lowering his voice, he leaned forward across the empty coffee cups.

"I may not know who Ben is my friend but I think that you have an excellent chance of fucking her if you wish. She has never pulled a dress like that out of the cupboard for me."

Fabio shook his head.

"No. I am sure that is not true, every woman likes to look good."

"Not that one." Why did he get such a perverse pleasure from putting Kate down? "She prefers to look sexless, not sexy."

The object of their discussion came back into the room at that moment with a tray of chocolates. Seeing them whispering she scowled and placed the tray on the table in front of Fabio with a slap. Looking up Fabio saw the green eyes fixed momentarily on his face. He smiled, feeling it unfair that this lovely woman should be the object of ridicule. Two pink spots appeared on Kate's cheeks ,and she smiled in return.

"Bang!" Said Declan loudly. "Do I hear someone pulling a cracker?"

"Declan," Kate said sweetly. "Do be an angel and fuck off."

"Really?" Declan pouted. "Can't I stay and watch the action?"

"Let me assure you. There isn't going to be any action while you're here." Kate snapped.

"Shame." Declan sighed. "I do love to watch."

As he spoke, he caught Fabio's eye. The Italian tried to look disapproving but failed and his shoulders began to shrug as he struggled to contain his laughter. He felt so mean, but Declan's wit always got to him. Kate, temper rising, spun away and went to sit by her father. Gerald seemed happily oblivious to the fact that his daughter was being ridiculed.

"Stars are coming out." He looked up at the sky. "Why don't we join them and sit around the pool."

"Are you sure?" Francine looked concerned. "It

is cold here."

"Not by Berkshire standards." Gerald smiled. "Come on. Anyway, it may make Declan put his shirt back on and cover up his chest."

"No chance." Declan was pouring himself another drink. "Cocktail, Fabio?"

"I am not sure." Fabio hesitated. "What is it?"

"Don't risk it," Carlo advised. "If it is one of Declan's inventions it will be lethal."

"I've got a new one." Declan proudly held his glass aloft. "Equal parts Bacardi, Vodka, a healthy splash of Pastis and some pineapple juice and some lemonade to bring out the colour."

"Ugh." Francine heaved. "What a mixture. What do you call this disgusting concoction?"

"Under the tyres." Declan smiled. "A few too many and you will be face down on the track."

"Not for me thank you." Gerald laughed. "But I'll have the Pastis with some water."

"Fabio?" Declan waved a glass at him.

"A small one." Fabio nodded. "Very small."

"Kate?" Declan called. "Drinkie?"

"No answer." Smiled Fabio. "I think that is a No."

It was late when the little party finally broke up. Carlo, having given in and started sampling Declan's cocktails, was incapable of speaking. As driving was clearly out of the question for anyone, Francine and Kate were preparing rooms for them all to sleep in. Declan, seeing an all-nighter opening up in front of him, was mixing more cocktails for himself and Fabio, who, as Francine had observed, was coping remarkably well with the amount of alcohol Declan was pouring down his throat. The only member of the party no longer drinking was Gerald. He was sitting by the pool trying to ignore his pounding headache. He didn't feel ill at all. Just tired and his head hurt. Perhaps he should call it a night and get some sleep.

"Time for bed." He got to his feet, hoping no one else noticed the unsteadiness in his legs. "Us oldies can't cope with the pace."

"Neither can the young ones." Declan pointed to Carlo who had fallen asleep on a lounger.

Gerald smiled wearily.

"Good night. See you at breakfast in the morning. "

He nodded at Fabio. "Go easy on him, Declan."

"Yup." Declan stretched. "Then in the afternoon, we'll give that car of yours a bit of welly, eh?"

"Maybe." Gerald laughed. "After a blood test to check your alcohol levels."

"Pah." Declan was settling down on his own sun lounger. "I will be fine."

He watched Gerald walking towards the villa with slow steps and, out of the blue, felt the cold hand of premonition drop suddenly onto his spine. For a second the hairs on his neck stood on end and he felt afraid.

"Are you cold my friend?" Fabio watched him

shiver.

"Goose walking over my grave." Declan shook himself.

"Pardon?" Fabio looked puzzled.

"Old English saying." Declan got back up. "Load of nonsense. The most practical translation for it is, 'time for another drink'."

CHAPTER 11.

The remaining time between the test session in Jerez and the departure to Australia passed quickly for all concerned with the Matros team. For Carlo and the mechanics, it was a period of intense activity as everything was checked; counter checked and repacked into crates. Moving was a logistical operation of immense proportions. Not only did the cars themselves have to get to Australia, but there were also the banks of technical equipment, the spare parts, the data, and all the other paraphernalia that played their own part in the F1 circus. Lorries with the Matros logo emblazoned on the side carried their precious cargo to its departure point. From here on everything spent its life in bits and pieces until it could be reassembled and fine-tuned in the days leading up to the race. There was no more time to test and query anything. This was it. The car's body parts had been covered from nose cone to tail fin in advertising, but stylishly done so as not to spoil the GM-4's sleek profile. In Carlos' besotted eyes, this was not just a car. It was a work of art.

Declan and Fabio, their friendship strengthening all the while, spent more and more time together; Declan even joined the younger man in the gym, something that had previously been unheard of. Fabio was fitter; there was no doubt that he led a far healthier lifestyle. Declan had a raw, natural, strength that Fabio could never hope to emulate. But he helped the Irishman sort his diet out, encouraging him to lay off the booze, stay out of the takeaways and far from the chocolate shelf in the local supermarket. In return, Declan told Fabio every last detail of the Melbourne track and about life on the circuit. They had both graduated through the lesser ranks of motorsport, but nothing could prepare a young driver for the baptism of fire that was their first Grand Prix. The heart-pumping moments on the grid, the first corner where panic could threaten to overwhelm the mind as adrenalin soars through the veins, the sheer physical exhaustion of completing your first entire race. These were things that Declan could talk about, his was the voice of experience. So, they sat up long into the night, growing ever closer but all the time aware that come race day neither would be prepared to give an inch to the other.

There were also no women to distract them in those last few days. They kept to themselves, the only chassis on their minds the mechanical kind and the only hands-on female touch coming from Francine in her official role as trainer. Gerald watched them, these unlikely comrades and felt a touch of satisfaction. He had thought to encourage a healthy rivalry between them, but they had naturally steered themselves in the opposite direction. As long as it worked that was fine. Gerald knew Declan of old and understood that if Fabio stood between him and the chequered flag, he would put everything on the line to take that position from him. It was going to be an interesting season and, he hoped, a successful one. He hid in the back of his mind every second of every day that it may be his last. He did not have time to think of illness. He had a team to run and it was time to get the show on the road.

The long flight to Australia passed swiftly for Declan as he spent most of it asleep. Fabio, on the other hand, was painfully awake for the whole journey and sat staring out of the window, fingers tapping on the armrest of his seat. It was not only the pre-race tension that made him unable to rest, it was also the knowledge that he was a passenger. He was not in control, and he hated it. Every twist and turn that the aircraft made set his stomach churning, his every nerve aware that his fate was in someone else's hands. Gerald's chartered aircraft was comfortable and luxurious. But the space and freedom afforded by even this customised craft could not ease Fabio's mind. Nothing, short of throwing the pilot out of his seat and taking the stick himself would soothe his trembling heart.

Carlo, watching the young man from across the aisle, was somewhat amused by his attitude. Fabio was not hiding his dislike of flying very well and it deeply intrigued Carlo that a man who launched himself at breakneck speed into the open arms of fate for a living could be so fazed by a more conventional mode of transport. Opposite Carlo Gerald had immersed himself in a pile of computer printouts studying the performance of his machines while Kate, two rows behind, was also staring out of the window with expressionless eyes. She had been very reserved throughout the flight, eating little and hardly speaking. Francine, like Declan, was asleep; her hair tangled behind her as she reclined in her seat. That was perhaps the reason that she got on with the Irishman slightly better than anyone else, they were very similar and had an inborn ability to just switch off from everything. At the rear end of the craft, Peter Trent and the rest of the crew were having a pre-season party that was growing in volume by the minute. Thanking the quirk to Gerald's management plans that allowed the team to travel together on long hauls Carlo got to his feet and went to join them.

A fleet of articulated lorries awaited them at the airport, all wearing the Matros livery. The crated cars and equipment were unloaded under the supervision of Gerald and Carlo and they finally set off on the last leg of their mammoth journey. The rest of the workforce bundled themselves into what would be their mobile working and living quarters for the rest of the week and headed off into the night behind them.

"Hotel for me tonight." Fabio was looking for his hire car. "I will see you all in the morning after some sleep."

"Who needs sleep?" Declan joked, after some twenty hours of it himself, was bright-eyed and raring to go. "Where's the nearest bar?"

"Ugh." Carlo, looking slightly pale, was sitting on a suitcase. "If you had not been snoring all the way from England you would have had enough alcohol at the party."

"What party?" Declan looked crestfallen.

"The one you missed." Carlo's head was starting to pound. "Here Fabi, we are together in this, you drive or my licence and I will soon be saying arrivederci."

The journey from the hotel to the track the following morning was a mere jog in comparison to the endurance run they had just completed. As they were driven in luxury the final miles to their destination, Declan and Carlo reminisced about previous Australian Grand Prix.

"Adelaide was the place." Declan grinned.

"It was." Carlo agreed, remembering dramatic finishes on the City of Churches circuit. "You are too young to have driven there surely?"

"Nope." Declan laughed. "I drove it. Junior

Series, just a baby-faced kid in those days. It's the parties I remember the most. Did you get to the Fosters bash with the snakes?"

"I would rather not." Francine shuddered. "I ran whenever they came close. I prefer Melbourne. Such a beautiful city and Albert Park is so tranquil; I love the lake."

"Typical woman." Declan watched a lizard scoot across the road in front of the vehicle. "Shopping first; sport second. Did you see that sign there Fabio? Kangaroos Crossing?"

"Really?" Fabio sat up and craned his head to look.

"Idiot." Francine grinned. "That is the name of a town."

"What?" Fabio laughed. "Is a stupid name."

"Take no notice." Carlo shook his head and then winced. It still hurt. "They are teasing you."

"Very funny." Fabio pulled his baseball cap over his eyes and slid down in the seat. He felt ill. He wasn't adjusting to the time change at all and his jet lag felt dreadful. Lying in his bed last night, he had felt every twist and turn of the aircraft in his mattress. Coupled with his mounting nerves it was making him feel physically sick. The closer they got to the city the more his stomach lurched. Beside him, Declan was munching his way through a bag of peanuts. How could he? Fabio looked at the stocky figure, unshaven, tousle-haired, relaxed, not a nerve ending on show. Fabio felt a pang of envy. Declan was so at ease with himself, so confident in his own abilities whereas he, Fabio, was plagued by self-doubt. He dreaded ending his first Grand Prix in a cloud of smoke, or worse.

"Are you okay?" Francine turned in her seat and patted his leg.

"He's twanging." Declan chuckled.

"What is twanging?" Fabio peered at him.

"Nerves." Declan beamed, a wicked light playing in his eyes. "Listen closely Francine and you will hear them going twang, twang, twang. I used to twang myself, believe it or not!"

"You still do." Carlos raised an eyebrow. "The hour before a race you are unbearable."

"I thought I was always unbearable." Declan raised his hands. "Thought it was my middle name!"

"It should be." Laughed Francine. "It would be very appropriate."

Declan's attention had already been diverted however as they drew into the outskirts of the city, passing houses surrounded by lush gardens that hid bright blue swimming pools. The Australian girls with their bleach blonde hair, driving past in open-top cars, wearing sunglasses and skimpy tops, further diverted him.

"Yum." He nudged Fabio. "Scenery has improved. Look!"

"No." Fabio shuddered suddenly. "I think we must stop the car; I am going to be sick."

CHAPTER 12.

It was an unhappy row of faces that greeted them in the pit lane garages a couple of hours later. Fabio's engine had not enjoyed the journey from England any more than its driver had and was refusing to start. Having dismantled it, more than once, the crew were waiting for Carlo in the vain hope that he would have a miracle cure. None of this helped the cause of the still queasy Fabio who sat, sour-faced, at the rear of his garage while his crew tinkered with the engine. The situation had no impact on the bubbling Declan who was tearing around the pit lane giving interviews and greeting old friends and rivals with equal enthusiasm.

"Look at him!" "Look at him!" Kate snarled as she brought ice-cold bottles of Coke out of the motor home. "He doesn't give a stuff about anyone else; all he can think of is potential parties and cans of Fosters!"

"Well, it isn't his problem." Gerald was checking that the computer equipment was working. "It's ours. His car is running well, so they tell me."

"He might be more concerned for Fabio. It's his first Grand Prix. What if he can't qualify?"

"He will." Carlo was trying to keep a cool head amongst the chaos. "There."

His voice changed as a familiar roar sounded from the garage. "It's away."

"We should carry more equipment, "Gerald looked back over his shoulder, "And crew. We are still a long way behind some of the other teams."

"No Dad." Kate interrupted. "NO more money!"

Gerald looked at her and gave a doleful smile.

"But we are understaffed darling. Think how much easier life would be if we all did one job instead of two, or in your case three. After all, it is only money, and as the old saying goes, you can't take it with you."

Before Kate could think of a reply Declan came bounding into view, wearing a Matros team t-shirt and cut-off jeans. With his cinnamon tan and white hair, he looked like a native Australian and very at ease.

"Do I hear an engine?" He looked into the garage. "Nice work Mr. Rossi. When do we get into one of these babies?"

"Tomorrow morning." Gerald looked at his watch. " More media for you this afternoon and the press conference. Before that Francine is making lunch."

"Oh good." Declan patted his stomach. "No healthy food I hope, I'm starving."

They lunched in the comfort of hospitality enjoying Francine's home cooking. Carlo chose to join the engineers outside. Francine, not offended by her husband's defection to the team chef, sat with them. Fabio ate very little, his mind already out on the track. Declan ate everything in sight.

"Cheer up" He waved a fork at Fabio, "You are about to enjoy that most wonderful of experiences the Drivers press conference. "

"Oh Declan," Francine chuckled. "You love them. You always get the limelight!"

"I do indeed." Declan grinned. "Always avoid a straight answer is the key!"

Fabio looked at him and smiled, one day he hoped he would have Declan's confidence, right now the thought of sitting in a media suite with his peers and answering questions terrified him. He wished that Declan would have been there with him but as the new face on the grid, he was the team representative.

"Right." Gerald put down his empty coffee cup. "Let's get on with this nonsense and then we can focus on what matters. Cars on the track."

The day ground on at a snail's pace for Fabio. He hated the media attention, the interviews, the meetings with VIPs.

"Better get used to it." Declan had bounced his way through the day with his usual enthusiasm. "All part of the job."

If Fabio's confidence had been tested by all the media attention the day of the first free practice sessions took his nerves to a whole new level. As he walked into the garage his fire suit hanging from his hips his face was completely drained of colour.

"Don't look so worried!" Declan laughed "This is practice. That's all. Get to know your way around, let yourself get the feel of the place. No one's expecting land speed records today, and no one's going to be watching you."

"Really?" Fabio's eyes were pleading with him, begging for reassurance.

"Sure." Declan patted his shoulder. "Everyone is too busy sorting out their own problems to think about anyone else."

He was wrong. Word had spread fast that the Matros rookie was pretty hot stuff, physically as well as in a race car, so all eyes and cameras were fixed on the Matros garage as Fabio's debut grew closer. The press, defecting from the potential World Championship contenders gathered around his garage only to be held at bay by the immovable Kate who, despite her personal opinions, would protect both her drivers with the same ferocity. Even so, Fabio drove out of the garage to a whirr of motorised film advancers and was watched out of the pit lane by all present. Taking Declan's words to heart he drove carefully, letting himself learn the track. He returned to the garage uninspired, but safe, and with an engine that was still running. His cautious path finding left the way clear for Declan, who, well used to press attention, both good and bad, drove with his usual flair and attack and clocked a very impressive time.

The rest of the day found Fabio very subdued and his times failed to improve. He was afraid to push the car and had no faith in the engine, which in his ears still sounded weak. He was disturbed by the aggressive intrusion of the press; he hadn't been born with Declan's natural ability to show off and thrive on attention. Declan seemed to enjoy having his every move recorded on film and walking through a barrage of microphones.

Sitting silent at the dinner table later that evening he stirred his coffee in silence and wondered if he had made the wrong choice of career.

Declan watched and saw the telltale signs of strain on the young man's face. It was the same old story. It wasn't the sport that beat these newcomers; it was the pressure, the fear of defeat, and the inability to adapt to living in a circus for nine months of the year. It created in them nerves beyond their control and drove them out of the sport. In the past, he had observed it all and watched with amusement as they packed their bags and left the paddock as quickly as they had joined it. But Fabio was different. Yes, he was his rival but he was also his teammate and despite his earlier thoughts he had endeared himself to Declan in a way that none of his predecessors had. He didn't want to see him fail and leave the track with his tail between his legs. He turned to Francine.

"I think our young friend could do with a helping hand to get him to sleep. How about offering him one of yours? Put those magic fingers to work?"

"I was thinking that myself." Francine smiled.

"Definitely." Declan smiled. "While you have your oily hands on, you can do me as well."

" Only if you behave," Francine spoke sternly but the laughter was visible behind her eyes. "And help me clear the table."

Kate watched Declan picking up plates and dropping cutlery, laughing, and joking with Carlo's beautiful wife and instantly thought the worst. She could not envisage Declan being merely friends with any woman and as he and Francine disappeared into the back of the motorhome, she found herself horrified to see Carlo laughing at them and making lewd comments about the uses of baby oil. She was paranoid. Alternatively, was she right and everyone else wrong? Preoccupied with her thoughts she sat at the table while the others dispersed. Looking up she saw that her sole companion was Fabio. Her eyes met his and she felt herself blush.

Fabio stared at her. He found her so attractive, this powerful young woman, but he had put all thoughts of any type of relationship firmly aside. But now, when his career seemed deemed to fail before it had even begun, what difference did it make? Why shouldn't he take her slim form in his arms and feel the comfort of her skin pressing against his? He emptied his glass and watched the pulse in her neck. He could kiss her there. Just once, and he knew she would open up like a flower and be his for the taking. Declan's voice broke into his thoughts and thankfully pulled him back to his senses, reminding him of the burning ambition that had brought him to this all-important point in his life.

"Come on Fabio." He yelled. "Massage time. I said you could go first but don't wear those fingers out."

Fabio gave a lifeless laugh and went to join Declan. Kate listened to the laughter and sighed. What was wrong with her? Why couldn't she just let go and laugh along with the rest of them? Was there something in her makeup that intended her to be miserable forever? Little wonder that Fabio would only look and not touch. Maybe her father was right; she was too like her mother for her own good. Irritated, depressed by her inadequacies she got up and went out into the still airless night.

She returned some hours later, having wandered around, stopping to talk to old acquaintances, and checking the garage security. Re-entering the motorhome, intending to have a drink before she left for the night, she found herself standing in front of Declan. Wearing only his boxer shorts, his brown body gleaming with oil, he was laughing loudly and glowed with satisfaction. Kate stood rooted to the spot. He hadn't seen her; he was talking over his shoulder to Francine who was still in the depths of the motorhome. When he did look around, he caught her watching him. He was surprised rather than gratified by the look on her face. Despite her attitude towards him, the sight of his near-naked body was obviously not a repulsive one to her, something that he had not expected. Continuing his path to the door he brushed past her, eyes never moving from her face. She looked up and her eyes met his, only briefly, but long enough for him to read the turmoil of emotions in them.

"Good night, Miss Matthews. See you in the morning."

Then he was gone, and she was still standing in the doorway, swallowing hard. He had brushed past her and had left oil all over her shorts and t-shirt and her nose was still full of the smell of his hot body. Taking a deep breath, she looked at her arm, still moist from his contact, and felt in her memory the hardness, the muscular power of his body as it had touched hers. She was hot and horrified. All the denial would be useless now; she had exposed just a tiny glimpse of the feelings that sometimes came to the surface. Could he really have that effect on her? The man she proclaimed to hate? The man who irritated her beyond belief? She felt as if she didn't know herself anymore. Leaning back against the door she slid slowly to the floor and wrapped her arms around her knees. Her whole body was aching, a strange cocktail of desire and despair. The loneliness she kept bottled up so deep inside her rose to the fore and emerged in a sob.

Francine stood in the rear of the motorhome and watched her in silence. She felt so sorry for the young woman in front of her. Kate had everything money could buy but that could never compensate for the desire to be loved by another human being. All her attitudes stemmed from a deep insecurity that she couldn't let show. Not wanting to upset her further Francine stepped back into the massage room and closed the door. Poor Kate. If Declan had been a torment to her before he would be the very devil to her from now on.

The devil, however, was concerned with nothing other than the clock the following morning. Any signals sent and received in the heat of an Australian night were forgotten and throughout the final practice session, he spoke to only Carlo and Peter. He did his duty by the team with the press and in hospitality, but his mind was clearly on his job.

By the end of Saturday's qualifying session, he had secured himself a place on the front row of the grid, only hundredths of a second behind his friend and rival Kurt Braun who held the pole position. Fabio, having settled in his car and regained his confidence, had driven far better than he had hoped and was five places behind. Not a blinding start, but a solid one, and good enough. So, the scene was set for the first Grand Prix of the season; all they could do now was wait.

CHAPTER 13.

The grid was swarming with people: press, camera crews, sponsors, mechanics, and celebrities getting some free publicity. There was barely enough room for the cars themselves. The drivers, being shaded from the heat by the beautiful grid girls; all wearing sponsors' logos and bearing large sun umbrellas, were sipping energy drinks through straws, and trying to keep a clear head in the face of all this activity. Carlo was checking his cars for the final time; the tyres were wrapped in their blankets to get them up to the right temperature. Fabio was silent, concentrating on keeping calm, Declan, true to form, was arguing with Peter.

"We've got the wrong bloody tyres on, I'm telling you. I shouldn't be on slicks, look at that bloody big cloud over there. It'll be pissing down after ten laps!"

"Carlo, will you talk to him?" Peter pleaded. "He thinks it's going to rain. Tell him he's wrong."

"The forecast is for a hot and dry day Declan" Carlo soothed. "It is not going to rain."

"If I lose my position because I have the wrong tyres on" Declan snarled in reply, "I'll shove the weather forecast up your fat Italian arse!"

"Declan," Carlo was untouched by the outburst. "Do everyone a favour and shut up!"

Turning to the amused Gerald, Carlo escorted him back to the monitors stand from where they and Peter would keep an eye on the race and study each car's performance. Kate, having completed a heated discussion with a track security guard, came to join them.

"Bloody Declan!" She gasped. "The pratt left his identity pass in his room and I've just had hell getting him into the pits. Would you believe that the man had never heard of him? Bloody idiot."

"Typical Declan." Gerald chuckled. "He's out there now giving everyone hell."

"Glad you find it so funny." Kate snapped her voice on the edge of breaking.

"It's a good sign." Gerald chuckled. "He's uptight. As long as his back is up, he'll be brilliant. Believe me."

"I bloody hope so." Peter joined them and reached for his radio. "He is absolutely foul today!"

The grid was cleared as the klaxon sounded; the formation lap was about to begin. The snake of vehicles began to move around the circuit; obliged by the regulations not to overtake on the formation lap, the drivers weaved to and fro across the track warming brakes and tyres. This was the dress rehearsal. When the red lights went out it would be opening night.

"Everything okay Declan mate?" Peter spoke

into the radio. "No problems?"

"I should bloody well hope not " Declan snapped, his voice taught. "We haven't started yet!"

"Good luck boys," Gerald spoke calmly. "Safe drive both of you."

Sitting, rigid in his cockpit, Declan tapped his fingers on his steering wheel and stared ahead; eyes fixed on the five lights that hung above the track. His heart was pounding, beating faster and faster as adrenalin flooded his system. He wanted to be off and racing, not sitting in the metal caterpillar waiting for everyone to get into position. This was the only part he hated, the part that freaked him out; these few, agonising minutes waiting for the red lights to go out. Then, after a few heart-stopping moments he would be fine. The final light turned red. He revved the engine, set the clutch, and waited. The lights went out; and in a deafening cacophony of noise, tyres screaming and engines roaring, the Australian Grand Prix began.

A statistician had once recorded that a driver's heartbeat at rest was some fifty beats per minute, but that on reaching the first corner of a Grand Prix it increased to one hundred and fifty. Fabio felt every thump of those one hundred and fifty beats against his chest as he was carried into the first bend and thought, frozen with panic, for a split second that he was going to pass out. Too terrified to be tactical, he just managed to hold his position and set out on the first lap, desperately trying to control his erratic pulse.

At the head of affairs, Declan and Kurt were streaking away from the rest of the field, and by the end of the first lap, they already had a one-and-a-half-second advantage. Declan, always the thruster, was trying to pass the Austrian at every opportunity; but Kurt was not world champion by chance, and although the blue Matros filled his wing mirror at every braking point he would not let it pass.

On the computers the car's telemetry readouts were good.

Carlo nodded in satisfaction as he studied the times.

"Stay on him Fabio, if you get a chance to pass take it, but don't get caught in his dirty airflow."

"He's doing okay." Gerald watched the car flash by on the screen. "Just keep him calm."

At the front, Declan was still fighting with Kurt, but could not break the Austrian, whose car was pulling away on every straight.

"Next time Declan." Pete watched another abortive attempt on the monitor. "Push harder; you can get past."

"Fuck off Trent" Was the reply. "Who's driving this thing, me or you?"

"Charming." Peter grinned. "You say the nicest things."

"Up yours." Declan retorted." If this bloody Austrian doesn't get out of my way soon, you'd better X rate this radio."

It was such a contrast, the banter with Declan to the cool, calm encouragement that was transmitted to Fabio. The Italian was driving a very solid race and had moved up into fifth position but was a long way off the leaders. "You're doing well." Carlo was pleased. "Just try and stay in the points."

With eighteen laps of the race gone, almost one-third distance, the teams whose drivers were on a two-stop strategy began to think of calling them in. Overhead, the black cloud that Declan had spotted had moved closer and was now sitting very menacingly right above the Melbourne circuit. The waters of the lake were beginning to swell as the wind increased.

"Oh oh." Peter looked skyward. "Don't tell me that he was right after all, please!"

But he was. At the start of the twenty-second lap, the first drops fell and soon turned the dry track into a greasy skating rink.

"It's raining." Declan roared. "I bloody told you Trent you prick! Why didn't you listen to me? I'm like fucking Bambi out here! "

"We're getting ready to bring you in, Declan," Carlo commanded. "We have intermediates ready for you."

"Like hell!" Declan yelled. "And let this Austrian get the run on me? No way!"

"Declan." Gerald was quite cool." Come in when you see your pit board. That's not a request, that's an order, you'll only be stopping a few laps early. We'll have you in the box first."

But as the mechanics stood ready the Matros flew past the pit lane entrance.

"What the hell are you playing at Hyde?" Carlo roared.

"I'm okay," Declan replied. "I can handle it, I'm staying out."

"Get in here!" Carlo shrieked.

"No!" Declan shouted back. "I'm coming in when I'm due and not before."

"Sod you, you arrogant English prick." Hissed Carlo.

Gerald's colour was rising.

"Get Fabio in. Let's have at least one car on the right tyres. If Declan spins off, I'll knock him out myself!"

Fabio obeyed his pit board and came in on the next lap. He was enjoying himself now and waited calmly while his tyres were changed, and fuel was added to his car. Back on the track he felt the improved grip of the fresh tyres and, full of confidence, set off to regain his position. The race was changing rapidly now as car after car came into the pits to change tyres and refuel. Only the race leader and his aggressor showed no interest in returning to the garages. Carlo, watching Declan sliding around every corner on the wet surface, wrestling with his steering wheel, was losing his temper. Spotting one of the rear tyres starting to blister he growled into the radio.

"Declan! Box, Box. Box this lap. Look in your right mirror, that tyres on its way out; unless you want to end your race on three wheels in the gravel pit, you had better get your cocky backside in here! Now!"

Out on the track, Declan, who was not replying to his radio, was aware of the problem and could feel his already tentative grip on the glass-like surface disappearing by the second. He decided to play it by the book and obeyed his pit board on the next lap. Seeing the Matros turn into the pit lane Kurt saw his chance and told his team he was staying out for another lap to consolidate his lead. It was a bad decision. Trying to put in a really fast lap Kurt came across a very out-of-control young Spaniard, who clipped Kurt's rear wing as he passed and took them both off the track. The news greeted Declan over the radio.

"Braun is OFF. Repeat Braun is OFF. You have P1."

Despite his early pit stop, despite all the defiance, he was now the race leader. A grin split Declan's face from ear to ear as he set sail for home. The race wore on into its final laps. Cars were retiring thick and fast as engines succumbed to early season problems and failed to last the distance. Little flaws that had not shown themselves in testing made dramatic appearances as car after car ended the race in a cloud of white smoke. Fabio found himself in fourth place and, encouraged, began to push harder.

"Easy Fabio," Carlo warned. "Don't overdo it. You are in a good position, nurse that engine and get home with some points on the board. It's been a brilliant first drive."

But Fabio, for the first time that day, wasn't listening. He was enjoying himself too much. He could see the red livery of the third-placed car in front of him and he knew he could catch it. Images of podium positions flashed into his mind, and he began to give chase. Turning into what would be the home straight in three laps time he flattened the throttle. The car jerked, shuddered, and slowed as a cloud of smoke billowed out behind it.

"Shit" Carlo put his hand to his head. "He's blown it!"

Fabio managed to cruise to one of the runoffs at the side of the track and got out of the car, slamming his gloves onto the track in temper. Standing back, he watched with a very gloomy face as his car was swiftly removed from the track under a safety car. At least he had a short walk back to the garage. He was incapable of speaking to anyone. He just stood and watched the final lap on the monitor in silence. Declan now had a staggering twenty-second lead. There was no way, barring accidents, that he could be caught; but with the memory of Fabio's engine fresh in their minds the pit crew held their breath as he embarked on his final lap. They need not have worried. Declan cruised into the home straight and with a triumphant salute to his delighted crew who were hanging over the pit wall waving and yelling like idiots, he took the chequered flag. In front of the monitor, Carlo was leaping up and down and hugging Peter, who in turn was slapping an emotional Gerald on the back. At the rear of the garage, Fabio stood alone. He was pleased for his team and for Declan but for himself he was bitterly disappointed. Francine, her eyes alight with excitement, appeared beside him.

"Remember." She said kindly. "It is the noble gesture that is always remembered. Swallow your feelings and go and greet him. He'll thank you for it."

Fabio smiled at her, kissed her cheek and, the forgotten figure amongst the celebrations, made his way to join the victorious crew.

It was a great party. The Matros team left the official post-race event and toured Melbourne's bars and clubs with an enthusiasm that didn't begin to wane until three a.m. Then, one by one, they straggled back to their hotel, to catch a few precious hours of sleep before the morning journey back to England. Declan, despite his aggression towards the Austrian on the track, loved Kurt's company off it and was involved in another tussle with him, this time at arm wrestling. Surrounded by a group of drivers who had tagged along for the fun they tussled through a few bouts until, this time, Kurt was declared the victor.

"Time to be gone." Kurt was having more trouble than usual with his command of the English language. "I think I am too much in the piss."

"So do I." Declan emptied his glass. "I am coming home to bed with you."

"No. No. " Kurt shook his narrow, high-browed face vigorously. "I am not this way I tell you; I have a wife."

"Idiot." Declan chuckled. "I didn't mean I am going to bed *with* you. I mean I am also going to bed. Alone."

"Ah." Kurt smiled. "This is good. I did not mean to make a fence with you."

"This conversation stopped making sense hours ago." Carlo looked over his shoulder. "We have lost an Italian. Where is Fabio?"

A quick search revealed that Fabio was in one of the darkest corners of the bar with his hand down the top of a pretty waitress.

"Oh, tut tut." Declan pulled him away. "Behave young man. Mustn't upset the boss's daughter, must we? I've seen the way she looks at you!"

"Why?" Fabio looked longingly back at his waitress. "She is not here to see it."

"And if she was, she wouldn't be impressed at a quick grope behind the optics. Miss Matthews is just not like that."

"Like what?" Fabio followed him, in not too straight a line, out of the club.

"Haven't you noticed?" Declan linked arms with him. "Little Miss Refrigerated. Fancy a bet? Think you can defrost her?"

"I would not dare." Fabio shook his head. "She would get me the sack."

"Instead of in it? I suppose you are right. I just wondered if a Latin Lover would be to her taste. Irishmen it seems are not."

"Why?" Fabio frowned. "Have you tried?"

"Wouldn't dare." Declan grinned. "She'd take my head from my shoulders. Where would I be without this masterpiece on top of my neck? "

They wandered through the streets of Melbourne for a little longer until returning to their hotel. Declan wished Fabio a good night and stood alone in the lobby for a few minutes. Tomorrow they would go their separate ways; but not for long, as they would be back at the factory for some time in the simulator in a few days, before the circus moved on to the heat and humidity of Malaysia. So it began, this would be their life for the next nine months, and with a little bit of luck, they would both still be standing at the end of it.

CHAPTER 14.

Declan loved his Monaco apartment, high above the marina overlooking the blue waters of the Mediterranean. From the right-hand side of his balcony, he could see the very road that would take the cars along the Marina straight on Grand Prix Day in a few months' time. He liked this place. He liked to sit out at the cafes and watch the beautiful people go by; he liked the food, the wine, the glitzy lifestyle, and most of all he liked his escape from the crippling grip of the British taxman.

His apartment had been kept in immaculate condition by his hired maid and when he walked into the kitchen, he found that the fridge had been freshly stocked with his favourite cheeses and a bowl of fruit sat on the work surface. Contented, he sat on his leather sofa, turned up the volume on his stereo to maximum and closed his eyes. He always had trouble coming "down" after a race, particularly a win; not that he had experienced that feeling too often in his career, or at least, not as often as he would like. Sunday's race was the best yet. He was very close to Gerald and was desperate to make him proud, it had been worth all the effort to see the satisfaction on the man's face. He knew that when it came to winning, he and Gerald were on exactly the same page. Closing his eyes, reliving that final, exhilarating lap, he drifted off into sleep.

He had not been asleep long when he was disturbed by his mobile. Hanging off the sofa to reach it he rubbed his bleary eyes and struggled with his still sleepy, uncooperative voice.

"Hello?" He croaked.

"Congratulations darling. How is the hangover?"

Declan paused for a second, unable to recognise the voice, and was afraid that it belonged to some forgotten conquest that he had made a rash promise to the last time he had stayed here.

"Declan are you there?"

Got it. He relaxed and sat upright. It was Bernice, Kurt's pretty devoted wife who was also one of Declan's closest friends.

"Sorry sweetheart." He apologised. "I didn't recognise the voice for a second."

"That's because it's been so long since you spoke to me." Bernice scolded. "So how is the new hero?"

"Tired." Declan yawned. "Is the man home?"

"I sent him to the shops." Bernice laughed. "To buy supper. Would you like to join us? A little celebration, just the three of us?"

"No blind dates?" Declan remembered Bernice's last supper invitation with a chuckle.

"None."

"Promise?"

"On my honour. Was the last one so bad? She liked you, a lot. Never mind, a pity. Still, see you in about two hours?"

"Lovely." Declan lay on the sofa and put his feet up on the armrest. "See you soon sweet cheeks."

After another half hour lounging on his sofa, Declan took a long, leisurely shower and dug some clean jeans and a cotton shirt out of his suitcase. He had a wardrobe full of designer chic in this apartment, but he seldom wore it, except on special occasions. Supper with Kurt and his wife didn't class as a special occasion. He could walk down the hill to their apartment, nearer to the water's edge than his own, and he strolled through the cool evening air, looking into the bars and restaurants as he did, checking out the town's new inhabitants. Ten minutes later he was standing outside the Braun's apartment, bottle in hand, listening to the chaos of two toddlers being ushered quickly to bed. Kurt answered the door, wearing only shorts, hair still wet.

"Come in "He led the way into the kitchen and opened the fridge. "The children are excited because I am home and will not go to bed."

"And they want to see the man who beat their father."

Bernice stood in the doorway, small, slim and with her brown hair cut into a bob that she hadn't had time to brush yet, her arms filled with two giggling, blonde-haired children.

"There. You have seen him. Shall we take him out on the boat one day? Yes? Okay, right bed. NOW!"

Sitting in the dining room that overlooked the bobbing, pale shapes of the yachts in the marina, Declan took the cold beer that Kurt offered him and looked around.

"Been decorating?"

"Bernice," Kurt explained. "She has to change the colour every spring."

"Bored." Declan chuckled. "Get her a job."

"I heard that." Bernice stood in the doorway. "I have a full-time job looking after those kids. How are you Declan?"

"All the better for seeing you. If you weren't married to this lucky bugger, I'd have to think twice about it myself."

Bernice, despite her European-sounding name, was in fact, English. She had met Kurt five years ago when she was his grid girl at the British Grand Prix. Unable to take his eyes off her slender figure and pretty hazel eyes, Kurt had tracked her down and pestered her until she had agreed on dinner. Within three months they were engaged, in another three married, and ten months later Bernice gave birth to the first of the mischievous imps she had just bustled into bed. They were blissfully happy together, a state that Declan, although he could not personally appreciate the benefits of monogamy, was frequently jealous of. He thought Bernice was the most generous, warm-hearted person he knew, and he could fully appreciate why Kurt wanted to spend the rest of his life with her. If Bernice had a fault, it was that she was intent on finding Declan his perfect soul mate and frequently kept producing likely candidates. Watching her serve the first course he realised how lucky he was to have two such good friends and how much he missed their company when he was away. Raising his glass, he nodded at Kurt.

"Here's to the season." Declan raised an eyebrow. "May the best man win."

"Sure." Kurt agreed. " As long as it is me."

Declan laughed. He wanted to win, he wanted to be the World Champion. But, if he couldn't do it himself, then he would be more than happy to see his closest friend take the crown.

CHAPTER 15.

In Rome, Fabio was keeping a very low profile. He was not finding life in the family home as easy as it had been. He had flown the nest; returning to it was not easy. Sitting in his room, the Sunday after Melbourne, he came to a decision. He had, as he could see it, only one way out of the situation. He had to move from Italy permanently and put distance between himself and not only his family but this ridiculous notion that he was still going to marry Sophia. Why on earth would he do that? He had his own life to lead and fulfilling drunken promises made by two men over dinner one night was not part of it. There would be repercussions, no doubt, but he would rather be disinherited than be forced into a marriage with someone he didn't love. The problem was where he should live. It would make sense to be closer to the factory, but he was wary of the tax system that would catch up with him. He quite fancied Monaco but didn't want to be thought of as copying his co-driver. So, he settled on Britain, to begin with. It was just a matter of where. Carlo was a little surprised when he received Fabio's call that evening.

"You want to buy a house here?"

"Yes." Fabio didn't sound convinced. "Or maybe I can rent one, but long term this time, something permanent."

"In this wet cold hole of a country?" Carlo chuckled. "If I didn't work here, I would be back in Milan on the next flight."

"Not forever." Fabio had a smile in his voice. "Only until I know where I really want to be. I just know I cannot stay here Carlo; it is a casa pazzo!"

Carlo quickly thought he could smell a rat.

"Fallen out with the family?" As a fellow Italian Carlo knew what being part of such a close unit could be like.

"Something like that. Let's just say that when we return from Brazil, I want to have my own place to go to. "

"Well, I'm not the best one to ask. If I was you, I'd try Kate. After all, she is your manager, she's there to advise."

"Mmm." Fabio mused. "I had not thought of her."

"Well do. But not tonight. Even Kate deserves some peace."

Fabio smiled as he hung up the receiver and grinned. His mind went back to the conversation he had held with Declan in Australia. What better way to seduce the lovely Miss Matthews than by looking at bedrooms all day?

His mother, as he had expected, was not at all happy at the thought of her beloved baby boy leaving home. He had thought of not telling her until the deal was done, but he couldn't hurt her like that. Sitting at the table, sipping a steaming espresso he watched her face changing.

"But why Fabio? Why cannot you make your home here?"

"Because I need to be closer to my job Mama. That is all.

"But all the other drivers, they do not live in England surely?"

" Some. At least for part of the year. Cheer up, you can come and visit me."

"But Raymondo will not like it. Having Sophia so far away."

"Sophia." Fabio took a deep breath. "Will not be with me."

" What?" Realisation dawned on his mother's face. "You are not going to marry her, are you?"

"No." Fabio took her hand. "It was never going to happen Mama. You must have known that."

His mother stared out of the window and took a deep trembling breath.

"Your father?"

"I will deal with him." Fabio squeezed her hand. "Don't worry."

"When do you leave?" There was a tremble in her voice now.

"Tomorrow. I am meeting Kate at the airport; she has some houses for us to look at."

"Kate?" His mother frowned. "She is your employer's daughter, isn't she?"

"Yes." Fabio could see an escape route opening

up as he spoke.

"You care for her mio figlio? "

Not in the way you think, Fabio thought, I don't love her, but if it helps me to get away, I will let you think that.

"Yes." He lied.

"In that case, you must go." His mother got up. "I will tell your father about this woman when you are gone. He will not like it, but there are many things that he does not like. Raymondo will have to look somewhere else for his daughter's fortune."

So that was it Fabio thought grimly. That was the real reason behind this lifelong insistence that he marry Sophia; his father's estate and what it meant for her family. Well, if they wanted it, they could have it, but not through him. He had his own life to lead, and it was only just beginning.

His mother watched him walk out of the kitchen and felt her throat tightening. Fabio was her youngest, her baby, and she had wanted to keep him home as long as possible. Once he was gone her reason for existing would begin to fade. But she could not hold him back; and although it would break her heart to see him leave, she knew she had to let him go.

CHAPTER 16.

Kate met Fabio's flight at the airport, and as promised, took him straight to the first house she had picked out for him. She had not considered any leasehold properties; Fabio could always sell when he had decided to move on or keep the place as an investment. As the team's manager, she felt it her duty to secure him the best deal; personally, and also from a work point of view, she was more than happy to encourage him to settle in England. Driving along the M40 towards Oxford, she thrust a large brown envelope onto his lap.

"All in there." She said shortly. "Have a look and see what you think."

Trying to keep her eyes on the road, Kate saw him flicking through the details out of the corner of her eye. She knew which one she would pick, but she mustn't influence him. Beside her, Fabio was completely lost. They all looked attractive, these country cottages she had picked for him, there were even some elegant Oxford townhouses, but the prices! He knew that house prices in England were high but had not quite been prepared for this. Of course, the money was not a problem, but it seemed a lot to pay just to get away from a clinging family and the threat of a marriage.

"I picked Oxford because I didn't think you would want to be living on top of us, and there are some other drivers living there so you would have company if you wanted it." Kate's voice broke into his thoughts.

"Thank you." Fabio was truly grateful. "But I do not socialise much with other drivers."

"You and Declan seem pretty close."

"That is just Declan." Fabio grinned at the thought. "I like him. He makes me relaxed. The only way to beat him, I think, is to join him!"

Kate laughed.

"You may well be right there Fabio. Maybe I should try that! Have you seen anything you like yet?"

Oh, what an opening. He couldn't resist it.

"Yes, I have."

"Oh really? Which one?" Kate glanced at him.

"You."

Silence. A silence that very quickly became embarrassing.

"I am sorry" Fabio shook his head. "That was a stupid thing to say and now I have embarrassed you."

"No." Kate's voice chose that moment to disobey her and came out as a squeak. "I am just surprised, that's all."

"Not pleased?" Fabio was beginning to feel a little hurt by this reaction.

Am I? Thought Kate. I'm not sure. Images of Declan danced before her eyes and the smell of hot body and oil poked at her memory banks.

"I'll think about it." She said lightly. "It's a very nice thing to say but I never think of pleasure when I am working. What about these houses?"

"I like them all. But I do not think I am a country boy, not if I am living on my own. I like the people."

"Right." Kate flicked the indicator. "Oxford it is then."

Gerald was pleased that Fabio had decided to come to England. He could call on his services more readily in between races, and he liked the fact that the boy was standing on his own two feet. Listening as Kate described the houses, they had visited he nodded in approval.

"They all sound wonderful darling. You've done a good job. Where is he now?"

"With Carlo. I would have asked him here, but."

"But what?" Gerald's eyes twinkled.

"Too awkward. He's happy where he is. Now, how have you been today?"

"Fine." Gerald lied. "Just fine. I've been looking at some aerodynamic changes Carlo wants to make; I think they will work well."

"Cars!" Kate snorted. "Bloody cars, that's all I get!"

"I know," Gerald admitted. "But it will be worth it when we have a title under our belt."

"I bloody well hope so." Kate shook her head. "Now where did I put my mobile?"

"In your bag." Gerald leaned across her and handed her the 'phone. "Who are you calling sweetheart?"

"Mother." Kate looked at him, awaiting a response and not getting one. "The whole bloody show will be back here in two days, and I need some space. As you insist on being well enough to manage, I'll go and see Mum and have a break."

"A break?" Gerald was amused. "We've only just got back from Australia!"

"Call babysitting your imbecile drivers a break?" Kate snorted. " I mean a real break without an engine in sight."

"Oh well." Gerald leaned back in his chair. "Go on then. A couple of days will do you good. But I need you here before we leave for Malaysia, the ship can't sail without the captain."

"Balls." Kate gave him a dirty look. "Some captain."

"You know what I mean." Gerald smiled at her indignant face.

"As long as you can take care of yourself." Kate frowned wondering just how wise the action to leave her father would be.

"Me!" Gerald laughed. "I was taking care of myself long before you came along, remember?"

The laugh sounded genuine enough, but inside Gerald's heart was quaking. He was good at being confident while Kate was here, while he had the security of another human being in the house. But once she was gone would he really be able to cope with the dreadful nausea he was experiencing without her presence? To be left alone in this big house unnerved him but he could not let her see it. Once she sensed his weakness that would be the beginning of the end. He wasn't ready for that, not by a long way. No one but Colin knew the extent of his condition. He had played it down to everyone. So, he let her make her plans, and pack her bags and only when she headed for the airport did he feel the pains in his head and realise the possible error he was making.

Lucy put down the article she had been reading, for the tenth time, and stared at the accompanying photograph. So, he had done it. Mr. Declan Hyde had won the opening Grand Prix of the year. Well done Mr Hyde she thought dryly. Thank you so much for letting me know, or for checking that I was okay after you left me thousands of miles from home. They obviously fixed that car you were so upset about. Until she had read the article it had seemed that he had disappeared off the face of the Earth. She had called so many times and had even left messages on his website. Nothing. He had obviously taken himself off to Monaco, lucky bastard; while she was here, in wet gloomy Cardiff, sitting about her flat and wondering what the hell she was going to do with her life. She still hadn't shaken the anger that his desertion had instilled in her. But how could she seek revenge when she couldn't even find him? It was such a bitter, twisted emotion: this stomach-turning, knife-edged jealousy that was eating her away. Not jealousy of any women Declan may be having, but jealousy of another kind. She was jealous of his life, of his power and his unsinkable confidence and single-mindedness. How could any one man reduce another human being to the depths of despair that he had driven her into? What right had he to be so successful, when everything she attempted was doomed to failure? She hated him. She was sure she did; although she could not fully predict what her reactions would be if he walked through the door.

Before, she had been quite happy with her life; plodding quietly on, with Declan Hyde as the ultimate fantasy in her life that kept her going. Even after the holiday fiasco, she had managed to live a normal existence; not as contented as she had been before without her fantasy to fill her days, because the reality of it was completely different, but that had faded, and she felt she had no life at all. She had lost the ability to go out, to communicate with her course mates. All she could think about was getting her own back on her tormentor. She was desperate to make him suffer, to have him experience the same hurt and rejection that he had put her through. But at the same time, she still felt the longing for him, a memory of her adoration, which made her even more unhappy. She had to reach him somehow, to try and maintain the contact, because if that contact was broken then there would be no way of getting back at him.

Unaware that she was becoming dangerously obsessive, she sat down and turned on her computer.

CHAPTER 17.

Malaysia was a disaster. Despite mammoth efforts from Declan in both practise and qualifying, he could only put the car into the sixth spot on the grid, being over a second off the pole set by Kurt, who had pinched the position with a canny piece of last-minute driving. It was a very humbling start for a man who had begun the year so well and it hurt. Fabio fared even worse and was way back in the sixteenth spot from twenty-two starters. It was easy to find places to lay the blame; unjustified though they may be. The tyre suppliers for trying out a new compound, Carlo for his new wing design which patently wasn't working as well as he had hoped and the pit crew, who were always the easiest people to blame in a crisis, even though they made no changes to the car and just spent long hours looking after it.

With all the flak that was flying about, the garage on race morning was an impossible place to be. It was hard to see either driver improving on their podium position and the disappointment after the euphoria of Melbourne was immense. Kate, never in the most accommodating of moods on race days, sick to the hind teeth of media crews and disgruntled sponsors reached the point where she could take no more.

"Will you all shut up!" She screamed, putting the noisy, rumbling garage into instant silence.

"It doesn't matter whose fault it is; the fact is that yesterday we fucked up, big time! We've all got to do something today to make a better show of it or I won't be taking any more shit for this team do you understand? I've got a bunch of hostile businessmen out there who want some return on their sponsorship. If they walked in here now, we'd lose them all, right on the spot. I've never seen such unprofessional behaviour. So, stop making this bloody racket and think about your jobs."

Behind her, Gerald was smiling. Kate would run his team very nicely if he was ever in a position to have to step down. He had always worried about her commitment, one of the reasons he had stayed out of hospital, but that little outburst left him in no doubt as to where her loyalties lay.

"Good shot girlie." He muttered in her ear. "That put them straight."

Not everyone was as impressed with Kate's speech as her father. Declan, the elastic of his nerves almost at breaking point, stared at her, eyes narrowing as he fought to control his temper. Not wanting to air his vexation in front of the whole garage he walked up to her. Carlo recognised the set of Declan's jaw and watched with interest. He had seen that look before and it usually accompanied scenes of near violence. The mechanics, whilst pretending to work on the much-maligned GM-4, were in fact straining their ears to hear every word of the impending conversation.

"Are you?" Declan spoke very slowly. "Accusing me of not doing my job properly?"

Kate looked at his face, read the stop sign and, with a pumping heart, ignored it.

"If the cap fits." She said shortly. "On yesterday's performance, you are lucky to have a job at all."

"What!" Declan hissed through gritted teeth. "Would you care to run that one past me again?"

"Let me be frank Declan." Kate's haughty voice was grinding Declan's fast-decaying patience into a pulp. "Yesterday you managed to put the car that won the opening race of the season in style a third of the way down the grid. Fact."

"It's in the points, isn't it?" Declan snapped. "And what the fuck do *you* want me to do about it anyway? The car was driving shit, a jellyfish had more spine than that thing yesterday!"

"You get paid three million a year!" Kate retorted "Plus perks and advertising. I don't care if the car feels like a dead tortoise, you give your best, always!"

"Are you saying I don't give everything to this team!" Declan's roar brought a reporter running to the garage entrance. "You bloody sanctimonious spoiled bitch! I drive my fucking arse off out there, and what do I get for support? A lecture from *you*!"

"Well make sure you drive your arse off today." Kate ignored the scarlet colour she knew was flooding through her cheeks. "Or you might find it being kicked out of the door."

"Kate" Gerald had spotted the gathering of people in the pit lane. "That's enough. No one's job is at stake here. Now is not the time, or the place."

"Oh, that's right" Kate deflected her anger onto her father. "I can always rely on you to stick up for him, can't I? You are always telling me to have more interest in how this thing is run; when I do you shoot me down. Maybe your spoiled little pet of a driver is right. We are a little short on support around here!"

Fighting to keep her composure in front of the stunned crew she strode out of the garage and back to her crowd of blissfully unaware sponsors.

The warm-up lap before the race did little to improve tempers in the Matros pit. Declan, still rumbling like a volcano at an erupting point, complained that his brakes were like toffee and had the reactions of a slug. Fabio, secretly agreeing with Declan that the cars were uninspiring chose to keep quiet and concentrate on keeping his on the track. His tyres did not feel as if they were doing their job at all well in the heat and he felt very precarious.

The beginning of the race did little to improve anyone's confidence as a car stalled in the middle of the grid and sent cars spinning wildly in all directions as they tried to avoid it, bundling into the first corner on top of each other. The red flag was out before the first lap was over and the cars were allowed to take their positions and start again. Something that made Kurt the least happy man on the track as he had missed the melee by being in front and had set up a scorching lead. Declan, who had also avoided the muddle, was grateful for the false start as his own had been abysmal, losing two places instantly. Fabio had gone into the gravel on the first corner and sat in position trying to rally his nerves and praying that the same thing wouldn't happen again. But after three laps he found himself dropping pieces of GM-4 all over the track and was forced to make a lengthy pit stop that put him at the back of the field.

Declan, hearing the news on his radio, was having battles of his own: he could not pass the car in front of him whatever he tried to do, he just didn't have the power. He had no confidence in his brakes so couldn't out brake his rival on the corners and had to be content to stay where he was, something that wasn't sitting well on his shoulders. After thirty laps Declan's labouring engine gave up the ghost altogether and he cruised into the garage with a very sour taste in his mouth.

The team's hopes now lay with Fabio who managed to stay on the track and despite badly blistering tyres finished the race in an undistinguished fifteenth place. Depressed by his failure and still rankling after Kate's outburst, Declan bucked the team rules and didn't stay for an engineering de-brief but left the track for the airport before the cars had even reached Parc Ferme. By the time Fabio emerged from his motor home that evening he was already in the air.

Fabio, feeling at a loss without Declan to lead the way post-race sat in the motorhome whiling away time before he returned to his hotel. He would fly home with the team in the morning and could see no reason for changing it. But he missed Declan's lively company, his knowledge of where to go to get the best food and entertainment and to help find a reason for those poor performances. Instead, he found himself looking at Kate who was sitting outside the canteen with a very red face.

"I quit." She said heavily as he stood beside her. "I can't take any more questions."

She was so harassed, so exhausted by her day that she could think of nothing but sleep. Fabio saw the shadows under her eyes and the stress etched across her face and felt a pang of sympathy. It must be difficult to shield the team from the prying eyes of the world. He and Declan got all the glory, not that there had been any today but for Kate, it was a never-ending day of talking and smiling and trying to keep everyone happy. Little wonder that sometimes she snapped. She must, he reasoned, be feeling every bit as bad as he was. She could probably do with a drink. Going into the motor home he found two cold bottles of beer and passed her one.

"I think you need this."

Kate looked at the outheld bottle and frowned.

"Not my first choice I have to say but thanks." She looked up and forced a smile. "Today I would drink anything."

"Is it that bad?"

"Worse." Kate leaned back in her seat. "The day from hell!"

Fabio took a mouthful of beer and shuddered slightly. He preferred wine himself or even the real ales they sold in Oxford, not this.

"So" He pulled over a chair and sat beside her. "Tell me about your day."

"What's to tell?" Kate had closed her eyes. "Same shit. Stroppy sponsors, all drinking too much and wanting miracles, people who have paid a bloody fortune to be part of the team "experience" wanting every piece of me they can get, bloody media wanting everyone's inside leg measurements and to top it all off Declan was supposed to do a pre-race with the British T.V crew and he didn't turn up!"

"Did he know about it?" Fabio was drinking his beer too fast and still slightly dehydrated from the race he could feel its effects.

"I don't know." Kate shrugged. "I am sure I told him this morning. It's been on the schedule all week. Although after that barney in the garage, well, you can't really blame him for ignoring me can you."

"No." said Fabio frankly. "I can't. You are too hard on him; he cannot be the best all the time."

"Got you in his pocket as well then?" Kate's face was heavy. "Why am I the only one who can see him for what he is?"

"And what is that?"

"Arrogant, conceited, bloody-minded. That's for starters." Kate's mind flashed briefly back to Melbourne. After today's furore, it was easier to quell her feelings of attraction and replace them with hate.

"I mean where was he today? He was at the airport before you even finished the race, not a word to anyone not even my father. Pig bloody ignorant. That's what he is."

"He needed to get away, that is all." Fabio knew how Declan must have been feeling. "This race was such a disappointment for him. Now he has so much work to do to be back on the front row. Already his place in the points has slipped."

"Does he think I don't realise that?" Kate was watching Fabio's dark eyes and wondering if he knew just how beautiful he was. "I do. Really, I do.

I just wish he could understand this is about so much more than just him."

Fabio shrugged. He knew how highly Declan thought of Gerald but felt that it was not his place to discuss Declan's motivations. Declan had been more than generous to him, and he knew how badly today's failure had hurt him. Declan was so driven by his passion that there were only highs and lows; that smooth contented place in between just didn't exist for him. Looking at his weary-eyed companion he thought how difficult it would be to make her understand the need to be first that was so strong in Declan's character. Finishing his beer, he slid down in his seat stretching his long lean legs towards hers.

"Another drink" He looked at her empty bottle.

"No." Kate shook her head. "I can't stomach another."

Fabio hesitated. He didn't want to leave the sanctuary of the motor home just yet.

"Coffee then. I will make it."

"Yes, please. " Kate smiled. Espresso, please. Two sugars. I need it."

Having made the coffee Fabio brought the two steaming cups outside. They sat there for a few hours, chatting idly about this and that until silence had fallen on the track.

"I should go." Kate looked at the sky and then at the engineers' wheeling racks of tyres and crates past them. "They will need to start packing this up soon, and Dad will be wondering where I am."

"I will walk with you." Fabio took her arm. "It is not safe for a lady in the dark."

"You are such a gentleman." She smiled at him. "Shame it doesn't rub off on Declan!"

Fabio laughed. If Kate knew some of the thoughts that had been going through his head the last few hours, she wouldn't think he was such a gentleman. The temptation to try his luck was very strong but something held him back. Even the thought of taunting Declan with his victory wasn't carrot enough to make the donkey walk forward. It was best this way. For now, at least. He could feel Kate looking up at him. It would be very easy, he knew that, but maybe not the wisest move he could make right now. It would keep.

CHAPTER 18.

Declan walked through the blustery wind, which tasted of salt, and drew a deep breath. It was so refreshing, and it wiped out all the negative thoughts in his head. What was it called? Positive Ions? Or something like that; whatever it was, it worked. Feeling brighter than he had when he had first left the cottage, he began to walk along the harbour wall, watching the waves crashing against the brickwork and sending the boats, none of which had ventured out on such a day, rolling, and tugging against their moorings. He enjoyed this turbulent weather when the sea was at its most potent; it reminded him of how mortal he was. One slip off this wall and those waves would pound his body against the stone, battering all the life out of it. Reaching the end of the wall he looked out into the horizon. The sky was dark, grey, and threatening, and where the water met it there was a pale glow. It would be so easy to believe in mystical floating islands on a day such as this when the sea offered up its secrets.

Turning slowly, he walked back towards the cottage, cold and wet, but not wanting to break this unusual affinity with nature. As he did, the heavens opened and did their worst. He was very quickly soaked to the skin, and he began to run, peering through the sheets of rain that swept across the estuary. As he reached his cottage he saw a figure, tall and slim with dark hair, at the door. He halted, hunched against the rain, trying to identify it. For an unwelcome moment he thought it was Lucy, back to demand answers for his actions; then it turned, and he recognised Fabio. What was he doing here? Feeling the usual displeasure at being disturbed that he always felt when he was here, he began to walk more slowly, almost hoping that Fabio would turn and go. But Fabio had seen him and was waiting, shivering in the wind.

"Ciao." Fabio's fingers were purple as he offered Declan his hand.

"Christ!" Declan was forced to laugh as he felt the icy digits. "It's not that bad!"

Opening the door, he showed Fabio into the kitchen and took his wet jacket, hanging it above the wood-burning stove that heated the cottage.

"I apologise," Fabio was practically sitting on the stove, his jeans steaming in the heat, "For arriving like this."

"No problem." Declan was filling the kettle. It isn't he thought, he had always encouraged the friendship between them and could not expect Fabio to be aware of the hermit-like attitude that took over when he was here.

"To what do I owe the honour?"

Fabio paused, then decided to come clean.

"Kate." He said simply.

Declan looked at him, narrowed his eyes, and then roared with laughter.

"You've done it!" He slapped Fabio on the back. "Round one to you! Cash, okay?"

"No." Fabio shook his head. "I have done nothing. I think perhaps I could have but I decide not to try. I think that it would be not good for me. But I think that now she has a, what do you say? A thing for me and she keep calling my house."

" Really?" Declan felt a pang of something akin to jealousy in his chest.

"I think so." Fabio looked at him earnestly. "I don't know what to do. I do like her, you know? But I do not want to tie myself down to her."

"With her," Declan chuckled. "Tie yourself down with her. Well, you don't have to do you? Nothing happened. You are in the clear. Don't worry she will get over it, women like Kate always do."

"I hope you are right." Fabio looked mournful. "This is my job, my life. I do not want to spoil it."

Declan could see that in Fabio he was dealing with a soul a touch more sensitive than his own. In a way, he was relieved. This thing he had for Kate Matthews was getting out of hand. On one hand, he hated her, on the other he could think of nothing more rewarding than enticing her into his bed. Or anywhere else.

"I know what you mean." Declan patted the younger man's shoulder. " And we have some serious work to do to put this job of ours back on the right road. Once Bahrain is out of the way I have a hell of a week. Nothing but appearances, interviews, and sponsor shit. Then I have to go fix the heating in Cork as my useless brother-in-law can't or won't look at it. I think I could do with a pint."

Fabio brightened.

"That sounds good to me. Maybe we can find a way to improve our performance."

"I find that a pint tends to affect my performance. "Declan laughed. "But as for the cars, all we can do is drive them. The rest is up to Carlo and the boys. But, as you seem to have made a headway with the Ice Queen that I have failed to do, the least you owe me is the chance to thrash you at a game of pool."

Kate drove through the lanes, her foot easing off the accelerator as she drew nearer her target. She was beginning to doubt the logic of this thing that she was about to do and was having second thoughts. But having driven this far, she may as well go through with it; after all, what did she have to lose? Pride, dignity, self-respect; but what were they compared to another evening with Fabio? Having waited patiently for some sort of signal from him, some promise that something was going to happen between them she had decided to take matters into her own hands. If the mountain would not come to Mohammed, then he must go to it. So, she found herself approaching Oxford, growing ever more wary, and slowing to a crawl as she entered the city.

She knew the way to Fabio's house well, after all, she had chosen it, virtually, and turned into the tree-lined road with her heart in her mouth. At the very end, where the road came to such an abrupt halt that it made it difficult to turn without entering someone's driveway, was Fabio's house. Set behind a huge lawn, and shielded from view by massive, ancient oaks, was the four-bedroom house that she had fallen in love with the instant she saw it. Turning into the drive she scanned the forecourt for signs of life. Her heart fell with a crash that made her stomach ache. He was out. All the soul-searching, the decisions, the nerves that had made her feel sick throughout her journey had been in vain. There was to be no meeting with Fabio today.

Turning the car around in front of the house she swallowed her disappointment. She thought of leaving him a note but decided against it; perhaps it would be better if he never knew that she had been here. Shaking her head, she began to feel irritated by her own weakness. How stupid! Driving all this way in the hope that he would be here, why hadn't she just asked him to dinner as any other female would have? Well, she thought, I may as well have something out of today. I can make sure that when we next meet, I look so good he can't fail to be impressed. Fishing into her bag with one hand she pulled out her credit cards, four in all; that should do it. Feeling better already she headed into the city centre.

CHAPTER 19.

The team flew to Bahrain with fingers crossed. Carlo and the crew had worked as men possessed since their return from Malaysia and were sure that they had cracked the problems that had ruined their chances there. It certainly looked that way as the times were improving throughout each practice session and Fabio in particular was scorching the tarmac as he pushed his car to the limit. Declan, fighting off a head cold that made him even more touchy than usual, was clearly below par, but he was happy with his car, and assured Carlo that come qualifying he would be back on the front row. Gerald, who was also suffering in the heat, didn't attend all the sessions, something that worried Carlo, but worried Kate even more, and she had a final attempt to get her father into the hospital when they returned.

"Please, Dad?" She begged. "You look exhausted. Please just go and have another check-up."

"No time." Gerald shook his tender head. "By the time I get an appointment, we'll be in Imola. I have a check-up due the Tuesday after we return. Don't worry it's just this cold dragging me down."

Kate shook her head and sat weakly on the chair, she had been so wrapped up in her stupid emotional battles she had failed to notice how ill her father was looking and was wracked by remorse. If she had been here instead of daydreaming about Fabio, or being eaten up by her hate of Declan, or running her cards up to the limit on clothes and makeup she would have seen what was going on.

"Cheer up." Gerald patted her leg, understanding her expression but not fully appreciating the cause. "I'll be right as rain in two days' time."

"I hope so." Kate's voice was heavy with depression. "I'm coming to the end of my tether."

"Why?" Gerald leaned forward and looked into her face.

"Oh, this and that. I hate you being ill, and I can't face another meeting like Malaysia."

"There won't be one." Gerald was full of confidence. "Reports from the track are glowing. Our Italian friend is flying, Carlo tells me. Why don't you pop down to the track and see for yourself? Then you can tell me if Carlo is lying or not!"

"No." Kate kept her back to him so that he couldn't see the tears in her eyes. "I'll wait. I don't want to find out that he is lying, depressing us before we leave."

Declan, once again the maverick, flew to Bahrain ahead of them. He had some friends who were visiting the country to watch the race and had made a holiday of it. He fancied catching up with them and renewing old acquaintances, especially with the daughter, who would be in her early twenties by now and fair game as far as he was concerned. The rest of the team flew out on Gerald's chartered 747. Fabio, on hearing about Declan's decision to leave early, had been tempted to join him, as he now faced a long flight in close proximity to Kate. He had not seen her since Malaysia and was wary of what her reaction would be on seeing him again. He felt bad that he had not even called her, but he really could not think of anything to say. So, he sat as near to the rear of the seating arrangement as he could, and avoided her eyes for the first few hours. Francine, who was watching him with interest, came and sat beside him.

"Don't be so mean." She smiled. "Can't you see what this is doing to her?"

Fabio didn't look at her but stared at the magazine in his hands.

"Non capisco." He shrugged.

"Rubbish." Francine jogged him with her elbow. "And don't speak Italian hoping that no one else will understand you. I mean Kate. Look at her."

Reluctantly Fabio raised his eyes and saw the red-headed figure in front of him; casually dressed, in jeans and a t-shirt, totally un-Kate, she was beautifully made up and had twisted her hair up into a pleat at the back of her head, letting stray curls hang around her face.

"Doesn't she look lovely?" Francine continued. "I don't think she has made that effort just to sit on a plane for hours, do you?"

"What has it to do with me?" Fabio shrugged.

"Oh, come on!" Francine laughed. "I wasn't born yesterday. I know what happened in Malaysia."

"What?" Fabio looked stunned. "What happened in Malaysia? Nothing happened in Malaysia. We talked. that is all.".

"Then there is no reason not to speak to her." Francine smiled. "Is it that hard?"

"Yes," Fabio whispered. "She thinks I want a romance with her now. She called me many times. I do not know what to say."

"Just go and say hello" Francine persisted. "It is not wise to play with the boss's daughter Fabio."

Despite Francine's urgings, Fabio stayed in his seat. He ran several openings of conversation through his head, but they all sounded contrite, and, he reasoned, he couldn't just get up and go and sit opposite her without drawing attention to them. Having sat in the same spot for nearly five hours he began to feel stiff, so he decided to walk to the toilet and wash his face. Moving slowly down the stairs and along the aircraft, wincing as the craft turned, banking steeply, he found that both cubicles were occupied. Hovering outside he looked out at the clouds. They were so dense that it was easy to believe that if you stepped out you would be able to walk on them. It was a peaceful sight, and away on the edge of his vision, he could see streaks of red, followed by midnight blue, where somewhere in the world there was a sunset.

The door behind him clicked open and shut and he looked over his shoulder straight into the eyes of Kate. She went scarlet and lowered her head, brushing past him.

"Kate." His words came out in a rush. "I am so sorry. I should have returned your calls."

"Yes." Her tone was brisk. "It would have been good manners."

"I am sorry" Fabio felt contrite. "But I did not know what to say. You are a beautiful woman Kate, so beautiful, but I cannot have a relationship with you, you know that."

"Why not?" Kate looked at him. "What's wrong with me?"

"You are the daughter of my boss," Fabio said calmly. "If I hurt you what would become of me."

"So, all my life I have to be the daughter of Gerald Matthews and no one can love me for being me?" Kate's voice cracked. "I would like the chance just to try. For just one man to take a chance on me. I know I can be a bitch Fabio, but my life is so hard and there are things..."

Fabio looked at her and saw tears seeping from her eyes. Cautiously he put his arms around her.

"Ssh." He whispered. "What is it cara? Tell me please don't cry."

Kate looked up at him, desperate to confide in

someone. His eyes were so sincere, so warm, that she could hold it in no longer.

"It's my father." She sobbed. "He's ill, Fabio and I can't make him get the treatment he needs, all he can think about is this bloody team."

"What is wrong?" Fabio hugged her.

She paused. No, she couldn't disclose her fears, the thoughts that haunted her in the deepest moments of the night.

"I can't say. I don't know. But I know there is something. He just won't tell me. But I'm so worried about him."

"Don't be." Fabio was stroking her back, desperate to comfort her.

"He is a wise man; he will not do anything stupid."

"I hope so." The sensation of his circling fingers was making Kate's legs weak. "I hope so."

Feeling his gentle fingers relaxing her tense muscles she dropped her head onto his chest and closed her eyes. It felt so comforting, the proximity of another human being. Being touched, being held, it was something that had been missing from her life for so long.

If only this moment could last.

CHAPTER 20.

Declan met them at the track. Red-eyed, he was suffering from lack of sleep and could not disguise it. The instant he saw Fabio, with Kate some feet behind him, he knew that there had been a new turn of events. If he hadn't struck lucky with the daughter, he might have been jealous. Instead, a little queasy, but otherwise bouncing with confidence, he went to greet them. Falling into step with Fabio he jerked his head in Kate's direction and grinned wickedly.

"Couldn't resist it eh?"

Fabio shook his head.

"It is not like that." He muttered. "She was upset, there is a problem I think but I don't understand."

Looking at him quizzically Declan shook his head and turned into the garage and faced the array of crates, nose cones and parts that could not be easily identified as a GM-4. Carlo, brow puckered as he concentrated, had beaten them to it and was sorting through computer equipment.

"What are you two looking at?" He raised an eyebrow. "Some of us have to work for a living."

In the chaotic motorhome, Francine was making coffee. Seeing Declan, she laughed out loud and handed him a steaming mug of hot, black liquid.

"Here." She gave him a knowing look. "I think you need this."

"Yup." Declan sat down. "I have strayed off the rails in your absence."

"Not too far I hope." Gerald's voice sounded behind them. "And don't do the same thing on the track."

"No chance," Declan said cheerfully, but on seeing Gerald his expression rapidly changed. He had never thought three days could inflict such a change in a man. Gerald's complexion was grey, and he had vast black shadows under his eyes. He looked gaunt and ill, a man in pain.

"Good God" Declan couldn't help himself. "Are you okay?"

"Perfectly." Gerald smiled as broadly as he could. "A cold that's all, and it hasn't taken all this flying too well. I'll be fine after a good night's sleep and some good lap times from you two."

Fabio remembered Kate's words and personally doubted that sleep was all that Gerald needed, but it was not his place to scare his colleagues, so he said nothing but made a mental note to do his very best for his boss that weekend. Gerald certainly did seem better the next day as he watched the first practice session. Both the cars seemed to be back on song and set up some blistering times. Optimistically, the whole team looked forward to Saturday's qualifying.

Declan set himself up for his qualifying laps in his time-honoured way, by spending the previous night with his friend's daughter, who he had decided was bordering on nymphomaniac. She was totally insatiable, and he loved it; a little short on sleep but on a real high he turned in a superb performance to share the front of the grid with Kurt, who was starting to dominate the season. Fabio, trying his hardest, found it all clicking into place at last and put up some good times. Carlo, an old hand at all this, held him in the pits until the very last minute and then sent him out to catch the flag in time for one last flying lap. The old ploy worked, and knowing full well what he had to do Fabio clawed his way with a fierce drive onto the third row in fifth place.

The whole team was jubilant, not least Gerald, who had a smile from ear to ear. He looked so much better today that Fabio thought Kate must be paranoid, Gerald was as healthy as the next man and was probably just working too hard. He had not had much contact with Kate during the sessions, but tonight they were going to have dinner together. He felt that he could at least enjoy her company if nothing else, it took the edge off the loneliness he sometimes felt at night and he knew she needed someone to talk to, desperately. He needed to be away from the track and hospitality and prying eyes so that they could get to know each other. Leaving Declan to some clandestine meeting he had arranged, about which he wouldn't comment. Fabio showered and dressed in eager anticipation of the evening's events.

Gerald, finding himself alone for once, which was a blissful change, also steered away from the busy atmosphere of hospitality and ate in his room. He was not really hungry as he had a constant sickness in his stomach. Foreign food and drink never did agree with him and even the water seemed too much for him in his current state. Sitting on the balcony of his hotel room he looked out over Sakhir and saw the Palace in the distance. Through the darkening sky, the city lights were already blazing in the early evening, and up above stars were beginning to appear in the dark blue expanse

The skies here seemed so close. Gerald thought of the open spaces of the desert and wished that the Grand Prix circuit took in fewer cities, it would be so pleasant to be looking at open spaces instead of the lights of the city and listening to the buzz of noise from below. He was not a city dweller by heart and longed for more tranquil scenes. The noise rising from the street was irritating him, a constant droning that made his head hurt.

He must be getting old.

Sipping his last glass of scotch, he settled back into his chair. This was tranquil he supposed, in its way; sitting here alone with the lights and the sounds of the city as his only companions. Narrowing his eyes, he watched the lights blurring and fading as the evening wore on until finally his eyes closed and everything went black.

CHAPTER 21.

Declan sprang out of the taxi, flashed his security pass at the heavily moustached guard and bounced past the assembled fans and media into the paddock. Sated, well fed, he was healthy, happy, and brim-full of confidence; the beast was back in action and Kurt Braun had better watch his skinny arse.

Mounting his scooter and making his way to the pit lane to touch base with Pete he was struck by how quiet the place was. He was late, not early, yet no engines hummed, there were no junior cars on the track, and everywhere he looked he was met with heavy eyes and solemn faces. Not a single smile. Approaching the Matros garage he saw Carlo hovering, stepping from foot to foot, looking up and down the row of garages with anxious eyes.

"Declan!" He caught sight of him and halted. "There you are. Where have you been for God's sake!"

"Sorry." Declan gave a cheerful shrug. "I'm not that late, am I?"

Halting outside the garage entrance he peered inside. The mechanics were sitting on the floor staring in gloomy silence at his GM-4 which was still wearing its cover. Pete had his head in his hands. For a second Declan felt the claws of panic grip him and his head spun.

"What's going on Carlo?"

He noticed the Italians' red-rimmed eyes for the first time and his heart began to pump faster.

"I have tried all night to call you." Carlo's voice was shaking. "Gerald is dead."

The world around Declan began to reel and he thought he would faint. Great rushes of heat pulsed through his body, and he breathed deeply trying to fight them off. His legs were suddenly weak, unable to carry him anymore and leaned against the wall.

"What?" He could barely speak. "How!"

"Kate found him last night. Sitting on his balcony just as if he was asleep. He died last night at the hospital."

"But how?" Declan's voice was beginning to break, and he knew he could not control it much longer.

"It was a brain haemorrhage. He had a tumour that no one knew about. Kate knew he was ill, but not what it was, only that he had been seeing a doctor. He wouldn't have the operations he needed or the drugs. He wanted to race."

"Oh God." Declan's mind was a maelstrom of emotions. A quagmire of sorrow, loss, anger, and pity. Kate had known that her father was ill and had kept it to herself. What must she have gone through? A wave of compassion washed over him.

"Where is she?"

"She is at the hospital with my wife. There are," Carlo paused. "Formalities."

Declan looked wildly round like a cornered animal looking for escape. This couldn't be happening. Not today. Not to Gerald, not to the team, not to himself. Horrified as he was at the thought, he knew that unless he saw for himself, he would never believe it.

"Declan!" Carlo called after him. "Where are you going?"

"To the hospital." Declan swallowed his tears and the fear that was welling inside him. "I have to see him."

"But Declan." Carlo shook his head. "There is nothing you can do."

"Yes, there is. I can say goodbye."

Kate hardly recognised the ashen-faced, red-eyed figure that walked slowly along the corridor towards her. All the bounce, the arrogance, the self-confidence had gone. He looked lost, deflated, broken. Letting go of Francine's arm, which she had clung to ever since they had arrived, she got to her feet. Declan's eyes were fixed on hers as he approached them and one glance told her that he was in as much torment as her. Declan Hyde was baring his soul to the world as he fought with his emotions. He stopped in front of her and she could see that he was shaking.

"Oh, Kate." Even the voice was different. "Where is he?"

"In there." She nodded to the room behind them. "I'm waiting for the doctor. They have to sign papers before I can make arrangements to take him home."

"May I?" Declan shuddered as he spoke.

"Of course." Kate looked at him and found herself overwhelmed with sympathy. She had never seen him look afraid before, but now he looked terrified.

And he was. Declan was more afraid of stepping into that room than he had ever been of anything in his life. He hated death and had avoided contact with it all his life, even staying away from his own father's funeral. He was horrified by the finality of it all. But the man who lay in that room had been more than a father to him: he had given life to all of Declan's dreams, had stood by him when things went wrong, and had kept his feet on the floor when he was being swept away by the adulation that followed him everywhere. But most of all Gerald had let him be himself. He could not begin to imagine an existence without him.

Taking a deep breath, steeling himself to face whatever lay within Declan opened the door and stepped into the room. Through narrowed eyes, he looked at the still figure on the bed. It was pale, but looked so peaceful, as if Gerald was merely asleep. One hand lay on the covers. With shaking fingers, Declan reached out to touch it and found that it was stone cold. With a gasp, Declan recoiled and stepped back. This couldn't be happening; this was a nightmare and at any moment he was going to wake up. It had to be; this could not be real. His eyes took in the machines, the now silent monitors and then looked back to the motionless figure on the bed. Sinking to his knees he laid his head on the bed and said a silent prayer to the God that he had never believed in. Kate stood in the doorway and watched him with a breaking heart. Looking up Declan saw her familiar face, no longer haughty, but lost and bewildered; saw the tears that slipped silently down her cheeks, and could contain his own no longer. With a great sob, he went to her, took her in his arms, and cried like a child.

They stood there, silent, and grim-faced and faced the choice they had to make. Carlo and Pete, both torn by their indecision. No one would blame them if they withdrew from the race. But unspoken among them was a wish to do this thing, to do it for Gerald, to put his beloved GM-4 in first place. But how? How could they do their jobs with their minds and hearts in such turmoil? To race would mean going out cold, as they had missed the morning's practice. But, and far more importantly, they did not want to appear callous to the eyes of the world which they knew were watching them closely. They needed someone to make the decision for them. To guide them, to send them into the battle. But they were lost, they were an army without their general. It was Carlo who finally broke the silence.

"We are running out of time." His voice was quiet. I have to tell the FIA if we will run or not."

"We will." A voice behind them made them all turn. Kate, white-faced but composed, stood in the corner of the garage.

"I have already told them." She continued. "It's what my father would have wanted.

"What?" Declan was sitting on the floor beside his car, his eyes swollen from crying. "You can't be serious? I can't drive with all this going on in my head!"

"I am serious," Kate said grimly. " There will be a minute's silence before the start of the race then you drive this race as if he was still here."

"I can't!" Declan shook his head. "No way. I can't concentrate, it will be too dangerous."

"Make yourself concentrate." Kate's voice softened. "It's the same for all of us, Declan."

"Is it?" Declan looked at her with eyes so filled with sorrow that she felt her heart wrench. "I don't think so. One slip, one moment of weakness, and Fabio and I are in big trouble. You have to focus on this job and right now I can't. I am sorry Kate but I can't drive that car today."

"Then you had better listen to me." Her voice was shaking. "Until my father's will is read, I am in charge of this team and I have told the FIA we will compete. So, consider it an order. You will drive or be in breach of your contract. My father gave his life to this team, it seems now he gave his life *for* this team."

Declan stared at her, not believing the words that had just come out of her mouth. Was this the same woman who, only a few short hours earlier, had stroked his hair and held him while he cried in her arms? The woman who was soft, warm, and compassionate?

"I am sorry," Fabio spoke quietly from his corner of the garage. "If Declan will not drive then I will not also. I think for respect we will all stay here."

"Carlo please!" Kate turned to him. "Don't you understand? My father died because of these bloody cars. He turned down something that could have saved his life so that he could be here for the season. Now he's gone, forever. I am sorry if you think I've done the wrong thing, but tell them please, if not for me then for my father. He can't have died in vain."

There was silence. They all stood, deep in their thoughts, each one waiting for another to react.

"It's okay." Declan got to his feet. Kate's words had moved him into action far more effectively than any threat could have done. "We'll drive. We will do our best for Gerald. But you can't be hard on us if we fail."

A full complement of cars took to the grid for the formation lap, and when they moved off all eyes were on the two Matros drivers, watching for signs of weakness. They showed none. For Carlo, at the monitors with an empty space beside him, it was a good sign. Perhaps in the heat of battle, they would forget everything.

He was wrong.

After two laps Declan, who started badly and moved back two places instantly, began to lose his way. He dropped steadily backwards through the field until he was almost last. Only then did he finally give up the battle with his emotions and turn into the garage. With the eyes of the world upon him, he sat in his car, helmet still on his head, and slumped on the steering wheel. He made no attempt to get out but sat there, a motionless figure, alone and lost in the world that was all that he knew.

CHAPTER 22.

Janice faced her daughter over the breakfast table the morning after Gerald's funeral and saw the signs of stress written all over Kate's shadowed face. Not eating, Kate was playing with the sugar bowl.

"Eat something darling." Janice pleaded. "You look dreadful."

"I'm not hungry." Kate snapped. "Just leave me alone."

"Kate" Janice raised her eyebrows. "I am only trying to help."

"I don't need your help." Kate got to her feet. "I'm used to coping on my own, remember? Dad was always busy with the team so I had to handle everything. Bills, accounts, solicitors, and that's what I am going to do today. Cope! On my own."

"But darling there's no need!"

"Why?" Kate's grief had slowly begun to be replaced by aggression. She wanted to take on the world single-handedly and punish it for the hand that it had dealt her.

"Because I am your mother. I want to help you, darling. This is too much for you to cope with alone. "

"You running off with another man was too

much for me to cope with!" Kate snapped. "But I did and so did Dad. We had to. You left us so we had no choice."

"Oh, darling." Janice shook her head. "It's not that simple. I did ask you to come live with me."

"Why should I want to? With another man that wasn't my father? Where is he anyway I'm surprised he's not here to help you gloat!"

"He stayed away as he knew he wouldn't be welcome. He has never done anything wrong to you Kate, his only crime is that he loved me and your father didn't."

"Don't you dare say that!" Kate screamed. "Don't you ever, ever, speak about my father that way! You've had everything you will ever get from him Mum there's nothing more left. No need for you to hang around so GO!"

"I'm not here for that." Janice's coffee cup fell to the floor and shattered. "I am here because of you. Yes, I left your father. But once I was very important to him and I loved him."

"Then why did you do it then?" Kate burst into tears. "Why did you do it to us? To me?"

"Oh, sweetheart." Janice went to her and took her in her arms. "Why did you come and stay with me only a few weeks ago? Think about it. Because you couldn't take any more. Cars, cars, cars that's all there ever was. Sometimes darling loving someone isn't enough. Time, attention, sharing, all the love in the world can't compensate for losing those things. And no matter how much you love a person if they aren't giving you that same love back there's no point. I was alone in our marriage so I decided I might as well not be in it. I admit my timing could have been better, but I did not run off with Richard. He just happened to come along as I was leaving and he gave me everything your father couldn't and still does."

"I know." Kate sobbed. "I do know. It's just so hard and I'm going to miss him so much. I'm all alone now. I don't have anyone to hold me when I'm sad. You do."

"You have me." Janice hugged her tight. "You have always had me, darling, you just didn't want it. But I am here for you now, and always. "

"Thanks." Kate looked into the green eyes that were so like her own. "I don't deserve it, not after all the things I've said and done over the years."

"Of course, you do, darling. Everyone hurts and says things that they don't mean. It's all part of being human and it helps to ease the pain."

Kate nodded and ran her fingers through her hair.

"I have to go to the solicitors about the will please will you come with me?"

"Of course, I will. Now go get tidied up and we will face this thing together."

"Okay." Kate took a deep breath. "Thanks, Mum."

Bernice laid a baguette and a cup of tea on the

table.

"Drink." She commanded. "Eat."

Declan raised his bloodshot, heavy-lidded eyes and gave a woeful smile.

"Looking after me, darling?"

"Someone has to."

Bernice sat opposite him and studied his face. It was incredible, really, the things that emotion could do to the human body. If she had passed Declan in the street, she never would barely have recognised him. The weight had fallen from him the past week, his broad, muscular frame had become lean and bony; only the big, powerful arms remained unchanged. His jeans, which were now inches too big, were tightly belted, hanging on his fleshless hips. But the most dramatic and shocking change of all was in his face. Sitting in hollowed, shaded sockets his bruised, tired eyes were huge above cheekbones that stood out over his pinched cheeks. He was unshaven and visibly exhausted. This was not the man she knew and loved; this was a stranger.

"Come on Dec." She tried to sound bright. "This won't do you any good."

"No?" Declan stared blankly back at her. "And what will?"

"Eating for a start." Bernice pointed to the untouched baguette. "I can't." He shook his head. "I want to. I'm starving, but it just sticks in my throat."

"Oh, my poor baby." Bernice took his hand. "It

will get better, Declan, believe me."

"I know." He squeezed her hand. "I've been here before. But it doesn't make any difference; knowing how much it hurts doesn't mean you get used to it."

"I should hope not." Bernice smiled. "Or the world would be a very callous place

Footsteps in the hall announced Kurt's return and he came through the door with a selection of wines and cheeses intending to put them to good use. He knew that Declan was not sleeping and thought that a wine-tasting session on the balcony might help. Declan heard the clink of glass and forced a wry grin.

"Sounds like I'm in for a night of it."

"Sounds like it." Bernice sighed. "I'll go see what he's up to. Someone has to keep him under control."

Declan listened to them talking in lowered voices in the kitchen and felt his heartwarming. They were good to him, these friends of his, but Kurt was wrong. He knew that drowning his sorrows may be a temporary solution to his heartache but in the morning, it would still be there. He wasn't sure whether he could trust himself either, drinking with only Kurt for company. In his current mental state, he would either end up in tears or try to fight everything in sight, probably the latter. A drink did sound tempting, the release it would provide would be merciful, but he needed to do it in his own time and in his own way. Getting quietly to his feet he picked up his jacket and slipped out of the door.

He started in a sensible enough manner, sipping cold beer in one of the small cafes that cluttered the side streets. No bright lights and casinos tonight, just himself for company and a glass of ice-cold beer. But as the night drew on the beer turned into Vodka and he found the gregarious side of his nature fighting to get out. No longer satisfied with quiet corners and passing conversation he set out in search of action. The casinos were not an option in his current state of dress but many of the clubs knew him well and would overlook his draggled appearance in deference to his status and bank balance. So, he headed for the liveliest club he knew, sipping a bottle as he went.

He rang Kurt, many hours later when he was incapable of walking unaided. He had fought off the girls who had attached themselves to him and made it to the doorway with the help of a few tables and a wall.

"Mr Braun." He slurred. " Help. I need you. Now."

"Declan!" Kurt was half asleep. "Where the fuck are you?"

"Not sure." Declan stopped his progress down the wall by grabbing a passerby. "Just come to the square and you'll see me."

"It'll take me ten minutes."

"Take me that long to get out of the door."

Declan giggled. "Cheers."

On the third attempt, Declan managed to stand upright and made his way outside. It was a difficult passage and by the time he made it Kurt was indeed patrolling the street outside.

"There you are." Striding across to Declan he grabbed his arm just as he was about to step in front of a car. "What the hell have you been doing for God's sake? We have been worried sick."

"Drinking." Declan smiled wandering all over the road. "But I need help getting home."

"My home," Kurt said firmly. "Closer."

"No car?" Declan peered around Kurt's shoulder.

"No. I thought the walk would do you good, and it appears I was right."

"Definitely." Declan stopped suddenly and rubbed his eyes. "I feel strange. Everything is getting lighter."

"That." Kurt said dryly, "Is because it is nearly morning!"

"Oh. Sorry mate."

"Forgiven." Kurt steered him around a tree. "Just don't do it again. My marriage won't survive it."

The mobile, ringing incessantly, woke Declan from his heavy slumber many hours later. Blinking his eyes against the light he moaned as the pain in his head started to register.

"Yes." He croaked. "Who is it?"

"Declan?" It was Carlo. "You sound ill."

"I feel ill." Declan moaned. "What do you want?"

"You. They are reading Gerald's will in two days' time. Kate wants us all here."

"Ah." Declan paused. "Well, it was nice knowing you Carlo, good luck for the future."

"Don't be so cynical," Carlo said sternly. "And lay off the booze."

"How do you know I've been drinking? " The room was spinning violently and for a moment he thought he would be sick.

"I know you and that's enough. I'll see you then. Sober I hope."

Declan lay on his side waiting for the nausea to pass and stared at the sea outside. It was pale and grey today under stormy skies. Like my future he thought, grey and uncertain.

After a moment's consideration, he decided that the only solution to his current problems was to have another drink.

CHAPTER 23.

Kate's eyes grew wider and wider as the solicitor continued. When he finished speaking, she stood open-mouthed, amazed at what she had just heard.

"Miss Matthews?" He leaned forward. "Are you feeling, okay?"

"Yes. No. I'm not sure." Kate shook herself. "It's all rather a lot to take in. I had no idea. Still, I know now. I just have to decide what to do about it."

Leaving the office, she paused in the corridor and pressed her hot forehead against the cool glass of the window.

"Oh, Dad." She murmured. "I'm not sure that I can do it. I'll try, but I really don't think I can."

They assembled. The two drivers, Carlo, Peter, and Francine stood in the conference room. Silence hung in the air as they all waited. The figure that came through the door was not the one they expected. Janice, stern-faced, was here as deputy. Looking at them all she nodded to the chairs lined up and waiting.

"Please sit." She spoke sharply. "No need to stand."

"What's she doing here?" Declan whispered.

"The wicked witch of the west?"

"Looking after Kate," Francine muttered. "She hasn't left her for a minute."

"And herself probably," Declan said sourly. "Just watch."

Kate looked impossibly small and frail as she came through the door. No longer in black, she wore a bottle green trouser suit that lit up her emerald eyes. She had hidden the shadows beneath them with makeup and scraped her unwashed hair back into a bun.

"Thank you all for coming." She didn't sit but stood, pacing back and forth as she spoke. "I'll come straight to the point."

Drawing a deep breath, she turned and scanned the row of faces. When her eyes reached Declan she stopped and her jaw dropped, seeing clearly for the first time his haggard appearance. But any sympathy she may have felt was nullified by the contents of the papers in her hand.

"Right." She paused again, then spoke quickly. "Dad has left the control of Matros to me. But he has increased Carlo's shareholding by twenty-five percent so Carlo now owns half of the company and I own the other half. Which was a wise move, because I know nothing about engines.

But he has rather cleverly put in a clause which means that neither of us can sell our shares or the company as a whole for twelve months; nor can we pull out of Formula One, so you can all breathe again, the team is carrying on and no one is losing their job. But."

Again, she looked at Declan.

"As the new, official head of this team, I can make changes, and I'm afraid I have to. Dad has obviously set things up pretty carefully but we can't keep operating on the current level without seriously cutting into our funds before the year is up. It appears that Dad had some extra, out-of-contract arrangements that will have to be cleared up."

Another pause. Declan had gone scarlet.

"As far as I am concerned, we will be at Imola next weekend. We've missed a bit of time so I need you all to put in the hours to get us back on track. That's all really. Pete, can you tell the lads there isn't a P45 with their name on it in this month's wage slip? I'll see you all here tomorrow but before you go my mother has arranged some refreshments for you."

As the group headed for the table and the food that Janice was laying out Kate stepped quickly to Declan's side and caught his arm.

"Declan." She spoke quietly. "Can you come into the office for a moment please?"

Once inside the office she closed the door and stood with her back to it. There was a pause as she struggled to find the words.

"My father." She stammered. "Was he really paying you more than your contract stated?"

"Yes."

The answer was simple and made her task so much easier.

"So instead of three million a year, you've been getting four?"

"Five." Declan nodded. "For the last two years."

"Why?" Kate's voice was tense." May I ask?"

"Sure. I was headhunted by another team. They offered me four basic, plus advertising and promotion work. Gerald didn't want to lose me so he made me a private arrangement."

"Generous of him." Kate shook her head. "But I can't afford to keep it up. Your pay will be what your contract states for this year, no more no less."

"Fair enough." Declan narrowed his eyes. "It's not like I need it, but I do need my drive. Thank you for not saying anything in front of the others."

"Remember it." Kate looked at him, eyes hard and unemotional. "Don't play me up, or question any of my decisions, or the rest of the team will all find out why they haven't had a pay rise for two years."

"Done." Declan hesitated. "But remember who has the experience here. Don't push me into a corner, let me do my thing, it's what I'm good at."

"You are in no position to lecture me Declan." Kate turned away. "But I do understand that if you get a better offer from another team, you may be inclined to take it. I won't be able to better it. Now or in the future. And please, for all our sakes, lay off the drink."

She didn't look around as he left the room. At last, after all these years of friction and pent-up emotions, she had Declan Hyde exactly where she wanted him. But strangely, now that the moment was here it was not as sweet as she had anticipated.

Carlo waited until the others had left and then went to find her. She was in the office, working her way through a pile of invoices. She looked up as he entered and gave him a welcoming smile. "Hello. How can I help you."

"Information." Carlo sat down. "What are these out-of-contract affairs that have to be cleared up'?"

"Oh, nothing I can't handle. Nothing to worry about. Just a bit of overspending, but it's sorted."

"Declan," Carlo said shortly. "It has to be."

"What makes you say that?" Kate said carefully.

"I'm not stupid. I heard all the rumours about the big deals he was offered a few years back when we were really under pressure. I always wondered why he stayed. I know he was loyal to your father, but everyone has their price in this game."

"I should have known better than to try and hide anything from you." Kate smiled. "But think no more about it, as I said, I've sorted it."

"How much?" Carlo raised his eyes.

"That I can't tell you. Even Declan deserves that.

But he knows that there won't be any more."

"Will he stay?" Carlo looked doubtful.

"Until this contract expires, yes, he has to unless he wants to breach it and then that will cost him money. Then it all depends on what offers he gets. But I shan't be holding out tempting extras for him. "

"It wouldn't pay to lose him, Kate," Carlo warned. "He knows this team as well as anybody."

"That is the one other thing that has to change, at least slightly. I wanted to talk to you about that." Kate paused. "I'm not going to make any big decisions without your help."

"Go on" Carlo was curious. "What do you have in mind?"

"Well, as I see it, the team has been run solely to achieve the best performance from the car, which I understand is what it's all about, but we are short on staff, people wearing too many hats, and I don't agree with my father's team policy. The little things such as having Pete as the only race engineer. He can't give his attention equally to two drivers in a race and we all know that Declan is his number one priority. It's not fair on you to have to step in and be on the radio for Fabio alongside everything else you do. I know Dad has left this team to me but you are the team Principal now, you will have so many other things to focus on. So, I want another race engineer for Fabio, someone good who can give him all the help he needs."

"It is a good idea cara" Carlo agreed, "Something we have needed for a long time. Always I have to delegate."

"Speaking of delegating." Kate looked at the pile of work in front of her. "I need help myself. If I'm going to be my dad then someone has to be me."

"Agreed." Carlo thought that personally, he did not think Kate was in a fit state to do anything at the moment. "You need an assistant."

"All I need is someone who can handle the media, the ordering, sending info back to the factory while we are away and making bookings. Stuff like that. A sort of personal assistant."

"Excellent." Carlo smiled. "Your father was in the middle of setting up a deal for some new technology to increase the relay speed around the system. What is happening with that?"

"I've pulled out." Kate smiled grimly. "I'm sorry Carlo. That sort of stuff is for the super teams and although we are frightening them at the moment, we have a long way to go to move up the paddock. Manpower first horsepower second I'm afraid."

"Okay." Carlo stood up. "So be it."

"Thank you. Can I leave it to you to sort out the new race engineer?"

"I already have an idea." Carlo smiled. "Italian of course, and he won't break our bank. Just think how it will rattle Declan when he cannot understand what we are saying!"

"I dread to think. I couldn't do this without you Carlo. You are the one man I can't lose."

"You will do fine," Carlo pecked her on the cheek. "You are your father's daughter."

Kate waited until he had closed the door and then went to the cabinet and pulled out a file. It was a thin file, containing a few CVs that had been kept in case they were needed in the future. The top one was new and neatly typed. Reading it through again, she nodded to herself. This girl was young, and inexperienced, but intelligent and looking at the attached photograph was very presentable. Just the sort of person she was looking for. No preconceived ideas, no habits, raw material that could be introduced to the sport as she wanted.

Picking up the telephone she dialled a number.

"Hello." She asked, "Am I speaking to Lucy Duggan?"

CHAPTER 24.

The rest of the team had already left for Imola, the fleet of dark blue lorries were heading across the channel when Lucy arrived at the Matros factory for her 'chat' with Kate Matthews. The move had been a tactical one on Kate's part. Getting the crew away from the compound early removed them from the familiar surroundings, and inevitably Gerald's ghost, before the boiling pot that was the San Marino Grand Prix. It also enabled her to conduct this interview in peace without the prying and critical eyes of the team looking on.

She had watched them go with mixed emotions. This was the crunch time for the whole team; how would they cope without the man who had made it all happen?

Her mother was still with her; but she needed her less, even now. The job of running this mammoth operation was taking up all her time and concentration, and the only hours when she thought about and grieved for her father, was when she lay alone in bed at night. She had avoided all individual contact with Fabio as in a twisted way she blamed him for her absence that night in Bahrain. If she had not gone out to dinner with him, then her father would not have been alone and maybe, just maybe, he would still be alive. She knew that it was unlikely, but it was a thought that she could not keep out of her head.

Her immediate impression of Lucy Duggan was that she would look very good in the hospitality unit, and would also make a very attractive grid girl if she couldn't do anything else. She soon found, however, that Lucy was a fiercely determined and very intelligent young woman. She had not decided to embark on a media career without the attributes to succeed. When queried as to why she wished to leave her course Lucy quickly replied that she felt she needed time to consider her options and decide if journalism was indeed right for her. This situation suited Kate perfectly as she could only offer a short-term contract while she complied with the terms of her father's will. Lucy's knowledge of Formula One was excellent and she was clearly a fan, which also suited Kate and she had plenty of common sense to go with her intelligence.

"Well." Kate took a last look at the C.V. and studied the dark-haired girl in front of her. "I think it will be best if we have a trial period, of say one month. You can decide if you like us and vice versa. This is a new position so there are going to be some teething problems."

"Fine by me." Lucy smiled. "Just don't ask me to

drive one of your cars."

"Not a chance!" Kate laughed. "You'd have to trample a few drivers first. Seats are in short supply at the moment. To be honest, I have never even sat in one myself, they scare the living daylights out of me."

"When do I start'?" Lucy was grinning from ear to ear, obviously delighted at her success.

"Now'?" Kate raised her hands. "I'll give you a guided tour, as the place is all but deserted, then I'll draw up "an agreement and put it in the post. I wish you could come to Imola this weekend but it would be throwing you in the deep end, especially in the circumstances."

"I don't mind," Lucy replied eagerly.

"Well." Kate thought for a moment. "Okay then. I'll ring you with our travel arrangements later today and you can plunge straight in. Francine and I will show you the ropes then we'll see how you manage it."

"Great!"

God this girl was keen.

"One word of warning." Kate got up. "Watch your backside in Italy; they are the world's best bum pinchers!"

After Lucy left, she drew up a preliminary list of duties that Lucy could undertake in Imola, things that would give her a taste of life on the circuit but would not cause problems if they went wrong. A meeting had been arranged for the following morning between herself, Lucy, and Francine before they left for the airport. Pausing outside her office she scratched her neck, concentrating on a nagging suspicion that she had forgotten something. Of course! She almost laughed out loud. It would be no use taking Lucy to Imola if she couldn't get into the track; she had completely forgotten to sort out a security pass for her. Hoping that this lapse of memory wasn't a sign of things to come, she went into the office and picked up the phone.

CHAPTER 25.

They assembled at the track the following day. Walking into the Matros motorhome Kate, struggling with ever-increasing nerves, halted in front of the seated group and gave Lucy, who was walking behind her an encouraging smile.

"Okay. For those of you who haven't met her, I'd like to introduce my new P.A. Lucy."

Fabio, ever the gentleman, got to his feet and offered Lucy his hand.

"Welcome." He smiled.

Lucy stared at him in admiration, a little overawed by the situation she found herself in now she was here, and, quite frankly, terrified of the introduction that would take place in a few minutes' time. She nodded but remained silent. Carlo greeted her in his usual friendly fashion as did Peter. Her eyes turned to the remaining figure of the group who was staring out of the window, his team t-shirt now too big on his wasting frame.

"Declan." Kate prompted. "This is Lucy."

"Hi." Declan didn't turn round, not displaying any interest at all in the newcomer until he caught a waft of perfume; light, flowery, it tugged at his memory and made him look up, failing to keep the surprise from his face as he did.

"Well, well. Lucy Duggan." He leaned back against the window and fixed his stare on her face, watching her colour rise with expressionless eyes. "What a surprise."

"Oh." Kate looked at Lucy. "Do you two know each other?"

"Not really." Lucy quickly regained her composure and smiled. "We have met once or twice."

"And you didn't think to mention it to me?"

"Well." Lucy flicked her hair and looked at Declan. "It didn't seem important."

"Believe me." Declan wasn't taking his eyes off her face. "It isn't."

"Right." Kate could feel the atmosphere growing tense around her and hastily tried to lighten it. "Well, it's your work that matters. No lovers' tiffs over the coffee machine, eh?"

"None at all." Declan picked up his cap and pulled it onto his head. "If you'll excuse me, I have work to do."

Breathing deep ragged breaths of relief Lucy took a seat beside Kate. Her heart was beating so hard that she was sure others could hear it. Having manoeuvred herself into this role she had to keep her head. It was time to get a grip, and quickly.

Looking around at the motorhome Lucy could feel something akin to awe. She had never imagined such luxury, and this all moved from place to place following the teams around the world. Through the window, she could see Declan speaking to a TV crew and wondered, and not for the first time, if this had been the right move to make. She was shocked by his appearance. The tragedy that had struck in Bahrain had been all over the press so she had expected an air of upset in the team but of all of them, it seemed Declan was suffering the most. Taking the drink that was offered to her she sat and listened to the chat around her, all the while painfully aware of the man who was only feet away.

The confrontation that she knew would eventually happen came sooner than expected. They had nearly finished the media day and were making their way back out of the paddock for the evening. She was tired and was looking forward to a shower and a few hours alone in her hotel room. During a halt at the security gates, she found herself caught up in a group of people from another team. Outside the gates, the fans were standing ten deep. Looking around frantically for Kate or Francine, she saw him approaching, bag hanging from his shoulders. He halted beside her and looked her straight in the eye.

"What the fuck are you playing at Lucy?"

"Pardon?" She said calmly, aware that all around her others were listening.

"What are you doing here?" Declan looked nervous, as if an illicit deal was being made and he feared getting caught.

"Working."

"Since when have you wanted to be a P.A.? I thought you were a student? The media thing? What happened to that?"

"We can all change our minds" Lucy forced a sweet smile. "Can't we? We certainly know that you can Declan."

Declan stared at her and felt his hackles rising. Aware of the crowd pressing in around them, of the fans beyond the gate who had spotted him and were calling his name already he steadied himself. Now was not the time or the place for a showdown, and if he was honest, he didn't have the strength.

"Just stay out of my way," He hissed. "Freak."

Lucy looked at the floor and when she raised her eyes he was gone, barging through the crowd, ignoring the fans that screamed and shouted as he passed. That last word stung, even more than his desertion of her on an Indian Island had. She had been under no illusion that he was suddenly going to have a change of heart and sweep her into his arms, but his animosity had taken her aback. She was the one who had been spurned and rejected, what right had he to be so venomous? Okay so she may have gone a bit overboard with the messages and calls but she deserved some kind of repayment for what had happened, didn't she? She shook her head. Her life had a habit of not sticking to the script. But she had plenty of time to rewrite it. She was here now, and like it or not Declan Hyde was going to have to tolerate her presence every day. A little smile of satisfaction lifted the corners of her lips and, flashing her pass at the guard, walked out of the gate to join Kate who was patiently waiting for her.

CHAPTER 26.

The atmosphere was so thick that it was almost impossible to breathe. Declan stood, snarling, and hissing in the back of his garage while Pete raced around trying to fix his ailing GM-4 which was refusing to cooperate and work at maximum power. Fabio, on the other hand, was having a tremendous start to Imola and was setting some really quick times as he winged his way around the circuit.

"Why the fuck does his car work and mine doesn't!" roared Declan as a blue flash sped across the monitor. "What the hell is going on here Trent?"

"Patience sweetheart." Pete had worked with Declan for far too many years to be fazed by this behaviour. "I'll get you on the front of the grid don't you worry."

"Forget it." Declan was peeling off his fire suit. "I'm done for the day. Just have her singing from the same hymn sheet as me tomorrow, okay?"

Pete stood up and watched in amazement as Declan, fire suit swinging from his hips, headed off across the paddock for the motorhome.

"Where is he going?" he asked Carlo. "He hasn't put in a proper lap time yet!"

Carlo shrugged. He had no idea where Declan's head had been since the day they had arrived at the track, but he knew it wasn't in the same place as his, that was for sure. He also knew that Declan was drinking heavily, and was concerned about his safety on the track. Without a word to anyone, he set off after the figure in the distance.

He found Declan drinking coffee in his driver's room.

"Fixed already, is it?" He snapped as Carlo entered.

"No." Carlo shrugged. "We are doing our best Declan."

"Are you? Honestly? Or are you and your little Italian *compagni* enjoying watching me fail?"

Carlo shook his head and sat down with a thump.

"What the hell has got into you Declan? Why do you think everyone is out to get you?"

"Well, aren't they?" Declan had spotted a red-haired figure walking across the paddock. "I've lost my partner in this one Carlo. He's dead and buried. I've got no one riding shotgun for me anymore. The only one in this team looking out for me is me"

"That's not fair," Carlo said calmly. "We are a team. But we all know you haven't been the best team, how do they say it, team player, yourself."

Declan narrowed his eyes at him.

"Told you, did she? Bitch. She's loving it, Carlo,

watching me fail, seeing me collapse in a heap. I'm right where she always wanted me and she's even hired a little lapdog to make sure I stay in my rightful place."

"There is no talking to you when you are like this." Carlo got up and went to leave. "Be back in the garage for second practice Declan, we have a race to win and you a car to drive. So do it."

Declan watched him leave and felt his stomach churning. He had watched Kurt setting lap after lap in his perfectly tuned machine all morning; he had finished for the session, and he could see him outside now, chatting to his sponsors, smiling, charming, benevolent and the fastest man on the track. Bastard. Why did he have to have everything? The car, the woman, the kids. He had it all. While he, Declan had nothing. Declan ran his hands through his hair and sighed. Life was out to get him at the moment that was for sure. So, they wanted him back in the garage that afternoon, did they? Well fuck it. They could wait.

He had no idea where he was. All he knew was that it was loud and dark. One thing was for certain, he was nowhere near the Autodromo Enzo e Dino Ferrari. Rubbing his eyes, he peered through the gloom and saw that he was surrounded by Italians, all wearing the red of Ferrari. He didn't recognise one of them. Pushing his way through the crowd he staggered out of the door and blinked as he realised it was still light. Where the hell was he? In Imola somewhere, hopefully. Flagging down a taxi he instructed the driver to take him to the circuit. He could feel the man's eyes on him in the wing mirror. After a while, the man spoke.

"You are Declan Hyde, yes?"

"I am." Declan nodded.

"I wish you very good luck for the race." The driver smiled. "Many Italians love the Ferrari but I love the Matros. Blue is my colour, see?" He pointed to his t-shirt which Declan now saw was a Matros team shirt.

"That's very kind of you." Declan was starting to feel sick.

"Now you have one of us at the wheel is better." The driver beamed. "But to me all Matros is good. You or him."

"Thank you for your kind words," Declan said dryly through gritted teeth. "Right now, I think you should stop the car."

Francine spotted him first, arguing with the security guards. Making her excuses she left the people she was talking to and rushed to his aid.

"This way." She steered him towards the motor home. "You need coffee and a shower. Where the hell have you been? Kate was going crazy!"

"On the warpath, is she?" Declan beamed. "Did she miss me?"

"I would be very humble if I was you." Francine hissed. "If you want to keep your seat."

"She won't sack me." He whispered. "She loves me, really."

"Really." Francine pushed him through the door. "And I've seen you looking at her also, Declan. Do you honestly think that this is the way to win her affections?"

"Don't know what you mean." Declan heaved. "Excuse me I'm going to be sick."

It took several cups of coffee to restore Declan to some sort of sobriety. Francine watched him head in hands, arms shaking and felt a wave of sympathy. Everyone knew Declan was a wild child, but this was different, this was bordering on self-abuse, and this looked like a deliberate attempt to hurt himself. He was crying for help in the only way he could.

"Tell me cara." She sat and put her arm over his shoulders. "What is it that makes you so unhappy?"

"I'm not unhappy." He lied. "Just frustrated."

"I know when you are lying." Francine hugged him. "I know how much you must miss him, but we all do."

"No, you don't" Declan held his breath for a moment and then let it out in a sob. "No one does. He made me, he guided me, he kept me going. Yes, we had our spats, but he understood me, Francine. No one else does, not like that. He let me be me. It's the only way I can work."

"And Kate doesn't?" Francine shook her head. "She is doing her best Declan, all that she asks is that you do your best."

"My best will never be good enough for her." Declan spat out the words. "Ever. She'll be happy when I'm gone and not before."

"I think you may be wrong there," Francine said calmly. "But for now, you have to try Declan. What do you think Gerald would feel if he could see you like this?"

Declan shook his head.

"I know. I'm letting him down."

"Then pull yourself together honey." She gave him another hug. "I'll tell everyone that you have been ill and needed some time to yourself. One thing darling, please eat, I have never felt your bones before."

A wicked grin passed across Declan's shadowed face.

"Bet you'd like to."

"Behave." Francine shook her head. "Now get in the shower. We are eating together tonight, so please try and behave. For me?"

"For you." Declan nodded. "And only you. Just keep that little weirdo Lucy out of my hair."

"What do you have against her?" Francine looked puzzled.

"Long story." Declan stood up. "We have a history. For some reason, and I can't work out why, I have a feeling her getting a job here is not a coincidence."

Francine looked at him and saw concern on his face. Something had happened here that she wasn't going to be privy to, but she intended to find out.

CHAPTER 27.

Fabio could not believe that he had got his car into P3, okay the session wasn't over but it was looking good for him. An Italian on home soil on the second row of the grid. Waving to his cheering race engineers as he pulled back into the pits, he smiled to himself. At last, he was proving himself, he had pushed his car to the absolute limits for that position and although he knew he would struggle to hold position in the race itself for now that didn't matter, not in the least, he had proved his place in the sport and that was all that mattered. He sat in his car and watched the monitors, praying that no one would knock him out of his spot. Kate leaned over the cockpit and spoke to him.

"Well done." She gave him a pat on the shoulder. "At least one of our cars will be in a good position."

"Careful," Carlo warned as he pointed across the garage to the silent form sitting in his car. "We want him to finish qualifying and be on the grid, not at the back with a penalty or in pieces in the Armco."

Declan was unaware of the conversation. His mind was focused on the task ahead of him, times and sectors ran through his brain as he visualised the track.

"He's fine." Kate shook her head as Declan's engine burst into life. He likes aggression and challenges; my dad told me that."

"There's a difference between that and being threatened," Carlo said wisely. "Right now, that is what he feels "

"Tough." Kate headed for the monitor. "It's not easy for any of us right now, he just has to grow up and deal with it."

Declan's eyes moved sideways behind his visor and watched Kate climbing onto a stool. He had a feeling that she was enjoying watching him slowly falling apart and had no intention of giving her the pleasure of seeing him losing it on the track. If the car performed well then so would he. He would show Miss Matthews who was number one in this team.

"Ready?" Pete's voice brought him back to the moment.

Yep. Let's send it."

Carlo leapt out of the way as a blue form shot out of the garage and away up the pit lane. Hastily running to the monitor, he watched as Declan sped around the track; almost losing it on every corner, tyres squealing in protest as he braked late and hard at every bend.

"Jesus." He muttered to himself. "If he goes off, he's in trouble."

Pete was thinking the same thing.

"Easy up out there mate." He pleaded. "Keep it intact for the race."

Declan ignored him and flattened the car through Tamburello, his eyes and mind were fixed firmly on pole position and nothing else would do. Kurt, watching from his car, read the signs and knew instantly what was going through his old friend and rival's head. Knowing that his pole position was in danger he saw that he had run out of time for another flying lap and leaping out of the car ran to the monitors to watch the times. If Declan could get it right through Rivazza he would have him. Kurt held his breath as the blue machine sped into the corner, and twitched sideways as Declan's foot rammed the pedal to the floor.

The twitch caused him the split second that lost him pole position and put him behind Kurt on the grid.

Kurt's garage erupted. Mechanics leapt in the air and patted their driver and each other on the back. In the Matros garage, similar poses were being struck, other than by Fabio who was staring at the monitor in awe. Never, ever, would he, Fabio, be able to drive a race car like that. If that was what he needed to do to get a pole position then he would never be able to do it. Declan had driven as if he was possessed and on this track of all tracks, where one of the greatest drivers of them all had lost his life. Humbled, he went to wait for his teammate and congratulate him.

Declan got out of the car and removed his helmet. He felt the pats of congratulation on his back but did not smile. He had wanted that pole position.

"Good drive mate" Pete beamed. "You nearly had him."

"But I didn't," Declan said shortly. "Pole goes to Braun, again. Sometimes I wish he would remember I'm his mate and give me a break. Just once"

"Hey come on." Pete shook his head. "Yesterday this thing wouldn't get past a skip!"

"True." Declan grinned. "Very true. You have worked your magic yet again Pete."

Feeling almost relieved that the qualifying session was over, Declan struggled through his press interviews and then headed for the motorhome to find Francine. His neck was seizing up and he needed help, fast. He burst through the door to find her sitting deep in conversation with Lucy. A television screen in the corner had been relaying the action to them.

"Out." He snapped, not even looking in Lucy's direction. "I need to get a massage."

"You drove well." The adulation sounded in Lucy's voice and made Francine look at her. "I was convinced you'd get pole."

"Well, I didn't." The flattery had mellowed Declan's attitude. "But I did my best."

"I'd better go." Lucy brushed past him, arching

her back away from him. "See you both later."

Declan narrowed his eyes at Francine.

"What's with the new best friend?"

"Oh, shut up." Francine scolded. "She's a sweet girl and very young. Kate is very pleased with her. Maybe you should learn to pick on people your own age, Declan."

"I don't think she's the one being picked on here." He said shortly. "But time will tell. Now get those oily fingers ready woman."

Lucy watched the door close behind her and stood rooted to the spot. She had forgotten, in her anger and her scheming, the effect that Declan had on her. Just a brush of his arm against her skin made her pulse race, made her heart skip in her chest. He still was, despite her hurt, the most beautiful man she had ever seen. She knew that she would never be able to switch off that attraction entirely whatever the outcome of her scheming. All she had thought about was putting herself into his line of vision so that he could not forget her. Then maybe, when he saw her every day, he would understand the mistake he had made; that he would warm to the thought of them being together. Just being close to him would, she thought, have been enough. That he would realise that he should never have deserted her on that island just because of a car. Now she was confused. His aggression and total dismissal of her had muddled her thoughts and she could already see her plans falling apart around her.

But she was here now, and like it or not Declan Hyde was going to have to deal with the consequences. One way or another.

CHAPTER 28.

Kate was taking no chances. She had no intention of letting her wayward number-one driver out of her sight the night before the race. They were all eating dinner together that evening and she had booked a table at a local restaurant and they all assembled there at eight once the usual round of engineering debriefs and interviews had finished. Declan had moaned and groaned but had been escorted there by Carlo, a jug of water placed firmly in front of him. Sitting at one end of the table Declan was aware of Kate watching him closely from the other. Raising his glass of water, he mouthed the word 'cheers' and drained it in one gulp. Carlo sat at his left shoulder, like a prison guard, watching everything that passed between his lips.

"There really is no need for this." Declan watched Francine sipping her wine and felt his mouth begin to water. "I am hardly going to get drunk the night before a race."

"Really?" Carlo shook his head. "You think not?"

"Of course, not" Declan looked horrified. "It's a dangerous enough sport as it is; anyway, what do you think I am, an alcoholic?"

"I don't," Carlo whispered. "But there are others who do. You are becoming slightly dependent, more so than usual."

Declan scowled at Kate and as he looked away, he caught Fabio's eye. Fabio shrugged and raised his own glass of water.

"You too?" Declan called. "She'll be having us get religion next."

"I have a religion." Fabio shook his head. "I am Catholic!"

Declan chuckled.

"Hear that, Kate? You needn't worry about Fabio getting lost in someone's bed tonight, it's against his religion."

Kate shook her head and turned back to her conversation. Beside her, Lucy was watching the two drivers and was growing increasingly aware of the fact that Fabio's eyes turned in her direction, often. Waiting for the right moment she met his glance with a smile. Fabio smiled in return and leaned across to speak to her. A few moments later Declan, who had been busy taunting Francine, noticed the two of them, deep in conversation, dark heads almost touching across the table. He narrowed his eyes for a second, debated with his better judgement and lost.

"Now there's a nice girl for you Fabio, your mother would like her, definitely no sex before marriage from that one."

"Declan!" Francine nudged him. "Leave the poor girl alone!"

"Poor girl my arse." Declan snorted. "She knows what she's doing. Don't you Lucy? Any racing driver in a storm is that it?"

Lucy blushed scarlet and sat back. Fabio, intrigued, but not wanting to cause this pleasant, pretty, girl any more discomfort, ignored Declan and focused his attention on Lucy. He had no idea what Declan was talking about but felt he would find out in due course. Until then he was quite happy to pass the evening flirting and taking his mind off what lay ahead.

"Ignore him." He smiled. "Declan is always like this before a race. It is nerves, he doesn't like to admit it but he has them. Sometimes he does not handle them well."

"Really?" Lucy seemed curious. "Declan gets nervous? You never would have thought it. He seems so confident about everything."

"Most things, yes." Fabio agreed. "But this is different. He always wants to win. To be the best. So, it is fear of failing that worries him."

"Oh, I see." Lucy smiled. "What about you?"

"Me?" Fabio laughed. "I am not the star! No one expect me to win, so if I fail it does not matter. Only to me."

"But are you scared?" She insisted. "Before the race?"

"Of course, I am," Fabio admitted. "It is dangerous sport. But the pleasure is bigger than the fear so it is okay. When I first came my nerves were too bad but Declan, he shown me how to, you know, manage them"

Lucy was listening but her eyes were fixed on Declan himself. He was laughing loudly at a private joke between himself and Francine. He touched her often, her arm, her leg, her face. Lucy felt jealousy twisting in her stomach and wondered how Carlo coped with such behaviour. He seemed to be laughing with them, something that Lucy found very odd; surely, he didn't like Declan touching his wife in that way?

"So, tell me?" She swung her attention back to Fabio, aware, as she did so that Declan's attention had drifted and he was watching her.

"Tell me, what is his girlfriend like?"

"He has none." Fabio narrowed his eyes. "Like me, he is free man. Why do you ask cara? You think maybe he like to be with you?"

"Oh no." Lucy blushed prettily. "He's not my type. I prefer my men to be more sensitive."

"Ah." Fabio beamed broadly. "In this case, I am the winner. I am a very sensitive man."

Lucy giggled and lowered her eyes. She knew that Declan was still looking at her, she could feel him glancing and then looking away. Well, Mr Hyde, she thought, if you don't want me, you will just have to watch me be with someone else.

The fact that her new P.A. was getting on rather well with her number two driver was not lost on Kate. In a way she was glad. Lucy was a nice young girl and Declan's attitude towards her was rather surprising, she had fully expected him to be the one playing for her attention. It seemed there was a past between them that neither one wanted to share. She watched them all, Lucy deep in conversation with Fabio, Declan taking note of it all and wondered what that past was. Should she care? It seemed that she did as she felt very uncomfortable that Declan should have had anything to do with this girl. Convincing herself that she was only being concerned for Lucy as a new member of the team she turned to Carlo and steered her brain back to the subject of winning a race, which really was all that mattered.

CHAPTER 29.

Lucy had spent many, many hours watching Formula One racing on television. From the very first moment that she had set eyes on Declan Hyde, she had been completely fascinated by him. She felt that there was nothing about this sport that she didn't know. Until the moment she stood in the garage and watched the team preparing for the San Marino Grand Prix. The crowds were huge and the atmosphere electric; fans roared every time a driver appeared, each one cheering for their respective hero. Her nerves jangled, butterflies roamed free in her stomach, and she was totally unprepared for the air of tension that surrounded her. Seeing so many famous drivers getting ready to race and facing the numerous television cameras was so different from the images she had seen that were portrayed by one camera lens. It was a rugby scrum on the track as reporters jostled and queued to get close to their nation's drivers and the man in pole position. She noticed that Fabio drew a good deal of attention in his own right but was very shy in front of the camera. Kurt was out of his car chatting and giving interviews in his time-honoured fashion. Declan was already in his car with Pete guarding him with the tenacity of a Rottweiler. He spoke to no one, other than Pete and Carlo and shook his head whenever a reporter tried to get near to him. Now and then he looked around him and she would see the electric blue eyes flashing inside his helmet. Her heart began to pump, faster and faster and without realising it she began to tremble.

She was scared.

For a moment she contemplated running, getting away from the garage and hiding in the calm of the motor home. What sort of fool would she look like if she did that? Her place was here, with her team, cheering their drivers' home. While her heart quailed, her feet carried her out of the garage to the edge of the pit lane where Francine was standing, watching the action with a tense face. As she stopped beside her, she saw Declan's head turn and for a second those eyes fixed on her face. Then a gloved hand reached up and lowered the visor. The eyes were gone. She gasped as adrenaline rushed through her body. The man was no longer there. There was just a motionless figure, seeming hardly human. Francine saw her shudder and patted her shoulder.

"Okay?" She asked.

"Not really." Lucy felt sick. "I think that is the

most eerie thing I have ever seen. The second Declan lowered his visor it was as if he didn't exist anymore. He was just part of the machine."

"Chilling, isn't it?" Francine nodded. "I felt the same the first time I saw someone in one of these cars. So much speed, so much power, so much machine and one fragile human body in command of it all. It is like a science fiction movie. But you get used to it. You see past the machine and the visor to the person inside. You remember they are in control and that they are being helped, helped by all these people here. But you are right. The first time I came to a race I was terrified. It was like looking at a nightmare."

The klaxon sounded and the track began to clear.

"Come on." Francine took Lucy's arm. "You should never watch a race alone, not when you know a man involved. Back to the garage and we will watch it together."

Declan counted down the red lights as they switched on. They were all lit. Five, four, three, two; they were all out and he was away in the same split second. Foot flat to the floor, tyres smoking as he made a mad lunge for the first corner. He got away well and sat on Kurt's tail as he followed him into the bend, through it and out the other side. In his wing mirror, he could see Fabio still in third but distant. Not wanting to give Fabio any chance of getting between him and his target, Declan stuck to Kurt like glue, trying to slip up his inside at any given opportunity. Kurt held him at bay until Rivazza where Declan finally out braked him.

"Yes!" Pete shrieked into his earpiece. "Got him!"

Relieved at having stolen the lead Declan locked into a rhythm, easing off slightly, but still determined not to let the thrusting red and silver arrow behind him resume its lead.

"Careful Declan," Carlo warned as he watched the GM-4 weaving all over the track. "Don't go breaking the law!"

Pete, while watching the same thing, was becoming aware of a slightly more serious problem than Declan's erratic behaviour on the track. The fuel consumption figures of Declan's car were not good. Something was wrong. He was not the only one to notice. Kurt, spotting something coming from the rear of the Matros informed his pit that he was holding back.

"I don't know what it is but it is misting my visor. I must stay off him for now."

It only took a few more laps for Pete's worst fears to become realised. After a hasty consultation with Carlo, he sent one of Declan's pit crew racing over to the pit wall with Declan's board.

"Dec, we have a fuel issue. Lower your settings."

"What?" Declan was struggling to hear his radio above the noise of the engine and a wall of interference.

"Read your board," Pete shouted. "Lower your fuel setting."

Declan's eyes spotted his board as he flew past the pit lane. What? What the hell was all that about?

"Pete." He shouted. "Why am I lowering my fuel setting?"

"You're using too much," Pete yelled back. "You won't make the distance."

"If I lower my fuel setting, he'll have me!" Declan roared, he's right on my tail for God's sake."

"Declan." Carlo intervened. "We want to get this car home and in the points. Lower your fuel setting. Now"

"She feels fine," Declan argued. "Let me ride it out until I'm due to stop."

Kate, who had been listening in to the conversation, grabbed the radio from Carlo.

"Declan." She said sharply. "It's Kate. Lower

your fuel setting. Now!"

"I will lose my lead," Declan shouted. "There is no way I am lowering my fuel setting!"

Kate looked at Carlo and could feel her temper starting to fray.

"You'll lose your job if you disobey me!" She yelled. "Drop your fuel setting now!"

"Fuck!" Declan screamed. "Let me pit first for God's sake. Once he gets ahead, I'll never catch him."

Pete watched the vapour trail that was now drifting out of the back of Declan's car.

"Dec." He said apologetically. "If you don't drop your fuel setting now you won't make it to the pits. Look behind you."

Declan looked in his wing mirror and saw a pale stream of white smoke behind him. Damn.

"Okay." He snapped. "Okay. But remember I didn't lose this race the bloody car did!"

As he had feared once he lowered his fuel setting and lifted off the power Kurt shot past him a flash of red and silver. Cursing and moaning loudly Declan pitted for fuel and fresh tyres and on pulling back out found that Fabio was now in front of him. Try as he might he could not make inroads on the Italian and began to lose his temper, snatching the car through the corners and pushing it to the limit.

"Dec" Pete said soothingly. "Cool head mate. You won't finish at all at this rate!"

But even as he spoke Pete had a feeling that Declan's car wouldn't make it to the end of the race anyway. The fuel consumption was still too high and he wouldn't get to the end of the race. With a heavy heart, he turned to Carlo.

"He has to cruise this home." He shook his head. "He's using too much fuel to race."

Carlo picked up the radio, aware of the backlash he would receive.

"Declan, we are maintaining our position. Lift and coast. Do not race, do not race. DO NOT try to pass Fabio. "

He winced at the stream of expletives that came down the radio.

"That's a team order." Carlo confirmed "Maintain position. We have to maximise points for the team.

"Damn." Pete shook his head. "There will be stormy weather ahead me hearties."

Declan watched his teammate ahead of him, within easy reach if he could only raise his fuel setting. But now he was being told to sit behind him and accept defeat. Think of the points he told himself. Just get home, you'll still be in the championship race with points on the board. Or would he? Kurt was heading for another win and he already had a "did not finish" on his record. Damn, damn, damn, the further into the race he drove the more the injustice played on his mind. If he was allowed to swap positions with Fabio, he would get more points. But he was being told to stay where he was. He was the number one driver, priority should be given to him, to his points, his position in the championship not Fabio's. Something snapped in his head and he swung his car into the gravel trap and turned off the engine.

"What are you doing?" Pete shrieked. "What have you done!"

Declan didn't answer but pulled off his helmet and his earpiece. Getting out of the car he pushed off the marshals who had come to help him and started making his way back to the garage. Kate narrowed her eyes as she watched the blue-clad figure on the television screen in front of her. Unable to concentrate any further on the race and not wanting the rest of the team to see the inevitable fallout that was about to ensue, she went and waited at the motorhome for him to arrive.

Herding him into the back of the motorhome she stared at him, cheeks flushed, willing herself to be calm. She forced herself to speak first.

"What the hell was that?"

"I retired," Declan said shortly. "A car that's losing fuel isn't safe. Shouldn't be on the track"!

"Damn you Declan." She hissed. "You will not get away with this."

"Oh, I know I know." Declan cocked his head to one side. "I know you'll fire me."

Kate stared at him, a million words fighting to get out of her mouth. Taking a deep breath, she turned and looked out towards the track where one of her cars was completing the race and one of her drivers was heading for the podium. She looked back at Declan.

Oh no, she thought to herself. I know a better way to hurt you than that. But not here. Not now. You will keep.

CHAPTER 30.

The piece of paper in Declan's hand began to shake. He stared at it. Read it again, and again, and then tore it into pieces.

The bitch.

Laying his head back on his sofa he stared at the ceiling. His phone was ringing but he ignored it. A message flashed on the screen before it rang again. Snatching at it he saw Pete's name on the screen.

"Yes."

"Is it true?" Pete didn't need to expand on the question.

"It is," Declan said bitterly. "Due to my behaviour at Imola, I am no longer the team's number one driver. That honour has gone to our dear Italian friend."

"Bloody hell." A pause. "Can she do that?"

"I believe so. Disciplinary action and all that."

"What will you do?"

"What can I do Pete? Walk? I'll just have to make sure that I start ahead of him in every race."

"I'm sorry." Pete sounded crestfallen. "Gerald would never have done that."

"Gerald isn't here." Declan sounded sorrowful. "She'll kill this team, Pete. To win a race you have to be allowed to race."

"Your car was messed up though."

"Probably. That isn't the point. I wasn't allowed to try. That's what I can't live with. I'm a racing driver. What good am I if I can't race?"

"We'll get there mate," Pete promised. "We've had some new parts today from a new partner. Lighter but just as effective. Maybe we can get a few more miles per hour out of her."

"Well." Declan took a deep breath. "My only consolation is that I know Monaco better than anyone, apart from Kurt. It's not the easiest track for a rookie. I have to win that race, Pete. If Kurt gets another win, I'm on the back foot for the rest of the season."

"We'll have him," Pete promised. "I'll work round the clock to make sure that car is perfect."

Declan ended the call and stared glumly at his trainers. He knew that he needed to get back to Monaco but for some reason, and for the first time in his life, he couldn't face Kurt. Kurt always obeyed orders, he would never understand why

Declan had done what he did and he would doubtless tell him how stupid he was. His phone rang again and he saw an unfamiliar number. His demise was already all over the press so he had no doubt this would be yet another reporter. He ignored it. Two minutes later it rang again. This time it was the number of the Matros office. In fear of having his career destroyed even further if he ignored Kate's calls he answered.

"Hi." It wasn't Kate. "I'm sorry to disturb you."

"What." Declan hissed "Do you want?"

"I just wanted to say I'm sorry." Lucy stammered. "For what's happened. I don't think it's fair."

"Why the concern?" Declan wasn't moved. "I thought you would be laughing all over your face to see me taken down a notch."

"No," Lucy said quietly. "Not like that. You are the better driver; you deserve to be number one."

"Well." Declan paused. "I suppose the least I can do is say thank you."

"That's okay. I am on your side, you know."

"Are you?" Declan was surprised. "I thought you and Fabio were an item now?"

"Hardly. We've had a couple of meals, that's all. Where are you?"

"Home." Alarm bells started to sound in Declan's head. "Why?"

"I wondered if you wanted company. It wouldn't take me long to get there and I could bring some wine. I'm only staying in a little bed and breakfast so I have to eat."

"Are you for real?" Declan sounded shocked. "You would come all the way here to keep me company!"

"Of course, I would." There was a note of encouragement in her voice. "You know I would."

"Lucy." Declan's voice had an edge to it. "I think you need to understand. We are done. We are different people. What you told me that night, well it's all very flattering, but you didn't know me. What you saw in the Maldives is what I am. I drink too much. I'm not averse to the odd illegal substance and I love sex. A lot. You do none of those things. Not even in moderation. Being with you would be the most boring relationship I could ever imagine. "

There was a silence that went on for a few minutes. He was just about to hang up when she spoke.

"Am I that bad?" He could tell she was crying.

"Lucy what the hell do you want from me?" He snapped. "I made a mistake. I should never have taken you away. After that night here I thought you were a different person. I should never have done that either. It was all a mistake. Then you show up working for my team! What did you think? That I'd come to my senses and realise that I was wrong about you?"

"Are you in love with someone else?" She sobbed.

His mind flashed back to that night and the reason he had thrown her out in the very first place. He had thought that maybe he could have been given the chance of being in love with someone else, but not now. Not after this.

"Myself." He said shortly. "The only person I am in love with is myself. Now go away and leave me alone."

Ending the call, he turned the phone off. He wanted no more disturbances. He contemplated walking to the pub but knew he would be the subject of stares and whispers even here. So instead, he went to the cupboard and opened a bottle of whisky.

Lucy stared at her phone long after the call had ended. She was shaking all over and had an overwhelming urge to lay her head on the desk and sob. Once again, her plans had gone wrong. She had thought by offering a comforting shoulder to Declan she could have shown him how much she cared and that she was on his side. But he had thrown her adoration back in her face. How much more was she going to take before she realised that he just did not want her? God, she was confused. One part of her wanted to get in her car and race to the cottage, throw herself on him and beg him to love her; the other part wanted to tear him down and laugh as he failed. She looked out of the window and struggled to compose herself aware that Kate was in the room next door. She had to be careful. If Kate ever found out that she had applied for this job just to be close to one of her drivers she would think she was a complete maniac.

Maybe she was.

Her phone beeped and she saw a message flash onto the screen. It was from Fabio. It said one word. Dinner? A smile played on her lips. Fabio was handsome and caring and he liked her. Why shouldn't she go and have dinner with him? Declan didn't want her and she had to grow up and face the fact. Maybe the wedding dress would get worn, after all, she would just be marrying someone other than the object of her fantasies. He was still a driver and now he was team number one. Tucking her glossy dark hair behind her ears she typed the word "yes" and clicked send. Looking at her computer screen she saw the half-written document she had been working on and noticed the time. Sod it. She would finish it tomorrow. If Fabio wanted dinner, then she should at least look good and she needed something to wear.

She was just about to shut the machine down when she noticed a little envelope in the corner of the screen. Clicking it she read the new e-mail message. It was quite short but to the point. It was from the new supplier they had signed a contract with. She had taken delivery of the parts the day before and knew that they were already in the garage ready for use.

' Product Recall. CER Carbon Fibre Brake Pads. Product Ref CFD 7601.

Dear Miss Matthews,

These parts have been removed from our range following an unsatisfactory test. We are recalling all these products. Please return your order and we will issue an alternative. It is recommended that you do not use these parts on your cars."

Lucy stared at the screen and read it through a few times. The email had been sent to the generic team email address, and so far, she was the only one to have opened it. Her heart skipped in her chest. She knew that the upgraded parts they had received were intended for Declan's car. Her hand hovered above the mouse for a second then her fingers closed on it. With her heart in her mouth, she clicked the delete button. Taking a deep breath, she stood up and closed down the computer. No one else would ever read that email now, and when Declan's car underperformed at Monaco she alone would know why. A smile spread across her face and when she walked from the factory minutes later, she felt happier than she had in weeks.

CHAPTER 31.

Fabio watched the door and waited for his date to arrive. When she did, he nodded in approval. She was wearing a clinging red dress that showed off her tiny frame and high-heeled glossy black shoes. She wore very little makeup, only mascara and gloss on her lips. He liked that. He got to his feet as she got to the table and pulled a chair out for her.

"You look beautiful." He smiled.

"Thank you." Lucy beamed. "Thank you for asking me to dinner. You are very kind to me."

Fabio laughed.

"I do not think that kind is the right word cara. I like you, so I like to be with you. That is all."

"Why?" In light of her earlier conversation, Lucy wanted to know what it was that made her attractive to Fabio. "Why do you like me?"

"You are beautiful." Fabio looked puzzled. "All Italian men like a woman who is beautiful."

"Oh," She sounded disappointed. "Is that it?"

"No." He laughed. "You are very sexy, and you make me smile. Is that enough?"

"I suppose so." She gave a little pout. "Now what are we having for dinner?"

The evening wore on pleasantly, although

Fabio noticed that she was drinking a little too much. As she reached for her wine glass, he caught her wrist.

"You are driving?" He asked.

"No." She shook her head. "I took a taxi."

Fabio smiled and released her hand. Maybe it was good that she had too much to drink. His hormones were working overtime and he needed a release.

"Maybe." He said softly. "You would like to come see where I live?"

Lucy froze.

"I don't know."

"I promise to be a very good boy." He smirked and raised an eyebrow. "Unless you want me to be a bad boy."

Lucy hesitated. What did she have to lose after all? Her long-standing obsession with Declan was getting her nowhere. Here was this handsome young Italian and he wanted her company, and more, why should she not welcome it with open arms?

"Okay." She nodded. "But let's have one more drink first."

It took a long time for her to relax. She had walked into his house and been taken aback by the expensive furniture, the white leather sofa, the black rugs, the massive television, and sound system. She had admired the glossy kitchen and stared at the paintings on the wall, then finally he had convinced her to sit beside him and lay her head on his shoulder. He had kissed her, gently, and she had responded as eagerly as he had hoped; but the moment his hand started stroking her body she tensed and pulled away. Reaching over her he turned off the light.

"Is better?" He murmured.

"Yes." Lucy felt herself relax now that he couldn't see her face or any other part of her.

"Tell me cara." He whispered. "How many men have you been with?"

"None." She was glad he couldn't see her blushing.

"Really?" She could tell he was surprised.

"Yes." There was an edge to her voice. "I am okay to a point then I just freeze up. Unless I have had too much to drink then I'm okay. But I've never managed to do it properly."

Fabio hugged her.

"It is okay cara. Is not a problem."

"It is." Lucy ran her fingers through her hair. "I've had a problem. I've been in love with someone for years and it's stopped me wanting anyone bar him."

"Who?" Fabio was curious.

"Oh, just some boy." She shrugged glad that the darkness could hide the colour rising to her cheeks. "It's over now. It's time I moved on. He doesn't want me."

"Then he is very stupid." Fabio kissed her neck and the action sent shivers down her spine. "You are very beautiful and I want very much to make love to you tonight."

Lucy hesitated. Memories of the night in Declan's cottage ran through her brain. She had been so ready for him that night and wanted him. He had always been the reason she had withdrawn from other potential lovers, then when she had the opportunity to have him it had felt different. Maybe now was the time to test the water with someone else who wanted her, not a figment of her imagination.

"Okay." She got to her feet. "If that's what you want."

Fabio stood beside her and took her hand in his.

"Come cara." He nuzzled her ear. "Let me love you."

She lay in his arms and felt him breathing heavily beside her. Her body was aching and sore but she had a wonderful warm glow spreading through her the like of which she had never imagined possible. He had been gentle and she knew that he had been holding back, but for her, it had been wonderful. She raised her hand and stroked his head, then kissed it. She felt special. Loved, cared for, satisfied. Something inside her told her that it would never have been this way with Declan. His was a raw, hungry, lust, not gentle and mild like Fabio's. He stirred beside her and she held him tight waiting for him to drift back into sleep. Instead, she felt him shift beside her until his hand was stroking her thigh. She turned her head towards his and kissed him, feeling herself pressing her body tight against his. Fabio murmured then started kissing her neck, her shoulders and down over her breasts. Lucy felt herself tense and then relax as his lips moved lower. So, this was what sex was all about. Feeling the fluttering sensations beginning deep inside her she let out a deep moan of pleasure and grasped his head with her hands. Giving herself completely to this beautiful man who wanted her so much she closed her eyes and lost herself completely in her emotions.

At the same moment, Pete straightened his back and eyed his work with a satisfied grin. He had promised to work around the clock on Declan's car to get him on the front of the grid in Monaco, and here he was. He had some ideas about altering the height of the wing and lightening the nose but he needed Carlo's approval to do that work. So, for now he had just finished assembling the new brake discs onto Declan's car. They were light and would give him a definite bit of an edge when it came to straight-line speed. Looking at the clock he admitted that he was too tired to do more and would have to call it a night. Turning to his computer he recorded that the CFD 7601 brake pads had been fitted to Declan's car and turned off the light.

CHAPTER 32.

The Monaco Grand Prix was not only the most famous race on the calendar it was also one of the oldest, and was renowned for its reputation as being one of the trickiest tracks on the circuit. It was equally famous for the glitz and glamour that surrounded the whole meeting. Normal racegoers found themselves being ousted by celebrities as this was the place to be seen. Film stars mingled with mechanics and the public could not walk down the streets without finding themselves passing a famous face. Celebrities were always two a penny in Monaco but this weekend took the population of the rich and famous to the extreme. Rooms were at a premium and many fans found themselves staying way outside the principality itself and travelling by coach to watch the practice sessions. The number of yachts in the marina tripled as millionaires hosted pre-race parties and provided unique viewing points for the action. The elevation changes and tight corners combined with the light change of the tunnel found Fabio struggling from day one. Declan, who knew these streets like the back of his hand, sailed through free practice without putting himself under pressure. He was widely recognised as one of the best drivers to have ever graced the circuit and it showed. There was no opportunity to use maximum speed here; this track demanded both skill and nerve from a driver. To win they had to have the courage to pass where lesser hearts would quake and back off. Declan took great pleasure in warning Fabio that some drivers had ended up in the harbour in the past and that he needed to fit a life jacket under his fire suit. Fabio smiled and took it all in good heart, but underneath he was getting increasingly nervous and his performance went rapidly downhill. Carlo called him to one side after his last free practice session had ended.

"Don't let this place get to you, Fabio. It is just another race."

"It is so narrow." Fabio shook his head. "I drive too slow. I am afraid I will be in the hotel with the guests."

"Well, if you do make sure you greet them with a smile." Carlo laughed. "You are number one now, remember?"

"I should not be." Fabio's eyes were watching a blue car returning to the garage. "He is the best. You know it and I know it."

"I don't doubt it." Carlo agreed. "But he is not behaving like a number one driver and that is a lesson he must learn. Gerald does not control this team now, Kate does."

Pete was helping Declan out of the cockpit.

"I wouldn't worry too much about being ahead of your teammate." He muttered. "He isn't getting to grips with the track at all."

"It's not him I am worried about." Declan stared into the track. "Kurt could drive this circuit in his sleep. I have only beaten him here when he has failed to finish. Which, the way his car is performing, isn't likely to happen this year."

"A little faith old man." Pete patted his shoulder. "How are the brakes?"

"Sluggish." Declan frowned. "I'm not convinced they are better than the others."

"Hmm." Pete frowned. "Well, they were very expensive, I know that much. Kate nearly had a fit when she saw the bill!"

"Well, if she wants to win, she has to compete." Declan shrugged. "That's up to her. You don't win Grand Prix races by taking shortcuts."

His eyes had spotted a dark-haired figure standing beside Fabio.

"Those two are getting pretty close, aren't they?"

"Jealous, are we?" Pete was about to laugh and then saw Declan's face. "Word on the jungle drums has it that they are now very much an item. To the extent that they are sharing a hotel room."

"What?" Declan raised his eyebrows. "Jesus. I never expected that."

Fabio was walking towards him. There had been an unmistakable air of tension between them since Kate had announced the team change but even stubborn, proud Declan had to reluctantly admit that none of it was Fabio's fault. So, he swallowed his feelings and greeted the younger man with a smile.

"Happy?"

"No." Fabio was frowning. "This track defeats me before I begin. I do not know how to drive it."

"Well, the quickest way is to learn it on a PlayStation." Declan laughed. "That's what I did!"

"Really?" Fabio laughed. "I must try this. Thank you."

"Fabio." Declan lowered his voice and became serious. "I know that none of this is your fault, okay? I don't blame you in the least. So, what I am going to say has nothing to do with the situation."

"What?"

"Be careful." Declan nodded towards Lucy. "That girl has some issues. Just be careful how involved you get."

"Is okay." Fabio looked wary. "She tell me about you two."

"Did she?" Declan looked puzzled. "What did she say?"

"That you have a few dates but nothing work. I am sorry if I do wrong thing for you in seeing her."

"You do me no wrong at all." Declan laughed.

"You have done me a big favour, believe me. A few dates, eh? Nothing worked? You seem to have succeeded where I failed Fabio. To the victor the spoils and you are welcome to them."

Fabio hesitated. He didn't like Declan's tone and wanted to say something but thought better of it. He was nervous enough; he didn't need to create any more tension. So, he smiled, nodded, and walked away. Lucy was waiting for him.

"What did he say to you?" She muttered.

"Nothing." Fabio put his arm around her. "Let us go."

The press loved them. The handsome Italian and his new girlfriend, the cameras flashed as they walked out of the garage. Declan watched them go and pulled a face. This was all playing into his hands. Between nerves about the track, the added press attention, and the demands of a needy girl such as Lucy there was no way Fabio would have his mind on the job tomorrow.

"Don't forget tonight Dec" Pete's voice brought him back to the present. "Sponsors dinner in hospitality. They are expecting driver talks."

"Fuck that." Declan laughed. "That's Fabio's territory now. Me, I'm just the number two.!

Pete laughed.

"You know full well that makes no difference. It will be you they want to see."

"Tough. I'm having dinner with Kurt." Declan smiled. "It's a tradition. I beat him on the PlayStation and then he beats me in the race."

Pete laughed.

"No booze." He warned.

"What the hell is it with you a lot!" Declan shrugged. "Can't a man have a beer with an old mate these days?"

"Not before qualifying he can't!" Pete shook his head. "Just be wary Dec, the red-headed demon has her eyes on you. One slip and you are gone."

The beer, as Pete had feared, turned into a few. Having, as he had predicted, beaten Kurt on the PlayStation, a fact that did not make him feel good about the race itself, Declan found himself at a pre-race party. He wasn't sure who the organiser was. Or who the blonde who ended up in his bed that night was. All he knew was that he arrived for qualifying the next morning looking a little worse for wear.

"Jesus." Pete steered him towards the coffee machine. "What the hell is wrong with you man!"

"Shut up Dad." Declan took the coffee and raised the cup. "I'll be fine in five. I just need something to wake me up."

"NO." Pete hissed. "NO drugs Dec. You want to get struck off?!"

"Who mentioned drugs?" Declan laughed. "I was referring to the coffee. Come on Pete; I might party the night before a session but I don't want to commit motorsport suicide, do I?"

"Sometimes I wonder. God, it's a good job I

love you, you old shit."

"Never knew you cared." Declan finished his coffee. "Come on Trent, get me in that car."

As expected, Kurt took the pole position later that afternoon in some style. Staying in the garage until the last possible minute he did one last, flying, lap and pushed Declan back into his customary second place. Fabio, still struggling with nerves, was back in tenth. If Declan felt relief about being eight places ahead of his teammate, he did not show it and conducted his interviews with his usual charm and wit. He had an air of confidence about him and the press lapped it up. But inside his head, he was being troubled by a nagging doubt. As soon as he had finished his interview, he went in search of Carlo.

"These brakes." He shook his head, frowning. "They feel so different."

"They look fine," Carlo assured him. "And you are driving well. I do not think there is a problem."

"It's just a feeling." Declan shrugged. "I can't explain it."

"All is fine," Carlo assured him. "Trust me."

"On your head be it." Declan laughed. "If I fly into the harbour, it will all be your fault. Still. At least I can walk home from there."

CHAPTER 33.

The morning of the race dawned bright and breezy with temperatures that rose steadily throughout the day. Smiling with relief celebrities donned short-sleeved shirts and dresses and completed their outfits with sunglasses. Looking good in the rain was a challenge they didn't want to face. The drivers thanked the dry weather but cursed the rising heat as they sweated through the driver's parade and wandered the pit lane with race suits hanging from their hips in an attempt to stay cool. Fabio, sipping an energy drink through a long straw, looked up at the cloudless sky and felt grateful that he wouldn't have to cope with a misted visor as well as dented confidence. This track was beyond him; he was still filled with self-doubt and even a session on a PlayStation had not lifted his spirits. He leaned against the pit wall and closed his eyes; trying to memorise every twist and turn of the winding circuit he was about to drive on. A hand touched his arm and he opened his eyes to find Lucy standing beside him.

"Are you okay?" Large round sunglasses hid her eyes.

"Yes." He lied. "No. I do not know. I do not think I can do this."

"You can." She reached up and planted a kiss on his cheek, a gesture that instantly caught the attention of the ever-attentive press. "And you will."

Fabio smiled down at her, he wished that he shared her faith in his abilities.

"I will try. Now cara I am sorry but I need to think, to focus my brain."

"I know." She gave him another kiss. "I will be in the garage watching."

Declan was, as ever, in his car already and he surveyed the scene with a scowl on his face. He hoped that little idiot wasn't going to spoil Fabio's concentration and put him at risk. Fabio's tension was so great he should have had a sign attached to his car saying "nervous driver". He, Declan, on the other hand was feeling quite cool. He knew this place so well that it was like driving in his living room. The twists and turns were so familiar he could do it with his eyes closed. Unfortunately, so could Kurt. His eyes went sideways and he watched his friend and rival going through his usual pre-race routine. Interview here, drink, interview there, drink, argue with his engineer, moan about downforce then get in the car and win the bloody race. Not today Declan thought to himself, his hands tightening on the steering wheel, not today. This one is mine. As if he had read his thoughts, Kurt turned and looked at him. A grin split his narrow face and he raised a thumb. Declan laughed and nodded. That was the beauty of their relationship. They were as thick as thieves off the track and as heartless as murderers on it. Once those lights went out neither one gave an inch. All around him, the excitement was growing as drivers started to strap themselves in ready for the formation lap.

Declan's eyes switched into focus and he lowered his visor. In his ear, he could hear Pete chattering away.

"Radio check Declan. Radio check."

"Trent!" He hissed in reply. "Shut the fuck up for five minutes!"

One by one, the cars headed out onto the formation lap. Twisting and turning, getting brakes and tyres up to temperature: this was one of the hardest tracks on the circuit for warming a car up before a race and for those at the front of the grid it seemed to take an age for the back markers to come through Anthony Noges and take their place at the rear of the pack. Then at last the lights came on and a hush descended over the crowd.

In his cockpit, Fabio took a deep breath and counted down the lights. His foot hovered over his throttle, ready to act. The lights went out and all around him cars took off and headed for the first corner at Sainte Devote.

Except his.

"I've stalled." His desperate voice sounded in Carlo's ear. "Get me started, quick!"

Within seconds his crew had fired the car back into action but their driver was already well behind the last car. Declan heard the news over the radio and suppressed a grin. One down. One to go. His eyes were locked on the silver streak in front of him; Kurt's car had flown off the start like a rocket and was already a second ahead, but Declan still had him in his sights and knew that every time they reached Mirabeau the cars would slow almost to a standstill as they negotiated one of the world's most famous hairpin bends. He had time, plenty of time. All he had to do was creep closer and then when the moment was right, he would chase him through the tunnel and have him there. Failing that he could out-manoeuvre him at Beau Rivage, they were his only options; there was nowhere else to pass.

It soon became clear to all watching the race that it was going to concern, barring mishaps, two drivers. Kurt and Declan had stolen a massive lead on the rest of the pack and the new Matros number one was tailing the field after his poor start. The first pit stop came and went and there was no change in the order. The crowd, lulled into sleep by the heat and alcohol became almost bored and watched the cars streaming past for another ten laps before a burst of excitement roused them.

"Safety car Dec." Pete was sounding very cool.

"Safety car is out. Watch your speed."

Declan groaned as he saw Kurt lifting off in front of him and drew up onto his tail.

"Who's off?" He moaned.

"Fabio" There was a pause. "Went straight on at Saint Devote. They are picking him out of the barrier as we speak."

Declan's eyes shot to the left as he passed the scattered remains of the GM-4. Fabio was standing by the Armco being attended by a paramedic but he seemed unharmed, irater, at having spun off.

"Not so number one now, are we?" He muttered. "Watch and learn Miss Matthews, watch and learn."

"Safety car coming in." Pete sounded in his earpiece. "Stay on him Dec this might be your only chance."

"As if I didn't know that." Declan retorted. "I am stuck to his arse like glue, believe me."

As soon as the safety car turned into the pit lane Kurt floored his accelerator, his eyes on his mirrors. As he expected the blue car stayed right behind him.

"Come on Braun," Declan shouted. "Let's duel. Pistols for two and coffee for one"

But try as he might, Declan could not get past Kurt. He tried to outmanoeuvre him at La Rascasse but knew that it would never work. Staying off his brakes until the last possible moment, he tried to cut through the inside at

Sainte Devote and nearly joined Fabio in the Armco.

"Ease up old mate," Pete muttered. "Let's get you home in one piece."

Declan growled something illegible and read his pit board. Damn.

"I want to stay out." He shouted. "If he pits, I'm staying out."

"You have two laps," Carlo informed him. "Watch your fuel."

In the car ahead, Kurt was all too aware that Declan was playing cat and mouse with him. He expected nothing less. He knew that Declan wouldn't pit until he did. He pushed his car to the limit of its fuel tank and caved in after a lap.

"Here I come. Declan in pit lane" Declan swung in behind him. "There's a grand for everyone if I get out first!"

The crew needed no bribing, they were armed and ready for action and wanted their man back on the track ahead, money or not. As his rear tyres were removed Declan glanced in his mirror and saw a cloud of dust billowing into the air.

"What the hell is that?" His eyes widened.

"Brakes." Carlo was bending over to inspect them. "This new compound breaks down quickly, that is all."

"Will they get me to the end of the race?"

"Of course; but try not to be hard on them."

"Did you hear that?" Pete quipped. "No more standing on them in hairpins!

"Bollocks." Declan was watching the fuel man. "Come on, get me out!"

Ahead of him, Kurt's fuel man was removing the nozzle. Declan slapped his steering wheel yelling at his crew to hurry up.

"Go!" Screamed Pete. "Go!"

Declan swung the nose of the Matros out into the pit lane and as he did so a silver car swung out in front of him.

"Shit." He snarled. "Bloody hell Braun, will you never give me a break!"

The two cars streaked back onto the circuit and the crowd began to sit on the edge of their seats. This was it. Twenty-four laps to the end of the race. That was all Declan Hyde had to get the nose of his car in front. Fifty realistic racing opportunities or it was all over. No one was more aware of that than Declan, who hugged Kurt tight at every bend trying desperately to get in front. He could feel that Kurt was getting rattled as he began to swing off the racing line to hold Declan at bay.

"Keep it up Dec." Pete's voice was calm. "You'll have him next time."

Accelerating through Portier with only fifteen laps to go Declan could feel desperation taking over. Kurt's car was not performing well, he was sliding all over the track, but he had the lead and with clever driving was holding Declan back at every opportunity.

"For fucks sake Braun!" Declan shrieked "Get

out of my bloody way!"

Through Mirabeau, hard on the brakes, to a standstill round the hairpin, the nose of Declan's GM-4 was almost touching the tail of Kurt's car. This had to be it. He would out brake him at Portier and then overtake through the tunnel. He saw Kurt's brake lights come on as he entered Portier.

Wait. Wait. Not yet. Wait.

Now.

Declan depressed his brake pedal to the floor, hard.

Nothing happened.

The events that followed took only seconds, but were implanted in his mind forever. He sat helpless, horrified, as his car headed for the cockpit of Kurt's car. The brake should have carried him round the corner, but he was going straight on, heading like a spear for the vehicle in front of him.

"Kurt!" He heard himself shrieking. "Move!"

Then, in a split second, it was too late. His nose crumpled into the side of Kurt's car, and they set off in a macabre dance, locked together, spinning wildly towards the tunnel.

"Oh Jesus, Jesus, Jesus!" Pete could hear the horror in Declan's voice. "Help me!"

With a devastating crunch, the two cars hit the Armco and separated. Declan's head snapped forward on his neck and he gasped for breath as pain shot through his head. In the edge of his vision, he could see Kurt's car spinning, out of control, into the tunnel. Then he blacked out.

Through a fog of pain and confusion, he felt himself being lifted from the car. He breathed deeply, once, and again. He was still alive. Then it hit him.

The smell of smoke and a sound that would haunt him through every dream he had for the rest of his life.

The sound of a man screaming.

Pulling free of the Marshall and the doctor, ignoring the blood that pumped from his right knee and the pains in his neck and head, Declan began to run for the tunnel.

As he reached it, his body mercifully saved him from the sight that lay inside, and he collapsed.

CHAPTER 34.

Darkness. Darkness, that was all that there was. But, somewhere in that darkness was a noise, a buzzing that got louder and louder until it began to fill his senses. Then through the darkness came light and a sensation of lifting. Slowly, he opened his eyes and winced as the light pierced into his eyes and made them hurt.

There were shadows, vague forms in the haze of his vision. The noises were coming from them. He began to recognise words and voices and began the uncomfortable process of waking up.

"Declan." Pete's familiar voice triggered a response inside his head. "Come on mate, wake up."

He groaned and tried to speak but all that came out of his dry mouth was a croak.

"Here." Pete held something to his lips. "Drink."

Nodding his thanks, Declan felt the cool water slip down his dry throat.

"Better?" Pete seemed to be holding his hand.

"Yes." This time the words came out of his mouth, quiet and timid. "Where?"

"The hospital." Pete offered more water.

"How?" Declan was frowning, trying to remember.

"You crashed." Pete hesitated. "You've been out for a bit."

Declan nodded slowly and then his eyes widened as it all came back. The sounds, the smells, the screams.

"Kurt!" He gasped.

"He's going to be okay." Pete pushed him gently back against the pillows. "Nothing for you to worry about. You just have to concentrate on getting better. It's just so good to have you back."

It was another three days before he learned the truth. They had told him, quite soon after he woke, that he had a deep laceration on his left thigh and that his patella was fractured but not completely broken. He had multiple bruises and had been unconscious for over ten hours. He had a heavy concussion but there was no long-term damage. Then slowly, they began to drip feed into his bruised mind the rest of the picture.

His car had impaled Kurt into the barrier and set them both into a spin. He had then hit the barrier side on and broken free. Kurt's car had continued its spin into the tunnel where it hit the wall shortly after entry and burst into flames. Kurt was, albeit briefly, trapped and still conscious. It had been long enough for him to sustain burns to his arms, hands, and upper body. His right leg and shoulder had been shattered in the impact. He was being kept sedated as the doctors operated to stem a bleed on his brain. But he was alive and extremely lucky to be so.

Pete sat by the bed as Carlo delivered the news calmly, and in as matter-of-fact a tone as was possible and watched Declan's heart shattering before his eyes. Tears streamed down his cheeks and soaked his pillow, and then he began to shake, shaking so violently that Carlo sent him running to fetch a doctor. Once the doctor had sedated Declan once more and he slept they went to the hospital canteen.

"When are you going to tell him the rest?" Pete stirred his lukewarm coffee with a gloomy face.

"I don't know." Carlo shrugged. "You saw what that did to him. One thing at a time is all he can take."

"Please," Pete pleaded, "Tell him before Kate does. That would be cruel. She's after his blood."

"I know." Carlo was looking out of the window. "In everything, someone has to take the blame. But something is wrong here Pete. I do not know what but my heart tells me it is, and I mean to find out what it is."

So, the next day, they told him the rest.

His car was in the hands of the scrutineers, but until their report was complete the FIA had revoked his licence; the length of his suspension would be decided after he was well enough to talk to them. They, like many others, blamed him for the crash and considered he had caused it through dangerous driving. He had endangered another driver's life and quite simply, he had to pay.

Declan, out of bed and sitting in a chair with his leg raised, took the news with a resignation that worried Pete far more than the hysteria of the previous day.

"Who cares." Declan stared at his bruised hands. "I deserve it. My closest friend is in a coma and I put him there. He's all that counts. They can lock me up if they want."

"Come on Declan." Carlo went to his side and laid a comforting hand on his shoulder. "You can get through this."

"Can I?" Declan looked at him, and his voice broke. "They won't let me see him. If Kurt dies then it will me who killed him "

"I think that is a little hard on yourself." Carlo shook his head. "We work in a dangerous sport, you know that."

"Give me that paper." Declan looked at Pete and pointed to the bedside table. "And a pen."

"What are you doing?" Pete held out the paper and narrowed his eyes.

"My resignation." Declan began to write. "I'm getting out before Kate Matthews can remove the one thing I have left. My right to make a choice."

CHAPTER 35.

In the Matros office, Kate paced the floorboards and read the letter over and over again. In the end, she threw it to the table in disgust.

"Bastard." She hissed. "Coward. Taking the easy way out!"

"I would hardly call it that." Carlo retorted. "His career could be ruined. His best friend is still in a coma and he blames himself."

"So he should!" Kate shrieked. "You were watching Carlo. You saw it. He drove straight at him. He wanted to take him out just so he could win a bloody race!"

"You forget," Carlo shouted. "That is why we are all here to win the bloody race as you call it, and Declan could be in a coma himself. So you and your team could win that race! Think of what you say!"

Kate stared at him and her colour rose.

"Why are you taking his side?" She shouted back. "Do you know what he's done? The FIA is investigating this, we are all in the spotlight, all of us. All my father's work could be ruined because he can't control his temper!"

Carlo paused and then nodded his head.

"I can see that Declan has done the right thing.

I did not expect this from you. I hate to say this too but your father was wrong to make you head of this team. You do not understand what it is to drive in a race; you have never sensed that split second of fear, the inevitability of what is coming when something goes wrong. You do not understand the focus that it takes to win. "

"Well, that's great" Kate screamed, tears spilling down her cheeks. "Now you are against me. This is not my fault Carlo!"

"No, it is not." Carlo was putting on his coat. "But I do not believe it is Declan's. When I have the proof, I will come back and speak to you again."

"Where are you going?" She shouted after him.

"To do some work." He shouted back. "Of my own."

"But I need you here. Carlo, please!"

Carlo looked back over his shoulder.

"You forget cara that this is my team also, and I for one will not stand by and let the best driver who has ever sat in one of our cars have the blame laid at his feet for an accident."

Kate watched him walk away and sank into her chair. On the wall in front of her hung a photo of her father and Declan holding aloft a trophy. She stared at the two men. The one she had loved more than anything in the world, and the one she hated.

"Oh Dad, Dad, Dad" She sobbed. "Why did you have to leave me with all this? I can't cope with it,

I can't!"

In the office next door Lucy had heard the raised voices, the slamming of doors and then the sound of Kate's tears. She felt sick. But then she had been feeling sick since last Sunday. The crash had been the most horrific thing she had ever seen and she had only just controlled the panic that had swept over her at the sight of Declan's car disintegrating as it ricocheted off the barrier. She had spent hours scheming ways in which she could shatter his dreams in the same way that he had shattered hers; then, in the split seconds before he crashed, all she had wanted was for him to be safe. She was horrified by what had happened to Kurt but it seemed unimportant compared to the news that Declan was being blamed for the crash. Worse, he had resigned from the team. Now she would never be close to him again and it hurt. Still. After everything that had happened, it tore at her heart.

She heard a noise in the doorway and looked up to see Fabio watching her.

"Oh hello." She smiled. "Are you okay?"

"No." Fabio looked defeated. "Declan has resigned from the team. How can I do this without him? He teach me everything I know. He takes the spotlight so that I can learn and for so long he was my friend."

"Yes." Lucy nodded. "It will be very different here now. But he didn't like me very much so I won't miss him as much as you."

Fabio looked at her with mournful eyes.

"We will have a new driver for Canada. Jean-Claude. He is test driver here at the factory. "

Lucy got to her feet and went to him.

"Don't look so sad." She hugged him. "You still have me."

"Yes." Fabio nuzzled her. "I have you. For that I am happy."

Lucy smiled to herself as she nuzzled into his chest. Every cloud, she told herself, has a silver lining.

In a hospital room many hundreds of miles away Bernice was trying to touch her husband and not hurt him. She had walked into the room, ashen-faced; red-eyed and gaunt from nights of no sleep to find him looking at her. She had clung to the door handle and screamed. The doctors had come running to find her both crying and laughing at the same time. Kurt Braun, it seemed was made of stern stuff and his fit body had fought its way back from the brink. Now Bernice faced the yards of gauze and bandages, the tubes and the plaster and wondered how she could get to him to kiss him. When she did manage to lean across and touch his cheek with her lips her tears started again and flowed downwards to mix with his own.

A few days later she was sitting in his room watching him staring at the ceiling and counting the tiles. She smiled. Typical Kurt. Even in his battered state boredom was already setting in.

"Can I get you anything?" She grinned.

"New legs?" Kurt looked at her. "So I can get out of this bed?"

"It won't be long." She promised. "They'll get you up in a day or two once the burns have healed a bit more."

"Great." Kurt scowled. "What will I do then? Knit?"

"Very funny." Bernice laughed.

"I wish they would tell me." Kurt stared back at the ceiling. "When I will drive again."

Bernice froze. This was the moment she had been dreading from the very second she had known that her husband was not going to die.

"Kurt." She said softly. "Don't think about that now. That's a long way in the future. You have to get well first and get home."

"But what will I do if I cannot drive?" Kurt's voice caught in his throat. "There is nothing else for me."

"You can be a husband and a father." Bernice sat on the edge of the bed. "We don't need the money. We can just live our life."

"Don't you listen to her." A voice sounded from the doorway. "You do need the money; she's spent it all."

Kurt's eyes looked past Bernice and locked on the figure that was hovering just inside the door. Declan was leaning on his crutch and had a large bouquet in his hand. Terrified of the reception that he may get he had put off this moment until today. He was about to go home and he knew that he would get no peace until he had laid this ghost to rest.

The silence that hung over the room cut him like a knife.

"I" He hesitated. "I had to come. I had to...I'm sorry. I'll go."

"I do not like roses," Kurt said shortly.

Declan looked at him, searching his face for the joke behind the words. For a moment the pale thin face was still, devoid of motion, and then, just as he was about to turn away, he saw the hint of a twinkle in the pale eyes.

"All they had." He said shortly. "It was this or a porn mag."

"And what would I do with that?" Kurt nodded to his mummified hands. "Use my mouth?"

"Well." Declan was moving forward slowly. "It's an option. Anyway, they aren't for you."

Turning to Bernice he held out his hand, wobbling slightly as he did.

"They are for you."

Bernice took the flowers, lifted them to her face and hid the tears inside them. Knowing that this was a moment that even she could not share she got to her feet.

"I'll get them put in water." She muttered.

They stared at each other, the two battered, bruised, and broken men, neither one knowing what to say.

"I." Declan was struggling with his words. "I don't know where to begin."

"Then don't," Kurt spoke softly. "There is nothing to say. What is done is done."

"Oh God." Declan's crutches fell to the floor and he sat heavily in the chair. "I'm so sorry. If I could swap places with you I would. I didn't, I mean I never..."

"It's okay." Kurt could barely speak.

Declan looked at him.

"I will never forgive myself." He choked. "Never."

"Declan." Kurt had tears rolling down his cheeks. "I need help."

"What? Anything?"

"Could you get a tissue and wipe my face? I can't use my hands."

Bernice came back into the room sometime later to find the two men laughing and joking. She smiled as she sat on the bed and watched them. Kurt looked alive and, in less pain, now that Declan was here and she realised that this was the moment he had been waiting for. He would no longer need to count the tiles in the ceiling. She was his wife, the mother of his children and the love of his life.

But his soul mate was sitting in the chair beside him.

Declan did not watch the Canadian Grand Prix. It was far too much for his precarious mental state to handle. So instead, he sat in Kurt's hospital room and played Scrabble waiting patiently while Kurt moved the tiles with his mummified hands. It was only later that he found out that Fabio had gone head-first into the barrier and had somehow, miraculously, walked away with only minor cuts and bruises. His only contact from his former team was a message from Carlo. It said simply.

"We can all make mistakes."

The scrutineers report lay on Kate's desk and she stared at it with horrified eyes. Carlo watched and waited as she read it again.

"This can't be true." She stammered. "It can't be!"

"It is cara. It is true."

"Declan crashed because his brakes had disintegrated? Jesus." For a moment she imagined what must have gone through his head when he had realised that he had no control.

"Exactly. He could have been killed."

"Kurt nearly was killed." She gasped. "But how can this happen, Carlo? Is it just bad luck?"

"I would say no," Carlo said grimly. "The brakes on Fabio's car had done the same. Just dust, nothing left."

"But why?" Kate was shaking. "They were new parts. Better. You said. Safer. You said."

"I know." Carlo had a strange look on his face.

"But there was this."

He handed her another sheet of paper.

"But I never saw this!" She got to her feet. "I swear I never did."

"I am afraid that Declan does not see it that way. He thinks that you ignored this email so that you could save money."

"You told him!" Kate stared at him, "In God's name why!"

"He had a right to know. The FIA have suspended him for the rest of the year. If this is the cause of the accident they need to know as they are telling him this news today. It is only fair."

"But he's resigned." Kate pointed to the envelope on her desk. "What difference does it make? What does he want? To get his licence back, for what?"

"You should see him," Carlo said quietly. "He is a broken man. You cannot expect him to carry the guilt for the accident forever. He has the right to know his innocence, and for everyone else to know it also."

"Oh God." Kate placed her hands over her eyes. "Will this nightmare never end? What should I do?"

"That is up to you." Carlo placed his hand on her arm. "It is for your conscience to deal with. Someone here in this building opened the email; the company it came from has checked that. If it was not you then I have to know who opened it in your place."

"Find them for me Carlo." Kate pleaded. "Please?"

"I will. For now, I must tell Fabio what happened. He also cannot think it was him. He leaves for Rome tonight."

"Carlo." A terrible thought had just registered in Kate's brain. "You believe me, don't you?"

"I do." Carlo smiled. "You are your father's daughter and you would not risk his name by doing something so stupid. But it is not me you must convince."

CHAPTER 36.

Someone was knocking on the door. Bleary-eyed, and sluggish from the medication, Declan struggled to get up. It was a grey stormy day and he could not wait to get back to Monaco and the sun. His work here was done now; tomorrow he could get on with rebuilding his life. Feeling queasy he stopped in the hall and saw he was too late. Whoever had been knocking had already gone, in their place was an envelope, pushed through the letterbox. Puzzled, he picked it up.

' Dear Declan,' it read 'I can understand if you don't want to see me. I am so sorry about what has happened. Carlo told me about the brakes and the scrutineers report. He also told me about the email recalling the part, please believe me when I say I never saw it.

I admit I blamed you for the crash, at the time, but I also admit that I was wrong.

I feel so guilty. You and Kurt could have been killed by our inadequacy as a team. This would never have happened if my father had been alive. He was better than I will ever be. Please you have to believe me that I knew nothing of this. We may have our differences but I would never want you dead. There has been enough of that in my life already.

Kate.'

He read it twice before laying it on the hall table. Kate Matthews had come here? To apologise to him face to face? That must have been hard for her to do. After everything that had happened. Opening the door, he looked out, there was no sign of anyone. He hesitated then reached for his coat. He had to find her. He had to let her know that in this, at least, of everything that had ever been said and done between them, he believed her.

Hobbling out of the front door he began to limp down the quayside, ignorant of the rain that lashed against his face. Halting at the end of the street he looked around wildly. There was no sign of her, no sign of any living thing anywhere; just rain and houses and dark grey skies. The lights of The Harbour were glowing ahead of him. Perhaps she had gone in there to shelter from the rain; as he went to cross the road he saw a figure, huddled against the wind, scurrying from the cover of the Harbour Master office, and running up the hill.

"Kate!" The wind whipped his words away before they reached her and scattered them over the water. "Kate!"

He began to run after her, his limp getting worse as pain throbbed in his damaged knee. The hill had never seemed so steep before.

"Kate!" He roared. "Kate. Wait!"

The road began to climb steeply and he followed it as it turned to the right, he had gained on her but she was still some way ahead. He could run no further, his breath burned in his unfit lungs and the pain in his knee was unbearable.

"Kate." He gasped in one last, desperate, attempt. "For God's sake, stop!

With the wind suddenly silenced by the houses that clung to the hillside and sheltered them she heard him. She stopped and turned slowly; squinting through the horizontal sheets of rain she saw him leaning weakly against a wall, soaked to the skin, his t-shirt sticking to his prominent ribs. She opened her mouth to speak but instead walked towards him, afraid to look directly into his big, emotion-filled eyes.

"You read it."

"I did." He gasped. "I had to tell you. I believe you. I believe you knew nothing."

"Why?" She looked up at him.

"I'm so sick of feeling guilty." He shook his head. "I can't take any more. I couldn't let you just leave without knowing if I believed you or not. It would have just been more guilt to carry."

He was breathing heavily; his body shivering as the rain ran down the back of his neck and soaked his skin.

"You should get inside." Her voice softened

She had never seen him look so weak, or so wretched and it touched her. In that split second, in the lashing rain and the howling wind, she began to realise exactly what all of this had done to him. All of it, her father dying, his removal from his number one position and then the knowledge that he had put his best friend on the brink of death; it was so much for one man to deal with.

"You look awful."

"Thanks." He grunted. "Actually, this is one of my better days."

She forced a smile.

"Go on then. Get inside. My car is at the top of the hill."

"I can't." He gasped. "You'll have to help me."

"What?" She looked puzzled.

"I can't walk." His face was tightening against the pain. "My leg."

Kate hesitated. Despite the awkwardness, she felt she couldn't leave him as he was.

"Okay." The reluctance sounded in her voice. "Here."

Nodding his thanks Declan took her arm and leaned on her heavily as they walked back down the hill. She could hear his breath catching in his throat with every step. When they reached The Harbour he halted.

"I'll be fine from here. Thanks."

"Declan." She hesitated. "You can't go in there, you can't drink in this state surely?."

"I'm not." He shook his head. "I can lean on the wall from here. I'm fine now"

"You look it." She snorted. "Come on, I've brought you this far, I can take you all the way."

A thousand smart answers flashed through Declan's head and a smile touched his lips.

"One word." She warned." And I let you fall flat on your face."

Declan grinned at her and a strange sensation washed over her. For the first time in all these years they were communicating properly, and it felt like the most natural thing in the world. Quite suddenly the barriers had dropped

"Lead on." He took her arm again. "Mine's a coffee with two sugars."

Kate chuckled and laid her hand on his. Slowly, aware of the pain he felt at every step, helped him back along the quay and through the front door.

CHAPTER 37.

Rome was everything that Lucy had imagined, and more. From the moment she had stepped off the jet and breathed in the hot air, feeling the scorching heat of the sun on her back, she had felt a sense of homecoming. For Fabio, it was a homecoming in the true sense of the word. Taught and nervous, he put off the moment of facing his family again; using the excuse of showing Lucy the sights. They did the tours, ate at the best restaurants, and spent small fortunes in the elegant and extremely pricey shops. Lucy felt spoiled, utterly, but she loved it and accepted every lavish gift that Fabio bestowed on her. But she also sensed his tension and could not understand why he was so reluctant to go home. Finally, the morning came when he could delay it no longer. Walking through the reception of the hotel he was hailed by the manager, who was holding a telephone call for him. It was his oldest brother, who had seen him eating out with Lucy the previous night. So now they knew he was here, and it was time to face the music. He did not move their things out of the hotel but bundled Lucy into a taxi and sat silently throughout the long journey into the hills. Lucy was too excited to notice his silence. The scenery was so beautiful, the villas so grand, and the sun so blistering in the cloudless deep blue sky that she was bursting with energy. To her, it was a whole new world and one with which she felt strangely unified. To Fabio, it was just the road home, to a very uncertain welcome.

Whether it was Lucy's presence, or whether it was his absence softening the wounds he wasn't sure. But his father greeted him without a single recrimination. His mother was ecstatic, especially with Lucy, who would pass for Italian at least with her tanned olive skin and luxurious black hair. Setting about the kitchen with a vengeance she began to plan a dinner to welcome her baby home. Fabio took his escape while he could and took Lucy for a walk through the vineyards, and showed her the ancient wine cellars. She was staggered. Nothing had prepared her for such wealth, such ancestry. To her Fabio had always just been the team's Italian driver; admittedly gorgeous, and thankfully very attracted to her, but she had never considered that he could have such standing in his own right. Even if there was never another race car in Fabio's life he would want for nothing; everything he could need for a lavish life was here, waiting for him. She just could not understand why being here could make him so withdrawn.

It all came out over dinner. Fabio's promised

marriage to Sophia, his sudden, unexpected flight to England, and his total lack of communication with any of his family since. Lucy listened; understood his reservations about coming home, but failed to truly understand the situation that he had fled. It made her curious, and she asked too many questions, resulting in their first real confrontation after dinner.

"But I don't understand." She was standing on the terrace, wearing one of the figure-hugging dresses that he had bought her. It showed off every inch of her slender body and made his thoughts turn to things other than family disagreements.

"Why did you have to leave this place? Surely if you didn't want to marry what's her name that was up to you? You didn't have to risk losing all this?"

"You don't know Italian families." He replied, standing back in the shadows. Not wanting to talk about the past, he was only interested in getting Lucy back home and into bed. "You are not Italian."

"I don't know so much." Lucy gave him a seductive look from beneath her eyelashes. "I feel quite at home here. Even your mother thought I must have Roman blood in me somewhere."

"The only Roman you will ever have in you." Fabio's voice was low, making the hairs on the back of her neck stand up. "Is standing behind you."

Lucy smiled. It was good to be wanted. Now that she had finally overcome her hang-up, she was more than ready to collapse into Fabio's ever-open arms, and bed, at any time. But tonight, her curiosity was getting the better of her. That could wait.

"Don't be rude." She stared across the valley; covered in shadow she could detect only the faintest twinkling of lights in the village below. "Tell me about Sophia."

"There is nothing to tell." Fabio sounded curt. "It does not interest me."

"It interests me." Lucy turned to face him. "What was she like? Why were you so desperate to get away?"

"It is none of your business." He put down his wine glass. "Come, we must go."

"Go where?" Lucy shook her head. "Why can't we stay here? Your mother is expecting us to."

"No." Fabio narrowed his eyes. "I am not ready to sleep under this roof again. Not yet."

"Please?" Lucy pleaded. "Your mother will be so disappointed, and your father wants to give me a full tour of the estate tomorrow."

"Ah." Fabio nodded. "You see? They are playing their games already. All they want is to see me married with children running around me. I have brought you here so they think, Ah, this is the one. Next, they will be telling me to leave motor racing and come back to the vineyard. But it will not work, I know them too well."

"Would that be so bad?" Lucy went to him, closing her arms around his waist and looking up into his face. All she could see, through the shadows, were his eyes. As she touched him she could see them gleaming softly. But, as she spoke, the light in them faded.

"What?" He looked at her. "Do you mean?"

"Living here." She looked back over her shoulder. "Would it be that bad? It's so beautiful"

"Until I am an old man then yes, it would be. But maybe when I am old man I will have family of my own, a wife and children and live somewhere that I choose for myself, for me and for my family."

"You wouldn't want to live here?" She frowned.

"Not for a long time." He slipped backwards out of her grasp. "Neither do I wish for a family, for a long time."

"Why?" She stepped after him, laying her cheek against his chest. He was so strong, so warm. She wanted him to take her in his arms, but he was holding back from her.

"I think." He said slowly. "That there are things you do not understand."

"What things?" She spoke into the cotton of his shirt.

"About me." He rested his chin on her head. "About my desires."

" Ah" She smiled to herself. "On the contrary, I know all about them!"

"My other desires!" He pinched her waist,

making her squeak. "I want to be a World Champion. I want to make a lot of money in becoming one, money of my own, I want to answer to no one."

"Sounds good to me." She looked up at him. "Isn't that what everyone wants? To be successful in what they do? To be rich?"

"No." He shook his head. "Some people just want to be happy, wherever they can find it. But that is not for me. Until I achieve what I want I will never be really happy. I think."

He paused, aware that what he was about to say may bring about a storm.

"You are not like me. You just want to be loved. You seek happiness and nothing else."

"Really?" Lucy gave a wry grin. "That is why I wanted to study media because I didn't want to achieve anything in life?"

"You gave that up." He narrowed his eyes. "I still do not know why."

"I had reasons."

Lucy's eyes narrowed and her face grew cold. "But that is all in the past. I only have a short contract and when that is over I will go back to college and one day I'll be so successful you'll want me to handle your affairs. You and all your millions in the bank."

"I hope so." He kissed her, very gently. "I hope that in the years to come we will still be friends."

"I don't."

"No?" He ran his lips idly across her forehead.

"If you marry someone else, I could never be your friend. I would be too jealous."

"Really?" Fabio smiled. "Then it is good that I do not plan to marry anyone else."

"I am very glad to hear it." Lucy leaned back against his arms and studied his proud, handsome face. Now he was in her life, how could she ever be without him?

"I will make you a promise." A similar thought was passing through Fabio's mind. "When I am World Champion, when I have the millions in the bank, then, if you still want me, I will marry you."

Lucy lowered her eyes, letting his words slowly sink in. A warmth spread through her, starting in her stomach, and rising into her heart. With a smile of satisfaction, she looked up at him.

"Why thank you, Fabio." She nuzzled his cheek. "I will keep you to that."

"I mean it. He hugged her close. "I love you, Lucy."

"I love you too." She breathed in the musky tones of his aftershave. "So, how long do I have to wait for you to be World Champion?"

"Not long." He laughed and swung her off her feet. "But now I try even harder!" "So does that mean we can stay?" She pleaded. "The guided tours won't do any harm now will they?"

"I suppose not." He let her down, gently.

"Fabio?" His mother's voice called down from the terrace.

"Telefono!"

"Who is it?" Fabio frowned; nobody knew that he was there apart from the girl beside him.

"Carlo Rossi."

Fabio's frown deepened. What could be so important that it had made Carlo track him down at this time of night?

"Go into the house." He turned to Lucy. "I will not be long."

Lucy nodded, avoiding his eyes. As she followed his mother into the kitchen, only half listening to the little woman's chatter, she felt her happiness rapidly evaporating. Inside, she had a feeling that the castle in the air that she had just built around herself was about to come crashing down.

CHAPTER 38.

It was a strange scenario and one that he could not have imagined only an hour ago. Kate Matthews sitting in front of his log fire, drinking his brandy, and running an eye over the titles in his bookcase. He had changed out of his own wet clothes and was standing in the doorway holding an old shirt and jeans that may with a bit of adjusting replace the saturated ones she was wearing.

"Here." His leg was still throbbing and he moved slowly. "Try these. Go have a hot shower."

Kate looked at him and a half smile flickered on her face.

"Thank you, Declan. That's very kind of you."

"Not really." He threw the clothes to her. "You are making a damp patch on my sofa. I'll make you some coffee."

"Thanks."

Kate watched him limp out into the kitchen and picked up the clothes. She was trembling, not with the cold that was working its way into her bones but with nerves. At any moment she expected this placid atmosphere to erupt and a mighty row to take place. But Declan seemed calm, and not at all hostile. It was throwing her off her guard and if she was not careful, she may let the feeling of sympathy that was bubbling below the surface rise to the top. Following her sense of direction, she found her way to the tiny bathroom and not wanting interruption locked the door behind her.

The room was so small that the sloping roof almost touched her head above the sink. It was clean and bare; no homely touches, no traces of wealth. Declan had no time for worrying about appearances, he wanted to get on with life not waste it standing in front of a mirror preening. She had over the years seen him looking stunning in his Armani suits and Gucci shoes, but the real Declan lived in his Levi's and that tattered old jacket. That was the man the fans recognised.

Stepping into the shower she pulled the curtain across and let the hot water run over her. There was a half-empty bottle of shampoo and a bar of soap so at least she could get clean; she washed her hair, bemoaning the lack of conditioner, and scrubbed at her feet. As she expected there was no sign of a comb so she pulled her fingers through her curls and dried herself with the one towel. Looking in the mirror she could see that her cheeks were streaked with mascara. Rubbing them clean with tissue paper she scowled at her naked reflection. Freckles! How she hated them, and there was no way to cover them up.

His shirt and jeans hung on her frame like rags on a scarecrow; she turned up the hem of the jeans so that they did not drag on the floor. She had never thought of Declan as being very much taller than herself but he must be or have long legs. Straightening up she looked at her reflection again and saw her cheeks growing pink. Her fingers touched the arms of his t-shirt, almost caressing it and she felt her skin burning. Wearing his clothes, smelling of his soap, and his deodorant, was like being wrapped up in Declan himself; having his muscular arms surrounding her.

She shook her head. What was happening to her?

With a groan, she laid her hot face against the mirror. It must be the alcohol; her heart was crashing against her ribs and she was nervous about walking out of this room and back down the stairs. There was something so sensual, almost erotic about the sensation of his clothes on her skin. It stirred a memory that had been overtaken by so many more since it had happened. She questioned herself, again, as to why she had been so desperate to absolve herself, to come all this way to make him believe that she had not set out to physically hurt him.

Shaking herself she put her hand on the door. She had to compose herself, to think of all the things that she despised about the man downstairs; of all the reasons why she had pulled against him for so long. But they refused to come, those fickle emotions, all she could see now was a shadow of a man with tired eyes, the life beaten out of them by sorrow and guilt. A man who she knew that, in secret, she had desired as much as she had loathed. To go downstairs now, with those thoughts in her head, would be leaving herself wide open, but it was a chance she had to take. With her head held high, she stepped out of the bathroom.

Declan was sitting in the living room, two steaming mugs of coffee on the table in front of him. He looked up at her as she entered and she knew, in an instant, that she had given herself away. He stared at her, taking in the wet mane, the flushed skin, and the wide, hazy eyes. He recognised the signs and looked away. His mental state was so injured, so delicate that whereas months ago he would have thrown himself on the chance to have Kate Matthews in his arms he now could not cope with what he saw in her.

He glanced at her as she sat opposite him and stared silently into the fire, the light of the flames dancing in her eyes. She looked better that way, with no makeup, more natural. She was running her fingers through her hair letting the heat of the fire dry it. He looked away again, afraid that she may catch his eye and see his confusion. It was she who finally broke the silence.

"I really should go." She placed her mug on the

table. "Thank you for the clothes. I will get them back to you."

"No need." Declan was still unable to look at her. "Throw them away."

"Declan," She began, then stopped.

"What?" This time he did look up at her, his eyes hidden by shadows as he leaned back in the chair.

"Your resignation." She swallowed. "I won't accept it. Or rather I hope that you'll reconsider it. I need you."

She heard him laughing softly.

"I never thought I'd say that." She continued. "But I do. We do. Carlo has tried to make me see sense so many times but I wouldn't listen. Nothing seems to work without you there. The lads, they haven't got the same heart and Pete misses you terribly."

"You don't" He moved back into the light of the fire and fixed his eyes on her face. They were back on familiar ground and his confidence was starting to return. "You don't miss me at all."

She looked at him and hesitated. What she said now would change things, forever.

"I do." She blushed and the colour travelled across her neck." I don't miss your cheek or your arrogance, but I miss your experience and your presence."

"I'll think about it." He got to his feet. "I'll get your coat."

She followed him into the hall and took her

still-wet coat from his hands. As she did so her fingers brushed against his and the contact sent a thousand tingles running across her skin. She recoiled and saw that he was watching her. This close, she could see the lines on his face that had not been there before. She opened her mouth to speak but could not trust herself with her own words. He laid his hand on her arm and her stomach lurched.

"What?" Her pulse was racing.

"What were you about to say?"

She hesitated.

Declan looked at her, the green eyes avoiding his own. Just say it she thought, don't leave all this up to me. You tell me you have been wrong about me all these years, give me a grain of hope to cling to. He was taken aback by the strength of his emotions. They came from deep inside him and they hurt. It was so different to anything he had ever known. He wanted to take her in his arms, to hold her, but far more than that he wanted her to know him, to understand his nature and what made him the man that he was. He wanted to share his pain, and his fear, and he wanted to share it with her. Because, somehow, he felt that only she would truly understand.

CHAPTER 39.

The call from Kurt's team came two days later. Declan's visit to the FIA had prompted not only another investigation but also a hasty court action by Kurt's team to back up his own. In truth, they were the ones who stood to lose the most; Kurt had been streaking ahead in the points table and had every chance of retaining his championship title. With him out of action, they were negotiating a lease from another team to perpetuate their construction title hopes, but without their star, their odds against winning were greatly increased. Also, Kurt had been the one most badly affected by the whole incident, his whole career hanging in the balance as he began his long road to recovery. So, they were looking for a worthy replacement, and, after lengthy telephone conversations with Kurt himself had come up with an answer. In their opinion, and their drivers, the only man who was anywhere near as fast, as talented or determined as Kurt was Declan himself.

The proposal stunned Declan, who felt as though he would be betraying his best friend by taking his seat for the rest of the year. With his resignation still in Kate's hands, and as he hadn't yet retracted it, his existing contract was no problem. But it was the moral of it all, it felt wrong. There was also the problem of his suspension; surely the team was not going to wait until the end of the year for him? Another surprise awaited him. Before their call, Kurt's team had spoken to the FIA about Declan's reinstatement. With the new evidence at their fingertips, the authorities had agreed, and Declan was now once again the holder of an F1 super licence. It was all too much for him to take in. Pleading time before he made a decision, Declan went to the only person who could help him. Kurt.

The day that Declan's jet touched down in Nice was the very same day that Kurt was. released from hospital. Overjoyed at seeing him back home, albeit pale and covered in plaster, Declan put off asking his multitude of questions until the next day. Leaving Bernice and Kurt to a homecoming dinner, he went to his own apartment and spent the evening wearing out the tiles on the balcony. Kurt, however, was eager to get into discussions and hear his answer so he called Declan before breakfast the next morning, inviting him to join the rest of the family for the first meal of the day. Declan agreed and subsequently found himself tucking into a cooked breakfast. Waving his fork in the air, he complimented Bernice on the bacon and asked for more tea. Kurt watched him teasing the boys and smiled; it was good to be home again, especially with Declan as a guest of honour.

"So" His appetite was still poor and most of his meal remained on his plate as he pushed it away. "I think you have something to ask me?"

"Do I?" Declan felt his cheeks burning.

"I think so." Kurt's eyes were twinkling. "It concerns a car, I believe."

"From that, I gather that you have already been approached." Declan put down his mug. "What do you think?"

"I think it is an excellent idea; in fact, it was my idea!" Kurt nodded. "As long as you give it back at the end of the year"

"Oh, I can't promise that." Declan grinned. "I might get to like it."

Kurt chuckled.

"Seriously my friend. I think it is your best chance of putting yourself back on top. Matros have so many problems, so many inner difficulties to resolve that they surely cannot give you their best? My team will back you to the last corner, I promise you. They recognise talent when they see it."

Declan nodded but hesitated before he spoke.

"That's not the problem."

"No? Then what is?"

"Me." Declan looked at him. His eyes were pale and red-rimmed and spoke to Kurt of his inner torment.

"You?"

"Yes, me." Declan lowered his eyes. "I'm scared."

"Of what?" Kurt was very still.

"Of having lost it." Declan looked out of the window. "Of coming into a corner and blanking out. Of not knowing what to do. Of getting into that car and not even remembering how to pull it off the grid without stalling it. But most of all I'm scared of betraying you. "

"Me!" Kurt raised his eyebrows. "Don't worry about me."

"But I do." Declan looked at him. One side of his head was covered in stubble where the shaven patch from his operation had regrown. It was comical or would be if he weren't the one responsible for it.

"I did that to you." He shook his head. "And even though I now know that it wasn't my fault I'll never forgive myself. I was still driving like a maniac, putting us both at risk."

"Rubbish." Kurt snorted. "You were trying to pass, the only way that anyone can, everyone does it."

"Well, I don't think that I can do it anymore." Declan put his face in his hands. "If I just think of getting in a car, I feel sick. I have never been so scared in my life as when I looked into that tunnel and saw the smoke. I thought I'd killed you."

He shuddered.

"It's only a vague, blurry memory, but it will stay with me for the rest of my life. I don't think that I can drive again with that fear in my heart."

He went still as his brain flashed back to that moment. To the smell of the smoke, the pain in his leg, the sirens and somewhere in the distance, someone screaming.

So what will you do?" Kurt spoke softly.

"Quit." Declan dropped his hands and looked at him with reddened eyes. "My time is over Kurt. Declan Hyde is finished. Time to stand down and let someone else provide the excitement."

Kurt narrowed his eyes and looked thoughtfully at his friend's tense face.

"Bullshit." He said, shaking his head. "You have more determination than any man I know, you can do anything you want to."

"Not this time." Declan shook his head. "It's over."

"No." Kurt leaned forward and looked at him, ice-blue eyes glittering. "It is not. As soon as I am out of this plaster, I want to get back into my car, and if I can do it so can you. I hope that all this." He looked at his legs. "Has not been for nothing. If you quit now, without showing them all that you are one of the best there has ever been, then I will be the one who will be guilty. I do not want you to quit because of what happened to me."

"But if it wasn't for me, it wouldn't have happened to you!" Declan shouted. "Don't you understand?"

"I understand that we both live in a very risky business," Kurt shouted back. "If it had not been us going through the Armco it would have been someone else, some other time. It is the way of the sport, and it is a risk we all take. It is not your fault Declan, and I will not let you quit!"

Declan stared at him, breath coming hard, face flushed, and bit his lip. His mind was in turmoil. The thought of getting back into a racing car terrified him, but the thought of distressing Kurt terrified him even more. Spinning on his heel, he walked out of the dining room.

"Where the fuck are you going?" Kurt roared after him.

"Out." Declan opened the apartment door. "I'm sorry Kurt, but I just can't handle this."

He closed the door behind him and hobbled through the apartment block, past the pool, and out into the warm, sun-filled streets of Monte Carlo.

CHAPTER 40.

The beach was quiet. He looked at his watch and realised it was still only nine-thirty. Collapsing onto the sand, he stared at the water rolling towards him in gentle waves. All his life, since he was a child, he had known what direction he was going in, what he wanted to do; until now. Now he was without direction, drifting, like the tide. He buried his face in his hands, taking deep breaths. The one thing that he could not get his head around was Lucy. Everyone at Matros was making excuses: that she did not know the importance of what she had read, that she had made an error and deleted the information by mistake instead of keeping it for Kate, but he knew her better. Or he thought he did, her and her obsessive fantasies.

Maybe he was wrong and everyone else at Matros was right. But in his heart, he knew that Lucy was not that stupid and that she had known full well what she had read and that she had just deleted it. But why? Lying back, he stared up at the sky. He wondered if she had fully realised the danger that she had been placing him in? He doubted it, but it still hurt, the knowledge that anyone could despise him that much. If it had been Kate, he could almost have understood. She had hated him so bitterly; he had been convinced that it had been her doing, but once again, in the complex saga that his life had become he had been wrongfooted. He closed his eyes and listened to the buzz of noise coming from the streets. It was diffused, muted, and had a distance to it: lulling and soothing it calmed his agitated mind. He was in a doze, only half conscious, his thoughts rambling through various scenarios when he was aware of a shadow across his face. Opening his eyes abruptly, he sat up, staring into the shy, awkward eyes of a young boy.

"Excuse me, but you are Declan Hyde, aren't you?" He said in a quiet voice. "Can I have your autograph?"

Declan stared at him for a moment, taking in the pen and paper in the little lad's hand. He could only have been ten or eleven, and his red skin gave away the fact that he was a holidaymaker. Nodding, Declan took the pen he was offering.

"What's your name?"

"Christopher." The boy's face grew redder.

"I have a nephew called Christopher." Declan scribbled across the paper, which was the back of a hotel menu. "He's about your size too. Are you on holiday?"

"Yes." The boy's eyes were gleaming with excitement. "Not here, in a campsite down the road. That way." He pointed back towards the French coast.

"We're on a bus trip. I saw you as we pulled in and ran down to find you before you went. I think my Mum will be cross."

"I hope not." Declan smiled and handed the menu back to him. "I wouldn't like you to be in trouble because of me. Have a nice holiday, and watch the sun, it's very strong."

"I know." Christopher nodded. "Thank you, Declan."

Clutching the menu to his chest, he ran back up the beach. As he reached the group of people waiting at the roadside Declan could hear his excited voice shouting to them.

"Look Mum! I've got it! Mum! Look!"

Declan smiled. It was the first pleasant thing that had happened to him in a long time. It felt good, knowing that he had made that little boy so happy, probably even made his holiday. He remembered Gerald's words when he had been new to the sport, and the attention that went with it. 'Be good to your fans' he had told him, 'They can make or break you. People's opinions matter, don't forget it.'

Wise words and they were words that he had taken to heart. He had not always been the model employee, he knew that, but when it came to signing autographs, or donating defunct pieces of clothing to auctions, or merely stopping to talk to the crowds that would often gather at the compound entrance, he had been geniality itself. His heart grew heavy as he thought of Gerald. He missed him, missed his experience, his affability, and most of all his unshakable confidence in Declan himself. What would he have said if he could have witnessed the events of the past few weeks? Or know that the one man he had always said he could stake his life on to deliver the goods was about to hang up his boots?

Declan got up, and walked through the water's edge, feeling the sun warm on his back. A breeze touched his face, and at the same time, the thought touched his heart that Gerald would never again feel the sun on his back, or smell the salt air on the breeze. It hurt, and he felt tears in his eyes, but his sorrow was softened by the knowledge that Gerald had lived his life doing what he loved best and that given his time again he would probably do exactly the same. His own personal regret was that he had not given Gerald the world championship he so badly wanted. Now it was too late, for both of them. Standing in the waves, feeling the water soaking through his trainers, cool and refreshing, he looked back at the buildings clinging to the hillside behind him. It was because of Gerald that he could live in this place. Because of Gerald, he had a Ferrari parked outside his apartment; because of him he could hop onto a private jet and take off anywhere in the world. He owed everything, from his financial status that would ensure his comfort for the rest of his days, to his lifestyle and every podium position he had ever had the thrill of achieving to one man, and his faith. His whole career had been built on the foundations that one man had laid, and on the money that the same man had poured into his future.

He couldn't let him down. Not now, when everything that same man had worked for, everything he had believed in, was poised on the brink of disaster. Gerald had never been a quitter; he had been an achiever, never admitting defeat even in the face of his greatest adversity, his health. If the spectre of death had not stopped Gerald Matthews from fighting to the very end, then his own, lesser ghosts could be laid to rest. For Gerald's sake; for the memory of the man who had been more than a father to him he would carry on, and give his memory the victory it had craved. If not this year, then the next, or the next, but he would carry on fighting until the Matros carried the Number One flag.

Then he would give up. But only then.

Turning away from the water, he began to walk back to Kurt's apartment, a new purpose to his slightly uneven stride. He would not take Kurt's position, not even temporarily; he wanted his own drive back, and with it, he was going to win.

CHAPTER 41.

If Kurt was disappointed that Declan had chosen to stick to Matros rather than take up the offered role with his team, he did not show it. He was outwardly delighted at Declan's change of heart and fully understood his reasons. Sitting together on his sun-kissed balcony, they plotted his triumphant return. Not immediately, as Declan's physical state was still precarious and he was in no way fit enough to do himself justice, so they decided to let Jean Claude keep Declan's seat for the next few races, then reclaim it in time for the British Grand Prix in July. He would have just over three weeks to recapture his physique and get some miles in behind a steering wheel. Feeling more confident now that an actual plan of attack had been laid out, there was only one more job for Declan to undertake, to let Kate know that she could throw his resignation in the bin. He hoped that her new change of heart towards him would mean that he would not only be reinstated as a driver but also not be thrown out of the team at the end of the year, but perhaps the best way to convince her that he deserved the chance to stay was out there on the track.

After an inner debate that lasted into the small hours, Declan decided that the matter would best be approached in person. Taking temporary leave of Kurt, he boarded a jet back to Britain and faced a confrontation with the woman who had for so long been his biggest adversary and who he now needed to be his greatest ally.

He found her at home, sitting, as Gerald had so often done, in the conservatory, staring out across the lake. Janice, who was back in residence following all the legal wrangles her daughter had become involved in, showed him through in stony silence. He stood in the doorway for a few minutes unwilling to speak, partly because he did not want to disturb her, and partly because he feared her response to his suggestions. What if after all his soul-searching she threw the concept back in his face? It was a chance he was going to have to take.

Stepping forward, he coughed and then spoke.

"Hello, Kate."

She spun, startled, obviously unaware that he had been watching her.

"Declan!" She looked surprised. "I didn't know that you were here. What." She paused. "What can I do for you?"

"You've got an envelope that belongs to me." Declan looked at her, straight-faced, calm, judging her reaction by the movement of her eyes. "I would like it back."

Kate took a deep breath, looked out of the window, and let the breath out in a long, relieved sigh.

"Thank you, Declan. In the light of everything that's happened, and is going to happen here, that is very good of you."

"It is, isn't it?" Declan grinned. "Especially when you consider my alternative."

"What alternative?" She frowned at him.

"Taking Kurt's seat for the rest of the year."

Kate's eyes widened.

"I had no idea." She shook her head. "Why don't you take it?"

"Well, if you don't want me." Declan shrugged. "I will."

"I didn't mean that," Kate said hastily. "It would be such an opportunity for you."

"Your father gave me all the opportunities I ever needed." He replied bluntly. "I want to drive for this team for his sake, no one else's. I owe it to him to make this thing a winner."

Kate lowered her eyes. There had been a time, not all that long ago, when she would have looked for every opportunity to get rid of Declan, indeed had; but now all she could feel was a deep sense of relief that he was back on her side.

"There's one thing." Declan narrowed his eyes on her. "This is a full-scale reinstatement. I'm back as a driver, understand?"

"I understand. I wouldn't expect anything less."

Kate was trembling. Her mind was doing cartwheels; racing through the rest of the season, trying to picture how they could possibly climb out of the hole that they had dug for themselves. Court cases, potential compensation, and the legal fights ahead were not as important as getting the car back onto the front of the grid. They had all made mistakes; she most of all, and they would have to be lived with, but they had to start challenging again, to regain the positions that they had lost. She looked into the eyes of the man in front of her and saw the determination that still glowed somewhere deep inside him. Maybe, with Declan back on board, they could succeed.

"We had better tell Carlo." She picked up her jacket, which was hanging on the chair beside her. "He'll be delighted."

"Jean-Claude won't be."

Another cheeky grin that made her heart skip a beat. Why was he suddenly having this effect on her? Perhaps it was guilt, or perhaps she was finally recognising what she should have seen a long, long time ago. Whatever the reason, this new attitude unnerved her, so she brushed past him, holding her breath so that she could not smell his aftershave, and beckoned him to follow her.

Carlo was busy in the garage setting up Jean Claude's car for a tyre test. Having flunked out of an earlier session due to their problems, they were now racing against time to have a competitive car for the next weekend. They were up against it, as the team would have to leave in a few days to drive over to France, and things were not working out as planned. Stepping into this hive of frenetic activity Declan smiled broadly. Some things would never change. Carlo was ranting in Italian at a bemused Essex-born mechanic who didn't have a clue what he was saying; Jean Claude was complaining about understeer to anyone who would listen, and amid it all Pete was quite calmly taking the front wing off the car, taking no notice of anyone. As he straightened, spanner in hand, he noticed the familiar figure in the doorway and his eyes widened.

"Jesus!'" He laughed. "Am I hallucinating?"

"You should be so lucky." Declan walked over to him and slapped him on the back. "Sorry to disappoint you but I'm flesh and blood."

"Believe me that's no disappointment!" Pete enveloped him in a bear hug. "It's good to see you!"

"Please, please." Declan laughed. "There's enough scandal around here already!"

Pete released him, a smile splitting his face from ear to ear. His eyes turned to Kate.

"Thank you, Kate." He smiled. "You've done the right thing."

"I hope so." Kate was embarrassed by the public show of affection she had just witnessed; she had underestimated the level of affection that the team had for Declan. They were all crowded around him now, even Jean Claude, patting him on the back, throwing jibes at him, asking more questions than he could possibly answer. Only Carlo stood back. His eyes showed his pleasure at having Declan back in his garage but his reaction was more constrained. He shook the man's hand, welcomed him back on board, and then turned to Kate.

"Bene." He said quietly. "It was good thing to do."

"I didn't do anything." Kate shook her head. "He came to me."

"But you listened." Carlo smiled. "It is good."

"I hope so." Kate looked at the floor. "We need our luck to change Carlo. Quickly."

"Yes. I know." Carlo lowered his voice and whispered. "What are we to do about Lucy?"

"We have to sack her." A shadow flitted across Kate's face. "Even if it was a genuine mistake, we can't be seen to condone it. It could have cost a life, even two, and we have to acknowledge that."

"I agree." Carlo nodded.

"I'll call her." Kate sighed. "And ask her to come in. Will you?"

"Talk to her with you? Of course, I will?" Carlo was puzzled by the expression on Kate's face. "What is wrong?"

"I don't know." Kate shrugged. "l think this is all getting to me a bit. My confidence is pretty shit at the moment."

"Which is understandable." Carlo put his arm around her shoulders. "I will deal with Lucy." He looked back at the group of men, now huddled around the GM-4 "But for now I must concentrate on putting this car onto the track."

Kate stayed to watch the test and was pleased to see that the car was as quick as ever and stood the rigours of a long-distance test without any hiccups. Declan watched as well, his eyes studying the printouts with Pete, passing comments as data flashed onto the screen. If anyone saw him flinch occasionally as the car swung wide on a corner, or twitched along a straight, no one commented. There was a buzz in the room. An excitement, a sense of optimism in the air that had been missing before he had walked through the door.

The status quo had returned, the warrior's banishment was over and he had come back to stand at the head of his army. Now they could not possibly be beaten.

CHAPTER 42.

Fabio had not intended to return to England before Magny Cours. He had decided to fly straight to France for the first morning's practice. But when he received his third call from Carlo in as many days, he changed his plans. It was not Fabio himself that Carlo had requested; it was Lucy, and Fabio had a feeling that he should be at her side whatever the reason for the proposed meeting. No one expected Lucy's actions, however innocent, to go unpunished but until now she had been left alone, as if her absence from the factory was going unnoticed. He had talked to her long, long into the night after he had spoken to Carlo. He had to know for sure that what she told him was true and he believed her. She could not possibly have realised the danger that she was putting Declan in, and more to the point, in his mind, she would have known that the same parts would have been fitted to his own car at some stage. Such was his confidence in her feelings for him that he felt she would never have carried out such an act knowingly. So, he flew with her to England, and, after a brief detour into Oxford, set out to the factory to meet Carlo. The place was strangely quiet, as the fleet of lorries had already left for France, taking the majority of the workforce with them. The factory was still ticking over, already working towards Silverstone and the next test, and the few remaining employees were too engrossed in their computers to look up as they walked above them to Carlo's office.

Carlo was alone. Sitting at his desk he had a grim face and a neatly sealed brown envelope in front of him. The minute she saw it Lucy knew what it contained, so she sat opposite him, the man who she had once looked on as being on her side in these days of doubt and accusations, and saw the cold edge of doubt and hatred in his eyes. She listened unflinchingly to his words, nodding acceptance as he explained that she must leave, however innocent her actions may have been: what she had done was dangerous, and could not go unpunished. Fabio stood beside her and watched the colour rising and falling on her face. She had gained so much confidence in this past week; it was as though knowing where her future lay had freed her from the insecurities of her past. He was not sure if he loved her enough to be faithful to her for the rest of his life, but he intended to try; something of his father's family values existed in him after all. On her left hand, she wore a sparkling diamond, so big that it blinded you when it caught the sunlight. He had felt it proper to back up his words with a gesture, and it made both her and his mother happy.

Carlo saw it too, but his expression remained unflinching. He dismissed them, and turned back to his work, not looking up as they walked out of the room. Only when they had gone did he fall back in his chair and let out a heavy sigh. This advancement in Lucy and Fabio's relationship was going to cause problems. She was going to be present at every meeting, a constant reminder of their turbulent year. It was something he could have done without.

Kate walked into them, unintentionally, as she left her own office. She stood, frozen to the spot, and stared at Lucy with horror on her face. She had wanted to avoid this encounter; she had such dramatic feelings about Lucy at the moment that she was not sure she could trust herself to keep it together. Lowering her eyes, she went to walk past them, and as she did so the diamond caught her eyes. Halting, she looked up at Lucy, then at Fabio. His eyes softened as he looked at her, kindness and compassion shining from them.

"Congratulations." She muttered.

"Thank you."

Lucy looked up at her man and Kate glimpsed, for a few painful seconds, the expression on his face as he took Lucy's hand. It was the look she yearned to see on someone's face when they looked at her. It burned deep inside her, and turning away she hurried back into the office, shutting the door hastily behind her.

Collapsing onto her chair she put her hands over her face. Stop it, stop it, stop it! She told herself. I will not cry; I must not cry!

She heard the door opening, heard the footsteps crossing the room but did not look up. ·She knew that she was being watched, but as hard as she tried, she could not stop the tears from spilling between her outspread fingers.

" Mon Amore." Carlo's voice spoke gently as he put his arm around her shoulders. "Do not cry."

"I can't help it." Kate sniffed. "I don't want to cry, I hate it. I'm sick of crying. I feel as if I've been crying forever, Carlo. When is it all going to stop?"

"I do not know cara." Carlo was rocking her gently. "But it will. I promise it will."

Kate nodded, pulling away from him as she wiped her streaming eyes.

"You must be strong." He stroked her hair. "We still have many battles ahead of us."

"I know." Tears welled in her eyes again. "But I just can't do it. I can't face any more."

"You can," Carlo said firmly. "And you will. Now we have to leave for France and show them all that we may be down, but we are not yet out. We must show them that we are not beaten cara."

"Aren't we?" She looked at him with huge, worried eyes.

"No." Carlo got up. "Come. Wash your face, and we will leave together."

"Give me two minutes." Kate forced a smile.

"No more." Carlo nodded. "And no more tears."

Kate smiled again, watching his short, round figure walking out of the door. She wished that she had his confidence. She had a feeling that this was the end, the end of the years of work, the end of all her father's dreams. When he was here, she would have sworn that she did not care, but now she did, deeply. Her personal life was a mess of confused emotions and endless grieving, and this place was all she had left. At least here she was somebody, not just another used piece of flesh that nobody wanted. Her self-esteem had never been so low. Going into the toilet she washed her face, and, without bothering to replace her smudged makeup she went to find Carlo. Who cared what she looked like? Formula One was so full of beautiful women that no one would look at her anyway. What did it matter? She worked in a jungle, a dog-eat-dog world where friends were rare and enemies were everywhere, a place   coming first was all that mattered, and faces came and went faster than the cars themselves. She paused in the doorway and looked up at the factory. If this building was going to carry her father's name into the next century, she had to harden her heart, shut out the painful memories of her mistakes and failures and recapture the self-belief that had left her. She was in control, such as it was, of this thing, and she had a role to play. Tightening her fists, gritting her teeth, trying to mentally steel

herself for what lay ahead she walked into the car
park and prepared to face the eyes of the world.

CHAPTER 43.

The French Grand Prix was not a complete disaster, but records would never show that it was a success. Jean Claude, thriving on the support of an enthusiastic home crowd drove into a creditable fourth, with no disasters, no close encounters with other drivers, just solid dependable driving. It was not the podium he wanted, but it was a good result for himself and the battered team. Fabio, ebullient and beautiful, floating around the paddock with Lucy ever at his side, was flamboyant in his attack; a flaw in the GM-4's gearbox saw him forced into premature retirement from the race. Not wanting to hang around in the atmosphere that Lucy's presence incited in the motor home, they boarded a jet and flew back to Rome, to hide away in the vineyards and cement their relationship with hours and hours of lovemaking.

Kurt and Declan watched the race together on the huge flat-screen television given to Kurt as a get-well gift by one of his sponsors. Kurt thought it was ostentatious, and offered it to Declan, who refused on the grounds that he wouldn't get it through the door of his apartment. They watched the race amid pleas for pity from Kurt's two boys who thought that the television had been delivered purely for them to use with their father's PlayStation. Keeping them quiet with promises of ice cream and extra-long game sessions when the race was over, Kurt and Declan watched with intense faces. Declan watched every televised move of the Matros, while Kurt watched his teammate Julian snatch another victory that should have, by right, been his.

Neither man was encouraged or elated by what he saw. Kurt was painfully aware that the world championship could have been his for the second year, as the car was invincible in its current form. He also knew that if Declan had accepted his team's offer, he could have won the championship in Kurt's car, which would have been the next best thing to winning it himself. Declan's thoughts ran along similar lines. He could have launched himself straight back into the number one spot with Kurt's team, but he faced an uphill battle with the Matros; not that the car wasn't good enough, it could be, but the team's spirit was dented and it would take some time to lift the crew back to their normal level of intensity.

That was how Bernice found them, sitting with glum faces, staring at the post-race press meeting. She could see that neither one was taking in a word, so she turned the television off.

"I was listening to that!" Kurt sat upright.

"Balls." His wife gave a smile. "And if you

were, you shouldn't have been. I've never seen such long faces."

"Do you blame us?" Declan's eyes were bleak. "It was hardly inspiring."

"And what would have been?" Bernice laughed. "Let's face it, you two are only happy when you're in the heart of the action. I don't know why you watch, I really don't."

"I do." Declan had spotted a small, blonde, figure, crawling towards the television, lead in hand, keeping low so that he could plug in the PlayStation without being noticed. "It's to stop Batman jumping across the screen for three hours at a time."

Bernice laughed.

"Well, it is their turn! Come on you two, there is food on the balcony."

Helping Kurt up into his wheelchair, she aided him out onto the balcony and sat him at the table. Declan sat opposite, staring without interest at the pasta in front of him.

"Sorry." He shook his head. "I'm not hungry."

"Eat." She commanded. "We've got some muscle rebuilding to do if you're going to win that race in two weeks' time."

"I wonder what would happen if I put this in the Matros fuel tank?" Declan chuckled. Would it give that a bit more muscle?"

"It doesn't need it." Kurt chuckled at the thought. "All it needs is you behind the wheel. But it would be interesting, a new violation of the fuel regulations!"

A wail from the living room told them that Batman had got a premature comeuppance.

"That one is going to be just like you." Bernice sighed. "He's too competitive for his own good!"

"Rubbish." Kurt smiled fondly. "There is no such thing as too competitive."

"That's questionable." Bernice looked pointedly at the yards of plaster that still covered his body.

Another wail from the living room announced the arrival of the second little Braun, who was trying to replace Batman with a game of his own.

"Quiet you two!" Bernice shouted. "Let Batman go first!"

Declan roared with laughter.

"You know what I mean." Bernice blushed. "Shut up Hyde."

"Sorry darling." Declan chuckled. "I just never knew one of my God sons was called Batman."

Bernice shook her head, laughing and turning her attention to her lunch. Remembering something she had heard in the Grand Prix coverage of the day before she paused, her fork hovering above her plate.

"Is it true?" She looked at Declan. "That Lucy Duggan has become engaged to Fabio Fratinelli?"

She spat the last two words out with venom. There was obviously no room in Bernice's heart for the glamorous Italian.

"It looks that way." Declan shrugged. "It's a wonder she can lift her finger, the size of the rock she's wearing. Fabio should watch out; one backhander with that and she'd ruin his face for good."

"Which would serve him right." Bernice snorted. "I never did like him."

"Why not?" Kurt looked puzzled. "Anyway, we have had very little to do with him."

Declan frowned and then narrowed his eyes at Bernice.

"I have the answer." He said slowly. "Your dear wife thinks he's betrayed me by getting engaged to my attempted assassin. She also thinks I am stupid for messing with the psycho bitch in the first place, but as she finds it impossible to do anything but love me, she's taking it out on poor Fabio who really deserves our sympathy."

"Do you believe she did it deliberately?" Kurt was quiet.

"I know that she's far more intelligent than people are giving her credit for," Declan replied, his colour rising slightly. "But that's all irrelevant now. She's had the boot, I'm back in, and properly his time; and as far as I'm concerned Fabio needs to watch his back. He's got his first multi-million deal safely in the bank. One false move and she'll do a proper job on him then hey presto, one little rich bitch."

"You liked her once." Bernice scolded. "You told me."

"She was there." Declan shrugged. "But it would seem, she failed to understand the more complex side of my nature."

"What side is that?" Kurt chuckled. "The one that demands a different woman every night?"

"Unfair." Declan retorted. "I am virtually a monk these days."

"Something else that will have to change." Kurt chuckled. "I know you well my friend, you do not drive well when frustrated."

"Who said I'm frustrated!" Declan's eyebrows shot upwards.

"Well, aren't you?" Kurt's face was serious, but his eyes were twinkling merrily. "But you can forget about borrowing my wife."

"Now there is a prospect." Declan sighed. "Are you sure Kurt? I mean I am, as you said, getting desperate!"

"Hands off." Kurt shook his head. "Seriously, I think it's high time you found a wife of your own."

"Pfft!" Declan snorted. "Me? Married? No thanks, I have enough trouble dealing with my own life! I don't need someone else's problems getting in the way!"

"Oh, come on." Bernice got to her feet and started collecting plates. "I need a new hat."

"There is one thing that Lucy did for me." Declan looked down onto the harbour. "For the first time in years, it seems I can be in the same room as Kate Matthews without having my head bitten off. For that small mercy," He looked back at Bernice, "Believe me, I will be eternally in her debt."

CHAPTER 44.

When Declan arrived back in his apartment, much, much later, he found a voicemail from that very same Kate Matthews asking if he would be fit for a session in the car next week. He thought about it for a long time before returning her call. He could not go back into action unprepared, he had to have a few laps under his belt before the first practice day of the British Grand Prix. To re-enter the sport cold was not only foolhardy but dangerous, to others as well as himself. He had to find out if he could regain his confidence in a racing car, and the sooner he found out the better. Picking up the receiver he felt butterflies dancing in his stomach as he waited for the answer. Thankfully no one was in the Matros office at that time of night, so he left his intention to be at the factory the following Tuesday with the answering machine and hung up.

His heart started racing as he thought about being strapped into the cockpit of an F1 car again. Taking deep breaths, he rubbed his sweaty palms together and paced around his living room, trying to block out of his head visions of flying wing and tunnel walls. He went into the drinks cabinet and was about to pour himself a Scotch but hesitated. Drinking alone was not good, he would drive himself further and further into the pit of his self-doubt. Drinking was not a good idea full stop, but he needed to do something. So, he washed and changed, picked up his keys and headed into the night in search of comfort.

He had no idea where he was when he opened his eyes the next morning. But closer inspection revealed a strange bedroom, midnight blue sheets and a cropped dark head beside him. For a moment his heart lurched with horror, until the owner of the dark head rolled over and displayed perfect cheekbones and a wide sensual mouth, still smudged with scarlet lipstick. Smiling at his paranoia, Declan tried to remember her name but failed. He peered at his watch and sat bolt upright in horror. Eleven o'clock! He should be in the gym now. If Kurt found out that he had missed a training session he would go crazy. Manners flying out of the window in his hurry, he pulled on his jeans, and, barefooted with shoes in hand and shirt over his shoulder, ran out into the street to find out where he was.

His one-night stand had done nothing to improve his confidence; particularly when it involved him emptying his pockets to pay the taxi, he flagged down in the street to help him retrieve his car. He was only half an hour late, but his harassed state of mind, and his sex-induced exhaustion, made the training session a waste of time. Calling it a day, he walked back to the apartment, feeling that some exercise was better than none.

A voicemail played Kate's voice, thanking him for his call and informing him that they were all looking forward to seeing him. Unless he was mistaken, and he had heard enough female voices in his time, Kate's matter-of-fact message was covering up a more personal emotion. Not even Kate could withstand the consistent hammerings that she had received in the past months without some sort of effect. Maybe for once, she realised that she needed him, maybe in more ways than one.

In a way he was pleased, it would be pleasant not to have her hounding him all the time, but he wasn't sure that it would be conducive to his best performance. He thrived on aggression when he drove, and in the past, it had always been Kate who had provided the irritant. That was until now. Sitting on the balcony, feeling the sun on his face, he pulled off his t-shirt and laid back on the sun lounger. Lucy was going to be a constant presence at the tracks now, and looking at her would provide him with all the venom-filled belligerence he needed.

They said their farewells a few days later. Kurt, sombre-faced, sincere, wishing him luck and every success; Bernice, tearful and nervous, seeming reluctant to let him go.

"For goodness' sake woman!" He laughed, one hand on the car door. "I'll be back in a fortnight!"

"You'd better be." Bernice gave him a suffocating bear hug. "I'll never keep him sane without you to turn to."

"Drug his mineral water," Declan whispered. "He'll be no trouble."

Bernice forced a smile. Now that the moment had come to let Declan get back into a car, she was afraid; afraid that he would have lost the edge that made him brilliant, but even more afraid that he would get hurt. It had always been a subconscious fear before, one that she had kept locked well away; but now, after Monaco, she could keep it at bay no longer. What would happen when Kurt was well enough to drive again, she could only imagine with dread. So, she let the second most important man in her life get into the waiting taxi and drive away, out of her sight and back into the dangerous, uncertain, world from which he made his living. She wished that the next eleven days were already over and that he was bouncing up the stairs with a beaming smile and a winner's trophy under his arm. But the trophy this time was unimportant; she just wanted him back in one piece, not only for her sake but for Kurt's. She looked at her husband's eyes, deep and thoughtful, and read the same tension in them as she was herself feeling.

"Come on." She laid her arms around his thin shoulders. "I know it's against doctors' orders, but I think we both need a drink."

CHAPTER 45.

Declan drove through the main entrance to the Matros compound with a pounding heart. Throughout his journey along the motorway, he had kept his mind occupied with thoughts of past British Grand Prix that he had driven in, but now that he was here, he could only think about the GM-4 Matros, and getting in it. As he halted at the gates waiting to be let in a prowling pack of journalists pounced on him before the gates could open. Stone-faced, refusing to reply to any questions in case his nerves sounded in his voice, he was relieved when a flame-haired figure burst through the crowd from the opposite direction.

"Mr Hyde has nothing to say." Kate snapped, holding startled reporters and photographers at bay like a snarling Rottweiler. "You'll get anything you need to know out of the press release afterwards. Now will you all clear off and give my driver some peace? He has a job to do."

"Thanks," Declan muttered. "I must be out of practice."

"No problem," Kate replied shortly. "If I let them get their teeth into you, they'll tear you apart. They've been following that little bitch Lucy around all week, pumping her for inside information. She's been loving it."

"Doesn't sound like Lucy." Declan shook his head.

"Neither does manslaughter, which is conceivably what she could have been looking at. Especially if she had done what she did intentionally." Said Kate dryly. "Thank God she didn't, or we'd all be for the FIA high jump."

"You believe she didn't know what she was doing?" Declan paused at the entrance to the factory.

"I believe what's best for the team." Kate looked at him frankly. "It's the only thing I can do. We're in enough shit with this court case as it is."

"Well, at least that's halved." Declan gave her a nervous smile. "You've heard from my lawyers?"

"Yes." Kate blushed. "Thanks. I would have understood if you had gone ahead, considering what came to light afterwards. Well, I'll let you get on with it. Carlo's in there somewhere."

She nodded to the metal shutters over the garages.

"We have to keep them down to hold the press at bay Believe it or not they are parked across the lake with zoom lenses. We have had to let a few in so that we can show the world you are fit to be in the car."

"Privacy." Declan nodded. "I could do with it right now, while I find my feet."

"Well, keep them that way until you are ready."

Kate was away from him. "Just don't drive through them for God's sake!"

The thought of the GM-4 bursting through the metal doors like a torpedo made Declan smile and calmed his nerves. With a deep breath, he walked to the garage and was greeted by the loudest cheer he had heard in his life. Staggered by such a reception he stood in the doorway scarlet-faced and shrugged his shoulders. Pete, sensing his embarrassment, rushed over and shook his hand.

"Welcome back Diocles" He beamed. "Your chariot awaits!"

"Who the fuck was he!" Declan laughed and walked slowly over to the gleaming midnight blue car to run his finger over the body.

It was such a beautiful creation; he only hoped that he could still do it justice. Carlo watched him from the back of the bay, noticed the reverent way that Declan touched the car, and also noticed the trembling fingers as he withdrew his hands. Carlo had been in the business long enough to recognise stage fright when he saw it and knew that the only way to cure it was to face the audience.

"Good afternoon, Declan." He walked brusquely across the garage, business-like, avoiding the sentiment that was being displayed by the others. "Shall we get down to work?"

"Yes." Declan scanned Carlo's face.

The Italian held his eyes for a moment and

nodded.

"Welcome back."

"Thanks." Declan looked around him, breathing in the familiar smells and sounds, and jumped out of his skin as the car fired up.

"Sorry!" Pete laughed. "Just checking!"

The staccato beat of the engine filled the air, sending tingles of anticipation across Declan's sweating skin. Half excited, half scared, he disappeared through the rear of the garage and into the driver's room. Francine was already there, pulling fire suits out of wardrobes and helmets out of lockers.

"Oh hello!" She smiled. "You want this?" She waved his blue suit at him. It was as if he had never been away.

"I guess I do." Declan took it from her slowly. "I didn't think I'd be wearing this colour again."

"For a while, neither did I." Francine hesitated, then planted a kiss on his cheek. "But I'm so glad that you are."

"Me too." Declan put his arm around her. "It goes with my eyes."

Francine smiled.

"Will you ever change, Declan?" She looked at him, almost serious.

"I already have." He squeezed her arm and went to dress.

He could not remember it afterwards; but somehow, he managed to pull on his suit, pick up his helmet and gloves and walk back into the garage. There, under the scrutiny of Carlo, and the privacy of the metal doors, he was secured into his car. His pulse was so erratic that he thought he might pass out. Pete, strapping him in, felt the throbbing heart through his chest and gave him a fleeting glance. Declan winked the old O.K. signal and tried to convince himself that it was. The shutters rose with a clatter, and the eyes of the world outside turned inwards; a myriad of photo lenses gleaming in the light as the blue car pulled out of the garage and onto the track.

He drove slowly on that first lap, trying to recall the best way to drive this so familiar track. Letting the sound of the engine fill his head he gathered speed as he went into his second lap; only when he had to use the brakes did his fear begin to show. Locking wheels, getting out of shape at every corner, corners that he had driven hundreds of times, he made his way back to the pits with bile in his throat. Turning into the garage he ignored the expectant eyes of the press and began to let himself out of the car. Carlo saw the blue eyes glittering as the visor lifted and hastily dropped the shutters. Stepping out of the car, Declan pushed his way through the mechanics and into the toilet.

There, away from the curious stares and the whispers he let his helmet fall to the floor with a thud and slumped against the wall, trying to catch his breath. All his nightmares had come true. Every dread, every fear, was now a reality. He had lost it. He could no longer handle his nerves and he would never be able to face the fear of driving in a race. The door creaked open, and he knew without looking who stood behind him.

"Go on then." He shook his head. "Tell me how shit I was."

"I would not do that." Carlo's voice was calm. "You have to settle in Declan, find your feet; you have not been away a long time, but you have been through a lot. A shaky start is understandable."

"Shaky start!" Declan gave a sarcastic laugh. "I've sunk Carlo. Lost without trace; another failure to go onto the pile."

"I don't believe it." Carlo laid a hand on his shoulder but tactfully avoided looking at Declan's face. "Take some time, compose yourself, and get back out there. There's no rush. We'll be ready whenever you are?"

Declan turned and looked at him, his reddened eyes revealing his feelings.

"Thank you" He muttered. "l hope I won't let you down."

"You won't." Carlo gave him a hearty slap on the back. "Any time you're ready Declan. Just say the word. "

Declan stared at the door long after Carlo had closed it. His heart was slowing now, his breath returning to normal. He banged the back of his head on the wall and stared up at the ceiling. Think of the great men who've gone before you, he told himself, think of the victories, the triumphs, the disasters. Not all of them had it easy, probably in truth not one of them. Everyone had days of doubt. If not about themselves then about their future, and the sport that they took part in.

You're not alone. He told himself. You've got people who want you to succeed, good people. You can't let them down. He closed his eyes, willing the confidence to return to his mind. This is not a physical thing, he told himself. It's all about your mind and controlling it. Push fear, and doubt, into the furthest darkest recess, and think about nothing but speed, and being the fastest man on the track. Think about saving split seconds, about timing every single move to perfection; and never, ever believe that you can fail. He opened his eyes, looked around him, and shook himself. Right, now is as good a time as any. Do it. Walking back through the door, he kept his eyes straight ahead avoiding the eyes of his waiting crew and got back into the car. The engine back burst into life, the shutters lifted, and he drove back out into the daylight.

Focused, his mind not leaving the car for a second, he drove through the lap, hardly blinking in his concentration.

Lap one, not bad but could be better. He was still way too slow.

Lap two, getting it together now, the brakes, use

them, that's what they are there for. A bit more throttle, brake later, trust the brakes they are fine. He said it aloud, not caring who heard him over the radio.

Lap three. Got it! At last, the old confidence was flowing through his veins, the coursing surge of adrenalin lifting his performance even more. Back over the timing line, floor the throttle, hug the tight left-hander, brake, right turn, then hard back on the throttle along the back straight.

"Now he's going!" Pete was practically bouncing as he watched the monitors. "Look at the time Carlo! Shit! That car hasn't worked like this all year!"

"Calm down." Carlo laughed. "Let us hope he keeps it up."

But Declan was in a groove now; pushing harder and harder and set up a blistering time as he passed the timing line once more. Lifting off the throttle, he put in a languid, leisurely lap, and toured back to the garage. He wanted to enjoy it, that old familiar rush and the familiar sensation of the car moving beneath him.

He was greeted by an ecstatic band of cheering mechanics.

"Why the excitement?" His amusement showed on his face as he stepped out of the car. "Anyone would think I'd won a race!"

"You've already won one race." Carlo shook his hand. "The one which, I think, is the most important."

Declan nodded.

"I agree." He said quietly.

"Fastest man on the track returns!" Pete whooped. "Look out you lot! My man is back in action!"

Declan laughed. Pete's excitement was infectious, and a buzz of anticipation lifted the atmosphere of the garage. Perhaps, at long last, they could repeat the celebrations of Australia. Joining Pete at the monitor, Declan began discussing technical problems with him; suggesting minor adjustments that may make the Matros even quicker. Behind him, he heard a door closing; and, as swiftly as it had been created, the buoyant, bubbling hum of noise in the garage fell silent. He turned, curious, and looked into the brooding eyes of a tall, dark young man.

"Fabio." He turned and stepped down, unsure of what his reaction should be.

"Declan." Fabio nodded. "A good time. Well done."

"Thanks." Declan hesitated, about to go over and speak to him properly, to break the ice. Remove the barrier that neither one of them had created when another figure came through the door. He stared, unable to believe the gall which allowed Lucy to stand, cool and composed, in the garage. He looked at Fabio and saw the embarrassment on his face; then he looked straight at Lucy. He held her eyes for a moment;

one heart-stopping moment before he turned away.

Looking back at the monitor he stood, rigid, and tried to keep calm. He failed. In the monitor's reflection, he saw not his own face, but Kurt's, thin and aged, wearied with pain; and Bernice, burying her tear-stained cheeks in his shoulder. He saw smoke, and wrecked motor car, and the memory of terror. A terror that he had only just begun to conquer.

"Pete." His voice cracked, betraying his emotions. "Get her out of here Pete. Please?"

"Okay." Pete frowned at him. "Take it easy Dec. I'll get rid of her."

Declan heard Pete talking in lowered tones and heard Lucy's voice raised in protest. He fought the impulse, tempting though it was, to go and slap her face and tell her exactly what he thought of her. Then he could tell, from the tone of Peter's voice that his persuasion was falling on deaf ears, and his impulses gained the upper hand. Spinning on his heel, he stepped away from the monitor and strode up to this girl who had so nearly ended everything that he was. He could not believe that once, he had been swayed by lust for her. Now when he looked at her all he could feel was revulsion. He stood in front of her, his high colour and laboured breathing leaving no one in any doubt about his feelings.

"You have got some nerve." He hissed and turned to Fabio. "And so have you, bringing her here."

"Lucy made a mistake." Fabio raised his arms and shrugged. "That is all. She has paid for it. She lost her job. She too has suffered. She had some things she still had here to collect so I escorted her."

"I can see how much she's suffering." Declan snapped. "Lost a job and found a millionaire lover. How quaint. Don't upset her Fabio. She's a dangerous little bitch under all that humility.

"You bastard!" Lucy threw herself at him, only to be pulled back by Fabio. "That's not fair!"

"Not fair?" Declan glared at her, watching her colour rising under his vehement stare. "What isn't fair is seeing Kurt struggling to eat a meal, seeing him unable to pick up his sons. Watching the woman, his wife, who is one of my dearest friends, breaking her heart every day, and hoping that no one can see it happening. That's what isn't fair."

"Shut up!" She yelled. "Just shut up! Do you think I wanted Kurt to get hurt? Do you think I would have deliberately put someone's life at risk?"

"Yes." Declan's voice was so cold, so quiet, but it immediately silenced the garage. "I know you better than him."

Declan cast a bitter glance in Fabio's direction.

"Far far better. That much is obvious. If he knew you at all he would never have put that ring on your finger. I am sorry I'm not the Superman your fantasies made me out to be Lucy but to try and kill me? Why? Because I wasn't the person you had created in your dreams? Because you knew I would never have put a ring on your finger? You came after me, remember? Put yourself on a plate and then don't want to be eaten. God I should have known something bad would come of your schoolgirl obsessions."

"Enough." A quiet voice spoke in his ear, and he felt Carlo's hand on his arm. "Enough Declan. Washing the dirty linen in public does no one any good. Least of all the team. Remember where you are."

Declan looked around him and saw the eyes of every engineer fixed on him. Mercifully the shutters were still closed, hiding the group from the eyes and ears of outsiders; but what a field day the press would have had if they had heard his little outburst. He lowered his eyes.

"Get a coffee and calm down." Carlo squeezed his arm. "Get a drink, eat and we will do some more work."

Declan looked at his composed insistent face and nodded. His eyes strayed back to Lucy who was still staring at him, tears spilling down her cheeks, eyes wide in her own, indignant, face.

"I haven't finished with you." He murmured. "You owe me an apology. But you owe the biggest one to Kurt. If you are any kind of human being, you'll deliver it."

Pushing her out of the way so violently that

she fell against the wall he marched out of the garage into the calming peace of his room.

CHAPTER 46.

Kate, blissfully unaware of what had been happening, came across her sour-faced driver as she came to the canteen in search of a late lunch. Feeling confident in the new accord that existed between Declan and herself she sat beside him. Noting his petulant mouth and furrowed brow she wisely said nothing. He looked at her, briefly, out of the corner of his eye, then turned his attention back to his empty coffee cup.

"Do you want another?" She ventured. "Or are you going back into the garage?"

"What?" Declan spun around; his look so intent that she moved backwards away from him. "Sorry." He shook his head. "I'm not mad at you."

"I should bloody well hope not." Kate snorted. "I haven't been near you all afternoon."

"No." Declan's attention had gone back to his cup.

"But I did hear." She continued quietly. "That you drove brilliantly."

"Did you now?" Declan gave a sarcastic laugh. "Did you also hear that I bottled it on the first run? That I nearly threw it all away there and then?"

"No, I didn't," Kate spoke slowly. "And even if

I had, I would have completely understood. But all that matters now is that you didn't throw it away; you went back out there and proved to everyone that you're still one of the best."

"Shit!" Declan looked surprised. "Are they putting something in the tea around here? I've never had so many supporters."

"Especially not me?" Kate smiled. "I know. I'm still getting used to it myself."

"You are!" Declan shook his head and sat upright.

"Everything in my life has been turned completely upside down. You always hated me. Even when I didn't deserve it. And Lucy! I wish I had run a mile when I saw that one coming. A crystal ball would have been handy these past few months!"

"Crystal ball?" Kate turned her fork over in her hands and shook her head. "Do they work I wonder?"

"If they did." Declan sighed grimly. "Kurt would be in this race with me."

"I don't know if I want to see the future." Kate's voice cracked slightly. "Sometimes it is just better not to know."

Declan looked at her and saw that the glossy red hair was not as immaculate as it used to be. There was a dullness to it and the long golden lashes hadn't been darkened with mascara. Freckles lined her pale cheeks, and he could see the bones of her shoulders through her blouse.

With a pang of sympathy, he realised that he was not the only one who had been to hell and back.

"No," he said softly." Perhaps you are right."

They sat there in silence, listening to the noises of the factory around them. Fabio's car was putting in a fast lap, its engine screaming as it passed the pit garages; Declan's car was barking noisily in the garage as Carlo fine-tuned it to perfection. They were the same noises that followed them throughout the year, wherever they went; they could be anywhere in the world. The sounds of engines were the one certainty in the ever-changing, turbulent sport they worked in.

"What a life." Declan sighed. "A cog in a great wheel. But a dispensable one. All cogs easily replaced. This sport should carry a health warning."

"Ouch." Kate winced. "That was a bit close to home, Declan."

"I know." Declan looked at her pinched cheeks. "Sorry. It's the new me. Declan the fatalist."

Kate saw the sparkle returning to the indigo eyes and laughed, lightening the mood.

"You nearly had me there." She narrowed her eyes. "You are very plausibly human all of a sudden."

"As I said." He got to his feet. "It's the new me. Dr Jekyll has left the building. From now on it's just Mr Hyde."

"Not sure I'm sold on that idea." Kate looked

up at him. "You can't have one without the other, can you?"

"Maybe not." Declan looked down at her and laid a hand on her shoulder. "But I can try."

He moved off first, leaving her to pick up the half-empty plates. She watched him walking back to the garage, still limping, just slightly now, but it was still there. Yes, he had changed. Only time would tell whether the change was for the better; the old Declan, the one who had driven her mad with his every word had gone, but she wasn't sure why. Or was it just that she saw him differently? Confused and unable to accept this new situation between them without dissecting it further, she wiped it temporarily from her mind and went back to work.

The rest of the day was an unmitigated success as far as Declan was concerned. He drove out of the car park that night comforted by the knowledge that he had driven faster than his teammate. Elated by the day's events he drove home to Mullacombe at a leisurely pace. It was a long way, but a night in his own bed was far preferable to the regimented order of a hotel. The only blot on the copybook of his day was his attack on Lucy. Deserved yes, but it had not been the right place or time. He should have bitten his tongue and waited for the right moment. He would confront her again, he knew he would, but it would be in a more private place and then he would have the truth. Turning up the car stereo he pushed all thoughts of Lucy into the back of his mind and let the satisfaction of his performance take the front. He had done it; he had proven beyond doubt that he still had what it takes to drive a race car. The race itself may be a different matter but he had got over the first hurdle. That was enough for now. All he had to do now was wait. Nine days until the first test session was hardly a lifetime, but it was long enough to spend fighting battles with nerves. He knew that the best way to fight off those nerves was with Kurt.

Relaxing in the cosy family atmosphere that Bernice created and absorbing the confidence that Kurt seemed to give him was just what he needed. Looking forward to their surprised faces when he arrived back so early, he began to drive faster looking forward to collecting his bag. He was so deep in thought that his mobile rang three times before he heard it. He was surprised to hear Kate's voice at the end of a rather crackly line.

"Declan." He could hardly hear her. "Where are you?"

"On the motorway!" He shouted. "Why is there a problem?"

"I should say so," Kate shouted. "You are supposed to be here!"

"What? Where?"

"The hotel!" Far from being annoyed, Kate was laughing. "I thought you'd changed! We have a pre-race promotion evening tonight, remember? One of our new sponsors is really keen to meet you after today's lap times."

"Shit." Declan sighed. "I forgot. I'll turn around."

"Would you?" Kate sounded grateful. "I'll keep them at bay until you are here. I do need you for this. I'll see you then."

Declan sped down to the next roundabout and did an about-turn. It looked as if his return to Monaco would have to wait. A smile touched his face. He was back, back where he belonged, doing what he did best. If smiling at sponsors and chatting up their wives was what it would take to keep him there then so be it.

CHAPTER 47.

The week that led up to Silverstone and the British Grand Prix was blessed with the hottest spell of July weather for the last ten years. The temperature outside the factory was equalled only by the fever pitch of excitement mounting inside it. There was a real optimism about the team as they prepared for their home race, an optimism that, it seemed, was shared by thousands upon thousands of fans, who bombarded the office with well wishes. It was noticeable that most of the Good Luck cards that arrived came addressed to one Mr D. Hyde. This was not just because of his nationality it was also a result of the long-recognised British tradition of supporting the underdog. The British fans along with many from abroad felt that Declan had been dealt an unfair crack of the whip by the authorities and they wanted to see his redemption. They had all watched the horror of Monaco, and although sympathetic to Kurt and his team had been outraged at the FIA's decision to blame Declan. They had witnessed nothing that they hadn't seen a hundred times before. Overjoyed at the prospect of seeing their hero back in action they jammed the factory switchboard and exhausted the local postman with their enthusiasm.

For Declan, it was just another shot of the drug that was needed to boost his shattered confidence, giving him an unbelievable high. His attempts to go back to Monaco had failed as more and more people tried to get a piece of his time. Interviews, chat shows, and television appearances; it was the busiest week of his life. He had never before fully realised the strength of public support behind him, and it made him feel good, really good. From Kate's point of view, it was something of a revelation. Overwhelmed by the response to Declan's reinstatement she found herself, yet again, questioning her long-standing opinion of him. Could she have really been alone in her feelings? Declan was renowned for wearing his heart on his sleeve. He wore no public mask; what you saw was what you got, so his personality and his temperament were well documented. Slightly bemused by it all, she could not help but feel sorry for Fabio, who had been suddenly cast as the bad guy which was not only unfair but untrue. He kept well away from the rest of the team in the days leading up to Silverstone; whether he sensed the air of animosity that prevailed towards Lucy or whether he was simply hiding from the spotlight Kate wasn't sure. Whatever the reason he was conspicuous by his absence. The Matros team had always operated in a slightly different way to the super teams, this was very much a family, so Fabio's actions further distanced him from the men who really should have been on his side. Particularly his mechanics, who needed his support and input as much as he needed theirs.

At last, the scene was finally set for one of the biggest sporting weekends on the British calendar. Fleets of brilliantly coloured articulated lorries headed up the Ml all converging on one historic spot in the Northamptonshire countryside. The journey was made by many of them at regular intervals throughout the year to get back home. But this was different. This was it. Thronging the roads around the circuit, mixing with the transporters and the team motorhomes were the public. Armed with cameras, radios, tents, and beer cans they didn't want to miss a thing, not a single turn of a wheel. They filled every campsite for miles around the circuit and boosted the takings of the local pubs to yearly highs as they settled in to watch and admire the best that the sport had to offer. No driver was safe in this fever of fanaticism; anyone who bore even a vague resemblance to one of the twenty-two Formula One drivers got assailed by autograph-hungry teenagers at regular intervals.

For the real drivers, it was amusing to read yet another article claiming that they had been spotted in a local supermarket when they actually had been sitting in their hotel room. Declan's coveted privacy had been lost completely and the residents of Mullacombe and the surrounding area turned out in their hundreds to wish him luck as he left for the track. He shared a helicopter into the circuit itself with a member of the British television crew, an ex-driver himself, and as he looked down on the colourful, ever-moving scene as they landed, he was overwhelmed by an emotion he had never felt before. It was getting to him, all this excitement, all this expectancy, and he just hoped that he wasn't going to let anyone down; most of all himself. Kurt had called him that morning and told him how to drive the circuit. It was an old joke between them, created by Declan's first-ever attempt at the track in an F1 car which had ended in a scenic detour at Abbey. Declan listened to his friend's advice and proceeded to rip it to proverbial shreds until his motions started creeping in as he realised that this was his first time at Silverstone without Kurt. He had cut the conversation short, pleading a headache. Doubtless Kurt had guessed the real reason and had let him go without a fuss. And now here he was, stepping out of the helicopter, and pushing his way through reporters, all jabbering at him in different tongues, and making his way to the paddock.

The Matros motorhome was already oozing sponsors, actual and potential, from every corner. It was only nine a.m. but the atmosphere was electric.

"This is getting out of hand." Pete was keeping photographers away from the Matros pit garages. "What do they want to take photos of a dismantled Grand Prix car for? Why don't they wait until there is someone in it for God's sake!"

"Just doing their job " Carlo soothed him. "As are we all. Ah, buongiorno Declan. How are you today?"

"Not sure." Declan stood looking at what would eventually be his race car. "I'll tell you at lunchtime."

"I hope you've got a strong stomach." Pete chuckled. "I wouldn't fancy it myself."

"What are you on about?" Declan looked puzzled.

"I take it she hasn't told you yet?" Pete's laugh deepened.

"Who hasn't told me what? Declan frowned. "What's happened now?"

"Nothing yet." Pete was enjoying himself. "But it will. Some bright spark has come up with the idea of you taking part in the Air Display team on Saturday. They asked Kate about it this morning."

"What!" Declan's eyes widened. "I hope she didn't say yes!"

"Aahh." Pete cooed. "Is the ickle diddums baby boy afraid of heights?"

"No, I bloody well am not!" Declan snorted. "But I don't relish the idea of being turned upside down and inside out a few hours before qualifying either!"

"That's exactly what I thought." Said a voice behind them. "That's why I said no."

Kate had been listening to the conversation with an amused smile on her face. It was comforting; knowing that Declan was only human after all. She had half expected him to jump at the chance of a new kick and end up performing dismally in qualifying as a result. The old Declan would have done it; putting up a thousand reasons why he should; and then explaining away his qualifying performance with the same gusto. But this was the new Declan, the responsible version, who was putting his team and his career first. She liked it and thanked him accordingly.

"What are you thanking me for?" Declan narrowed his eyes. "I thought you would have enjoyed seeing me defying gravity at ten thousand feet while upside down."

"I probably would." Kate smiled. "And one day I probably will. But for now, it's a sight I can wait for. All I want to see is P.1 next to your name on Saturday night."

"God protect us from ambitious women." Declan smiled back. "Because they always want the best."

"Of course." Kate nodded. "Because nothing less will do."

"Car." Carlo interrupted them. "Suit, change,

car, track. Now, please."

" I take it that's my cue." Declan laughed. "Okay, okay I'm going."

The remaining trio stood by the car and watched him ploughing through reporters and cameras to the privacy of the motor home.

"He must be taking something." Pete shrugged. "I've never known him so bright before a race."

"We still have two days to go," Carlo commented dryly. "But, as long as he drives as well as we all know he can I don't care if he smiles, cries or screams the place down."

"No," Kate said quietly. "And do you know, for the first time, neither do I."

There were Union Jacks at every corner, waved frantically by cheering crowds at every British driver who passed them throughout the two practice sessions. The glorious weather boosted even the normal crowds for a Friday, but there was also something else, something more personal, that roused the bulldog spirit and made the fans want to turn out early to spur one particular man onto victory. Declan, bemused by it all, expected the hordes to start singing 'Rule Brittania' as he passed, and laughed loudly into his radio at the thought of it.

"Got to be on drugs!" Pete was also laughing. "He's giggling now!"

"Leave him alone." Carlo smiled. "He's enjoying himself."

Which is more, he thought to himself, than can

be said for Fabio. The young Italian's confidence was getting a constant battering in the face of all this patriotism. Fabio knew that in the eyes of the crowd, he was the usurper, the traitor, the man who had almost taken their darling's seat. They were not against him, he knew that that was not the way of the British Motor Racing public, they appreciated and admired all drivers too much to be so bigoted, but he knew there would be no tears of sympathy for him should he fail. Added to this the media had somehow gotten wind of the fact that Kurt's team and the FIA were investigating Matros for the use of faulty parts. Even worse was the fact that someone had got hold of Lucy's name and details of her part in the affair and now that they were officially engaged the eye of suspicion had started to turn onto him as well as her. Had he been party to this? Had he wanted Declan's seat that badly that he had put her up to it? The same questions were being asked everywhere and to such an extent that he began to doubt his own innocence. It was far more than he could handle, and he began to think going back to the vineyard was the only future he could now have.

Lucy was unaware of his erratic mental state and leaned on him heavily as support from the media assault that she was suffering herself. Her earlier confidence had gone, and now she bolted in terror whenever she saw a press badge. It was going to be a very long and difficult weekend for them both. The inevitable confrontation between herself and Declan came on the Saturday morning after the close of the final practice session before qualifying. Declan had been driving superbly, all the old attack and panache had returned, and he was looking forward to the afternoon's event with relish. He was sitting under the motorhome canopy, eating a very light lunch at Francine's insistence, when he saw Lucy approaching. The press pack that had followed her throughout the morning had gone in search of their lunch, so she walked to a table unnoticed. Except that is by him. His initial revulsion passed, and he stared in the opposite direction. Forget about it, he told himself. Keep your confidence; keep the good mood. You have to nail this one, not just for yourself but for Kurt, and for Gerald. Even if you don't win you can at least grab that pole position and give them something.

But thinking of his absent friends was not his wisest move and soon he found his attention turned back to the lone, dark-haired figure sitting at a table not too far away from his own. It was probably the wrong thing to do, and it may well ruin his chances of success that afternoon, but he had to have this thing out with her once and for all. He got up, very slowly and walked over to her. Keep calm, he told himself, no need to yell and cause a scene. His shadow fell across her and she jumped. She looked up into his eyes, the intense blue eyes that had held her hypnotised for so long. Once he had been her dream, and she had seen the hope of a future in those eyes. Now all she could see was hate. She closed her own weary eyes and lowered her head. She couldn't even look at him anymore.

"Why?" His voice, the voice she had heard in her dreams for so many years, was stone cold.

She looked at her hands, the always moving nervous hands that betrayed her mental state. There was no point in claiming ignorance, not to him. He understood her too well.

"I wanted to get at you." She still couldn't look directly at him. "You used to be my everything, my idol. All I have ever wanted in my life was you and you rejected me. Used me and threw me away."

"So, you thought you'd try and finish me off, is that it?" Declan's voice was barely more than a whisper. "You can't have me so no one can?"

"Of course not!" This time she did look up at him with her tear-filled eyes. "I didn't know those things were dangerous. I just thought they'd slow you down or force you to retire. That's all, I just wanted to see you beaten, brought to your knees. To let you see how it feels to have everything you've ever wanted taken away from you."

"And to see your new lover wearing the victor's spoils?" Declan sat opposite her, aware that a group of the catering staff were watching them.

"You always throw yourself in headfirst don't you Lucy? I wasn't the hero that you'd fantasised me to be, so you've picked out another one. What will you do when Fabio doesn't live up to your romantic expectations? Go and look for another idol. Life isn't like that. People aren't like that. People have flaws and history, and you have to live with them. Nobody's perfect."

"I know." She glared at him. "But some people try. But you, you don't care for anyone, you don't care who you hurt, who you destroy, as long as you get what you want. I was a toy to you, something to play with when you had nothing to do, easy prey or so you thought. You never stopped to think that I could have loved you and wanted you as more than a cheap roll in the sheets. So, when I didn't play as you wanted you threw me back in the toy box with the rest of your playthings. Whatever I have become Declan you made me. This is all your fault."

"Bullshit!" He banged the table with his fist, sending her coffee cup crashing to the floor. "Don't you dare try and dump this on me! Okay, you wanted to get back at me, that I can understand, you wouldn't be the first woman who's dreamed of slitting my throat and you probably won't be the last. But I never promised you anything! That was all in your sick twisted little head! I offered you a good time for a while and it wasn't what you wanted. So, because I didn't rush you down the aisle you tried to kill me!"

"I told you." She was sobbing now, taking great uncontrollable gasps of air. "I didn't know you would crash. I would never have done that, to anyone, and then it was too late, there was nothing I could do."

"Of course, there was you callous bitch!" He roared. "You could have told Carlo I was sitting in a death trap before he sent me out to race! What about Fabio did you get a kick out of him coming off in Canada?"

"No!" She was also on her feet. "Everyone was blaming you! Everyone said you caused the crash, that you had put Kurt in hospital. I had no idea those brake pads were the cause of any of it!"

"But you still didn't own up to it." He shook his head, "You knew the effect Kurt's accident had on me, everyone did, but you let me go on sitting there, blaming myself for his injuries, wishing it was me and not him. Gave you a buzz, did it? Getting what you wanted, seeing me fall apart?"

"It didn't." Her voice was barely a whisper. "I still don't know why, but it hurts. It didn't feel good at all. Not because I felt guilty, but because I didn't enjoy seeing you suffer after all. I'm sorry for what happened to Kurt. I'm sorry for putting your life in danger, I never intended to do that. But I'm paying for it all now, aren't I? Paying for being in love with you in the first place, paying for letting my heart rule my head and making such a bloody fool of myself. I suppose it's what

I deserve. But when all this is over, and I go back to being a nobody, you'll still be the hero, the one everybody loves, and somewhere out there will be another Lucy Duggan so be careful who you hurt next time, or it might all happen again."

"Oh, it won't." He stared into her eyes. "I'll know the signs next time."

She couldn't answer him. She couldn't think of anything, not one single word that she could say to him. So, this was the result of her obsessions. Standing here, locked in hatred with the one man she had been so sure was the love of her life. You sad pathetic creature, she told herself. You pursued him, you caught him and then couldn't handle what you got. He was right. None of this was his fault. Oh, he was a bastard, there was no doubting that, but you should have had the maturity to walk away from it all, to let him go. Then none of this would have happened. Another tear slipped out of the corner of her eye, and she wiped it away with her trembling fingers. Declan watched her and something similar to sympathy moved inside him.

"I believe you." He said shortly. "I won't ever forgive you and I will be happy to see whatever punishment you get handed out and I'll have a smile on my face while I'm watching. But I do believe that you didn't realise what you were doing was dangerous."

She looked up, wanting to thank him and reiterate that it had been a mistake, and not what she had planned to do but her eyes met the steely coldness in his and the words died on her lips as he turned and walked away.

Fabio was coming out of a stint in the hospitality tent when he found her. One look at her blotchy face told him all he needed to know.

"Where is he?"

"It's fine." She shook her head. "It's done. Over. He believes me now that it wasn't a deliberate attempt to kill him. That bloody message. Why didn't anyone else open it first instead of me!"

"Yes." Fabio felt an inward rush of relief. Perhaps now he could recapture some of his lost friendship with Declan. Life would be so much more bearable if he could.

" I wish." Lucy sounded wistful, "That I could turn the clock back and undo it all. Every bit."

"But you can't." He hugged her. "We must move on."

"I know." She kissed him, very gently. "I'm so lucky to have you."

"True." Fabio smiled. "Just keep remembering that."

"Oh, I will." Lucy closed her eyes. "What a mess my life has been. Like Romeo and Juliet in reverse. My only hate sprang from my only love. Except that I know that it isn't my only love, not really."

"No." Fabio looked smug, knowing the answer to the question before he asked it. "What is?"

"As if you have to ask." She gave him a playful

pinch with her fingers.

"No, I don't." Fabio looked up, as a growl from the pit lane told him that engines were being started and that the qualifying session was imminent. "I must go."

"Good luck." She kissed him.

Fabio nodded, and they walked together into the garage. He felt as if a weight had been lifted from him, and now he didn't feel the need for luck. He just had to relax and be himself, and let it happen. For the first time since he had arrived at Silverstone, he greeted his mechanics with a smile, saw their puzzled faces at this change of heart, and laughed as he crossed the pit lane to speak to Carlo. Carlo saw the relaxed face; the stress lines disappearing beneath the smile and was relieved himself.

"I am so glad to see you smile again Fabio." He patted his shoulder. "Perhaps now this can be a good race for us all."

CHAPTER 48.

Declan sat in his car, hands resting on the steering wheel, watching the times as they flashed onto the monitor in front of him. Pete was rattling away, bending his ear as usual, calculating a possible lap time, and where they would have to make savings to get onto the front of the grid.

"Pete." Declan's voice was serious, but his eyes, as he looked up at him, sparkled with humour. "Shut up."

"Sorry mate." Pete smiled back. "Am I giving you earache'?"

"You are indeed" Declan nodded. "If you don't mind, I'm going to bugger off for a while."

"What'?" Pete looked puzzled. "Where?"

"Out there." Declan was pulling on his gloves, smiling as he did so. "Unless you can run very, very fast you'll never keep up with me."

Pete shrugged; pleasure written all over his face.

"Your wish is my command." He beamed. "Fire her up."

He pointed to the waiting crew.

"It's time to get this show on the road."

It was a wonderful sight, the midnight blue machine performing at its best, shaving hundredths of a second off the leader's lap time with every trip. It took the full session, but eventually, they were there.

Pole position.

Declan cruised back to the garage, waving to the ecstatic fans as he went.

"Show off." Pete hugged him as he got out of the car. "You haven't won the race yet!"

"No" Declan pulled off his helmet. "But it's a bloody good way to start."

"Well done, Declan" Kate was in front of him. "I can give you a bit of time to recover later, but right now you're wanted for the television, and there's a roomful of sponsors waiting to pat you on the back."

"The television I can do." Declan rubbed his sweating face with a towel. "But the sponsors can wait. I have something to do. Tomorrow when they have something to crow about, they can pat my back as hard as they like!".

"Okay." Kate nodded. "If that's what you want. I have to ask if you still want a ride to the hotel after dinner tonight?"

"No." Declan shook his head. "Not tonight."

"Did you enjoy the pre-race party last night Kate?" Carlo smiled at her. "I have not asked you before."

"Yes, I did thanks." Kate smiled. "Although it wasn't the same without my Dad."

"Did you go?" Pete squinted at Declan suspiciously. "Was that why you were so high this morning? Still drunk?"

"No!" Declan laughed. "And no, I didn't go, not this time."

"Bloody hell!" Pete raised his eyebrows. "Were you sick?"

"Nope." Declan laughed. "Just didn't feel like it. But I want to get away early tonight."

"Anywhere good?" Pete peered at him.

"Just somewhere." Declan laughed again. "Now shut up and mind your business."

Carlo noticed the fleeting look of curiosity in Kate's eyes as she heard Declan's words and was surprised. Things were changing here, and fast. Declan, who hadn't noticed the look, stared out at the track and took a deep breath. He had to get out of here, he had a jet to catch. He could not explain why and did not fully understand it himself, but the only person he could spend the evening with and not fall prey to the nerves which were already lining up to attack him was Kurt Braun.

CHAPTER 49.

The first thing that confronted Kate as she drove into the circuit the next morning was a life-size cardboard cutout of Declan Hyde being carried by a group of fans clad head to toe in Matros team colours. Hoping that this was an omen, she negotiated the Fort Knox that was the Silverstone security system and made her way through the paddock to the motorhome. The gates had been open since early morning and the faithful hordes had been pouring steadily through them ever since. There was a full card of entertainment on offer to keep them occupied. As well as two supporting races, as important to their participants as the Grand Prix race was to her and the team, there were air displays, minus one Formula One driver thankfully: army bands, parachute teams, and even a fly past by the Red Arrows. The crowds were going to get their money's worth today. Only time would tell if they could get a British win to go with it.

The catering team were serving breakfast to the starving mechanics, who had already been hard at it since dawn. Nothing left to chance in this game, a place for everything and everything in its place. A quick scan of the canopy told her that Carlo was noticeable by his absence, so she went to the garage to find him expecting him to be poring over his beloved GM-4. It was quite dark, with the shutters down and the lights off, so at first, she did not notice the figure in the number one bay. Only when she turned to leave did she see a shadowy form crouching in the corner.

"Jesus!" She jumped out of her skin, banging into a stack of tyres with D.H. written all over them. "Who's that?"

"Well, it's certainly not Jesus." Replied a familiar voice. "Although I could do with some help from him right now."

"Declan?" She peered through the gloom and as he rose from his squatting position recognised his shape. "What are you doing?"

"Thinking." Declan stepped forward so that she could see his face. "And praying."

"You? Pray!" A smile passed across her face. "That's unusual."

"Isn't it?"

The shadows were hiding his expression from her, but she could see his eyes clearly, glinting in the dim light. Beside them, the GM-4 was ready for action. It had been polished to perfection; its gleaming paintwork immaculate.

"New nose." Declan nodded to it. "I managed to dent the other one in practice, don't ask me how as I really can't remember."

"Plenty more where they came from." Kate slid a finger along the cool, smooth surface of the car.

"Ready for battle." Declan's hands were deep in the pockets of his jeans, his face immobile apart from one muscle that twitched slightly in his jawline.

"You okay?" Kate laid a hand on his arm.

"Yes and no." Declan leaned against the wall. "My head says yes but my heart says no."

"Oh dear." Kate paused. "Doesn't your heart normally get its own way?"

"Normally." Declan nodded. "Or at least my body does. But today it can't. Today I have to listen to my head and win. Because it knows that I can, the problem is the rest of me doesn't quite believe it."

Kate leaned beside him. A shaft of light came through the shutters and lit up his face. A taught tense face, pale, drawn and unshaven He glanced at her, embarrassed that she could see his tension so plainly.

"It's okay to be nervous." She pushed at him with her shoulder.

"Nervous!" He laughed, a high ungenuine sound. "I'm not nervous. I'm scared. I've never been so scared in my life. No," he hesitated, "That's not true. I have been. When Kurt was in that tunnel, I couldn't see what was happening to him. Nothing will ever come close to that."

His frankness took her aback. She nodded but couldn't think of anything to say. Perhaps he was better alone, alone with his car and his thoughts. She turned to go.

"Don't." He pulled her back. "I need company."

At any other point in their turbulent history, she would have pulled away from the hand that clasped hers and walked away, but now she stepped back and looked into his wide frightened eyes with her own.

"Need to talk?" She offered.

"No thanks." Declan sat on the floor. "Although I probably will. I bent Kurt's ear all last night, I don't know how he puts up with me."

"Kurt?" So that was where he had been last night. Kate breathed deeply, feeling something like relief seeping through her. "So that's where you had to be."

"Yep." Declan closed his eyes. "He is a good listener."

"I don't really know him that well." Kate sat beside him.

"He's the nicest person I know. The best friend: the hardest worker and the fiercest competitor." Declan looked at her. "The only other person who came close to him was your father."

His last comment brought tears to her eyes. Flustered, she looked away.

"It's okay." Declan placed his arm over her shoulders, a natural gesture that didn't seem so prohibited now. "I miss him as well, you know."

He stared at the car in front of them, the end result of the dream of a man who would never see it race again.

"I want this one so badly." He blurted." Not for

me, I don't matter, but for him, and for Kurt. When I decided I would stay here, that I wanted my drive back, all I wanted was to win this race and that constructor's title. Not for me. But for Gerald. So that he could have his dream and then I could walk away. But I don't know if I can."

"Can what?" Kate heard the doubt in his voice.

"See it through. If I can win this race today, then that will be enough. I will have paid back my debts, to them, to you, to the team, to myself. Then I can walk away from this sport with a happy heart."

"Walk away?" Kate looked at him, not believing what she had just heard. "You mean you still want to quit?"

"Not quite exactly. More sort of retire. Maybe."

"But why?" She was confused. "What will you do?"

"Who knows? Live." He shrugged. "Go shopping, get a dog, maybe even a wife. All the things I don't do now."

"Will that keep you happy?"

"I don't know. I doubt it. But one day it will have to, so maybe I want that day to come sooner rather than later. But I do know one thing." He hesitated.

"What?" her voice was little more than a whisper.

"I can't live with this fear for the rest of my life."

His honest, candid eyes met hers and her heart went out to him.

"They are just nerves. You'll be fine when you are out there. You know you will."

"I know. But this is the first race since Monaco. It's not being in my car that worries me; it's being surrounded by others."

"Then don't be." She squeezed his hand. "You are in P1 remember? Get a flying start and stay there."

"Now that would be nice." He laughed. "I'll have to try it!"

With an impulse that took him as much by surprise as it did her, he lifted her hand to his mouth and kissed it. The sensation of his lips on her skin made her heart lurch and sent heat pouring through her body. He was looking at her steadily and his eyes were changing, the fear being replaced by a familiar gleam, the gleam she had been avoiding facing for such a long time.

"I've got to go." She said hastily but didn't move.

He nodded, but his face was drawing closer, closer until his breath was brushing her cheek and his mouth was caressing her own. She sat, eyes closed, breathing deeply for some time after he moved away. She was afraid to open them, afraid of breaking the spell that she found herself under. When she did, looking upward through her lashes, she saw his eyes fixed on her face. Oh God, she thought, why have I fought against this for so long? Why has it taken me until now to realise how beautiful he is? Shaking her head, almost laughing at her lack of control she threw her arms around his neck and kissed him frantically. Declan was pleased, if a little startled at this reaction to his gentle question of a kiss. Her hand tugged at his spiky hair then dropped to explore his hard, muscular chest beneath his t-shirt. The thought crossed his mind that it would be good to have her, here now, on the floor of the garage next to his car and his tyres; on the cold hard floor lying next to her father's other beautiful creation. The thought of Gerald instantly took all sexual fantasies out of his head. Kate was Gerald's daughter and deserved more respect. Sex would give him a high, particularly in such a risky place, but he would need to get his confidence boost elsewhere. Gently pulling her arms from around his neck, he lifted his head and planted a gentle kiss in her hair.

"What?" She mumbled. "What's wrong?"

"Shh." He hugged her to him, tight, feeling her narrow body hot and taught against his own. "Any second now this place is going to be teeming with mechanics. You have a job to do and so do I. Let's get it done. There is time for this later. Lots of time."

"I suppose so. She took his face in her hands. I am so, so sorry for all the times that I was a bitch to you."

"Don't be." He said firmly. "Don't ever be sorry for who you are."

"But all the time, the way I treated you." She

murmured. "If I had known that it would feel like this..."

"All in the past," Declan said lightly. "Right now, we have to deal with the present."

"There you are!" A voice echoed loud and strident around the garage. "I thought you'd gone A.W.O.L!"

"No, I'm here." Declan got up and stepped forward, giving Kate a brief chance to compose herself before Pete spotted her. "Just having a word with my machine."

"Did it answer?" Pete chuckled, looking at the car with a look of love on his face. "Oh. Hello Kate, I didn't see you there."

"I was looking for Carlo." Kate smiled "But all I found was Declan in conversation with his car."

"Carlo is stuffing his face as usual." Pete grinned. "But there are plenty of people looking for you."

"I dare say there are. Well, I'll see you both later. I had better go and find them all."

"You old dog!" Pete hissed as Kate's figure disappeared out of the back of the garage. "What were you up to?"

"Nothing at all. Honest"

"Yeah, yeah." Pete was heading for the shutters. "That's one pairing I never thought to see!"

"And you probably never will." Declan took one more lingering look at his car and turned to go.

"I've seen that look on your face before Hyde. Now piss off and warm up or I'll have to drive the bloody thing myself!"

CHAPTER 50.

The displays were over. The driver's parade had been and gone, the grid formation had taken place, and the Red Arrows had blasted through the skies leaving a trail of red, white, and blue behind them that mirrored the red, white, and blue masses on the ground below them. God Save The Queen had been sung beautifully by an opera singer, tunelessly by the crowd. Helicopters had landed, taken off and landed again until all one hundred and twenty-eight spaces were filled. The sun beat down on the scantily clad spectators who began to turn pink and open their beer cans, drivers milled around the grid too warm to get fully clothed yet, fire suits hanging as ever, drinks in hand.

All except the one.

Declan was shielded from the heat by an umbrella being held by his grid girl. Unable to cope anymore with the press, the fans, and the expectation he sat, silent and motionless, a man prepared to meet his maker, to look fate in the eye and thwart it.

Carlo crouched beside him, muttering comforting words as he made last-minute checks. Pete was already at the radio, cracking jokes, and singing, anything to ease the tension.

Suddenly there was a wave of activity, the sound of the klaxon and the grid began to empty. Declan's heart began to thump. Carlo looked at him and gave him the thumbs up. Declan nodded and raised his own hoping that no one else could see his hand shaking. There was no need for words. Declan swallowed and felt bile rising in his throat and his heart skipping about in his chest. He closed his eyes and willed himself to calm down. Focus. Concentrate. All around him visors were being lowered and bodies twitched nervously in cockpits. He raised a blue-gloved hand and lowered his visor. Now no one could read his soul through the mirror of his eyes.

He was alone. Just him; the machine and the track shimmering in the heat before him.

Red lights.

One, two, three, four, five. Wait. Select first gear; push up the revs, more, more, more, that was it. Watch the lights. Watch. Watch!

Lights out.

Dip the clutch, control the wheel spin. Go! Go! Go! More throttle, faster, faster into Copse, clear track ahead, check the mirror, nothing, they were already way behind. The flying start had happened.

"Yes!" Pete shrieking in my ear. "Great start Declan. Keep it up, my son!"

Becketts, next corner.

Sixth gear; into the turn, take it flat, then downshift for the left-hander. Watch the kerb, through the final sector and away down Hangar Straight to Stowe. Stop the car going left, over the rise, check the mirror.

Red and silver car. Who is that? Julian. No problem, I've seen him off many times in the past. He isn't Kurt and never will be. Focus, hold the racing line, don't give him space, don't let him through.

Careful, careful, watch the back end and on with the power.

Bridge, Priory, what the hell is that? Christ, there's a cut out of me in front of the fence. Take no notice of that Declan Hyde concentrate on the real one. Watch Julian he's stalking now. Sneaky bastard, I know your tricks.

Brooklands: into second gear, Luffield One and Two, take it in one big sweep then up the gearbox and around Woodcote. Over the start. Was that only one lap? Haven't I been driving forever?

"Nice work." Pete again. "Only sixty more to go!"

This is starting to be fun. The nerves have gone. No doubts in my head. Only the beautiful music of this engine. Where's Julian? Still there. What's that behind him, red? Ferrari. Then blue; Christ Fabio must have had a flyer himself to be in P4.

Watch the pit board. As long as it says P1 we are in business. Wish Pete would shut up. So, what if there are fifty laps to go? Julian is getting closer, need to work harder, and build that gap.

Box. Watch speed. Stop. Don't hit the lollipop man. Oops, sorry John nearly had you with the nose that time. Nice stop fellas. Back out, watch your speed, back on track, check your mirror.

Shit! Shit! Shit! Julian's ahead. I'm sweating. Now it's hard work. Aching arms: shuddering spine, burning breath and neck being pulled at every corner. Slow down Jules for God's sake, I can't get to you at that pace.

"Fabio's off!" Stop shouting Pete. "Fabio is off. Down to you Hyde. Julian hasn't had his second stop yet, but we need more speed to hold position. We need you to push."

Push? Where does he think he is, the maternity ward?

Pit board. P2 L35. Time for another stop. Hah! Missed you that time John. Red and silver car is in the pit lane ahead of me. Something's wrong, he should be on his way back out by now. Come on, hurry lads, hurry. Perfect! Great work boys, bloody perfect stop. Speed, speed, careful, back on the track, now where is he?

"Yes!" Cue Pete. "He's behind you! It's all yours Dec. Go for it"

Keep calm. Don't think about winning, not yet. Keep it together, keep the car on the road.

Pit board. P1. 2.3

What? Two-point three seconds? Julian must have a problem. Kurt would never be that far behind. Kurt would have been here, snapping at his tail, challenging. Don't think about Kurt, not yet, or Gerald, or anything except this last lap.

God, look at the crowd! Shut up, Pete! I know we

are nearly there.! Let me enjoy it.

Here it comes. Deep breath, sweep through Woodcote. Breathe again,

Chequered flag.

Now you can shout Pete. Now I can wave. Wave to the crowd, wave to the boys on the pit wall, wave to the sky. Now think of Kurt, now think of Gerald, and now let it all out, safe, hidden, behind my visor.

Where no one can see the tears.

CHAPTER 51.

Pete was at him as soon as he reached the barrier, both embracing him and slapping him on the back. The mechanics were behind them and somehow had got hold of little Union Jacks, which they were ecstatically waving at him. Declan broke free from Pete and went to join them. The noise was deafening. It was not until he was making his way onto the podium, sweat still running down his flushed face that he saw a red-faced, red-eyed redhead running towards him. He picked her up and swung her around in the air.

"Thank you." She gasped through her tears. "You were brilliant."

"Thank you." He gave her another rib-crushing hug. "For letting me be."

On one hand, he would have liked the ceremony to last longer; but on the other, he was glad that it didn't. As soon as he had completed his duties here he wanted to get on the 'phone to Kurt, and into the shower. Julian had drenched him in Moet, and everything was sticking to him; and, as champagne did, it would soon begin to smell. But as he expected, it took several interviews before he could be given the peace to get into the shower. The motorhome was positively jumping, a party starting to brew that would continue long into the night. He could even hear Pete from the sanctuary of the shower room.

Good old Pete. Every driver needed an engineer like Peter Trent. Better for him perhaps that they didn't, or he wouldn't be standing here letting the warm water wash away the sweat and champagne.

Someone was banging on the door.

"Hurry up Declan," Carlo shouted. "Everyone is waiting for you!"

"Let them wait." He shouted back. "I've been flat to the boards all weekend; I'm entitled to slow down now. "

"Someone is putting together a band for the circuit party." Carlo was still there.

"They want to know if you can play an instrument; the guitar, the drums?"

Declan's wet head appeared around the door.

"No." He grinned. "And I can't sing either. But tell them I play a mean electric triangle!"

The cardboard cutouts in the crowd had been breeding, as there were now four of them facing the stage when Declan walked onto it. There was an enormous cheer, and somebody started letting off fireworks. The 'band', made up of a group of frustrated musicians who had instead become drivers and mechanics, were part of the post-British Grand Prix ritual and traditionally started the circuit party. The music was not bad, and the songs were recognisable, but if the singing had been completely flat and the musicians tone-deaf the crowd wouldn't have cared. They had been given the one thing that they had all come to see and had revelled in the pleasure of singing along to the national anthem. What happened next didn't matter; their favourite British driver had won, and that was enough. Even when the band broke up, and the drivers moved on to the post-race party the crowd stayed. Somewhere in their midst was Pete, who had become detached from the rest of the team. Leaving him to celebrate for a little while longer, Carlo returned, a little lightheaded himself to the motorhome and considered the packing-up procedure that had already begun.

Kate was already there, sitting under the now empty canopy, completely oblivious to the fact that it was being dismantled around her. She had a glass of champagne in one hand and a programme of the day's events in the other. She smiled when she saw him; she looked completely drained.

"Party over?" She looked in the direction of the circuit, from which a lot of noise was emanating.

"Hardly." Carlo laughed. "The security men will have a real problem emptying the circuit tonight!"

"And where's the hero of the hour?" Kate rubbed her eyes.

"Giving one last interview. Pete was last seen on the stage and has now disappeared."

"Ahem!"

Carlo turned to see Pete, a Union Jack in each hand, weaving a little unsteadily through the jumble of tables. "I'm here and ready for duty."

"Really?" Kate laughed as he stumbled over a chair and clutched at Carlo's shirt to save himself. "You don't look it."

"Go and do something simple." Carlo turned him in the direction of the out lane. "I will be there soon."

"I must find Declan." Kate put her empty glass into a crate. "He'll be wanting to leave soon, and I would like to see him before he goes. I won't be gone long."

"No hurry." Carlo patted her shoulder. "If the rest of the team is in the same state as Pete, we will still be here in time for next year's race!"

But before she managed to track Declan down Kate bumped into Fabio, who was removing his bag from the motorhome. Surprised that he was still at the track she paused, wanting to say something to him, but couldn't think of the right words. He saw her as he stepped out of the door; and was about to walk away, when he hesitated.

"A good day." He said quietly. "For the team."

"Yes." She nodded. "But not for you."

"It was my fault." Fabio shrugged. "I got it wrong. But I will learn from it and not make the same mistake next year. If," He looked at her. "There is going to be a next year."

"What do you mean?" Kate looked puzzled. "You

know there is a seat for you here."

"I know." Fabio's eyes had a distant expression in them, as if he was remembering something. "But things must change."

"What things?" Kate stepped closer to him. "Fabio, you can't throw away a career that's only just begun! You've too much talent to give it up now! "

"Have I?" He smiled. "I wish I had such faith in myself."

"Look." Kate took his arm. "This has been a nightmare of a year for us; all of us. I've made a really bad start in running this thing, and I have to do better. But things will change, today was only the beginning. We'll get back on the right track and then you'll have all the help and opportunities you need. If you step away now, you'll never know what you could have become."

"Maybe that is best. I too have made a bad start."

"Was it?" Kate blushed. "I don't think so, not really. It may have been the wrong start, but it wasn't all bad."

"No." He nodded. "It was not all bad. But we have all changed, in such a short time."

Kate looked over his shoulder and spotted Declan approaching, a cardboard cutout of himself under one arm.

"I agree. But now we all have to move on. But we should move on together Fabio, there are things ahead that we can only face as a team."

"I know." He nodded.

Looking down at her Fabio saw her eyes fixed on the approaching figure and saw the excitement in them. So that was where her heart lay. He wondered if Declan had known that all those months ago when he made his light-hearted bet. It all made sense now, the animosity and the friction that had always surrounded them. One was drawn to the other and the other didn't realise it. That was why Declan had always affected her so much. It seemed to him that at last. Each drawn to the other and fighting against it. Now it seemed Kate was facing up to her desires.

"I must go." He picked up his bag. "Lucy is waiting."

"Yes." He saw Kate's face change at the mention of Lucy's name. She looked up at Fabio and he tried to hide the doubts that must show in his face.

"If you love her," She said quietly, "Then stay with her. No one expects you to give her up because of what happened. But no one expects you to give up your career because of what happened either. If you do, then she really will have caused far more damage than she would ever have dreamed of."

"Thank you." He stooped and kissed her cheek. "Ciao."

Kate watched him walk away with the sensation of his mouth still tingling on her skin. A figure stopped beside her, and she turned to it.

She looked straight into the vivid, blue eyes of a life-size Declan Hyde.

"Which one do you prefer?" Declan's head appeared over the cutout's shoulder. "Him or me?"

For a moment, Kate stared at him in horror. Then the wiggling cardboard figure made her understand his meaning.

"Him." She nodded. "Cheaper to keep and less hassle."

"True." Declan scowled at his likeness. "But there are things that I can do that he can't."

"Such as?" Kate raised an eyebrow. "We could always glue him into the car and run it on remote control."

"Probably." The cardboard Declan fell to the floor and the real one stepped over it, standing so close to her that she could feel his body touching hers. "But it can't do this."

Slowly, gently, he took her in his arms and kissed her. She went rigid, then relaxed against him. So, what if people saw them? Did she care? Running her hands through his spiky hair, she felt him hugging her more tightly. They stood there, wrapped in each other's arms, doing what they both now realised they should have done long ago, until he finally broke free, laughter dancing in his eyes.

"Right." He picked up the cutout. "Now we've got that sorted out. I have to go."

"No." She whispered. "Not yet."

It was easier than he had ever expected it to be. After a few moments of initial resistance, he found her in his arms, melting against him, her slim frame pressed against his. She responded to his every touch, arching her back in pleasure as his hands slowly explored her body. She was soft and warm and smelled sweet. He undressed her slowly, watching her eyes hazy and unfocussed, as he slid his hand down her body and across her thighs. His fingers began to probe, exploring and she gave a little moan burying her face in his chest. He held her tight until she shuddered against him and then laid her on the seat of the motorhome as he undressed himself.

Kate watched him revealing his hard, powerful body and ached with longing. She knew he was taunting her with this hands-off show, and it was working. When he lowered himself on the seat beside her she reached for him and pulled him to her with almost frenzied desire. Declan smiled broadly but remained cool, almost detached as his fingers traced every line of her lovely body. He played this game until her eyes started to plead with him. Then, when there was desperation in her voice, he let himself go.

He had never known such pleasure. Losing all control, he surrendered himself totally to his desires, emotions he had kept hidden for so long that he had forgotten when they started.

"I'm sorry." He gasped; his fingers entwined in

her hair. "I tried so hard to be gentle, but I failed."

"Don't be" Kate cradled his face with her fingers. "It's fine. I think we have both waited a long time for this, even if we didn't realise it".

Declan shook his head and laid his head on her chest, feeling her heart racing. Why had it taken so long to get to this point? All those wasted years. But they were here now, and he wasn't going to turn away. He knew where his future lay, in these passion-filled moments, it had all become clear. With legs like lead he fell asleep where he was and when he woke, she was still there, arms entwined around him. He was cold and outside he could hear the sounds of lorries starting and pulling off. He had no idea what the time was, but what did it matter? A movement in his arms made him look at her and he saw hazy green eyes on his face. A smile spread across her face, and she nuzzled his neck. They lay there, both realising that they were doing what they should have done long ago.

"Now" He stroked her head. "I really do have to go."

Kate nodded. She understood. Kurt. She knew where his heart would want to be tonight, and it didn't matter. There would be plenty of time for this relationship to grow; what mattered now was for him to be with his closest friend and to share his triumph. Getting to her feet she reached for her clothes and saw the other Declan, the cardboard one, leaning against the door.

"What will you do with him?" She nodded.

"Give him to Kurt" Declan chuckled. " He can use it for target practice when I get on his nerves and Bernice can take him to bed when she misses me. "

"I am sure she will." Kate grinned. "I, on the other hand, will only be happy with the real thing. I think I should go find Carlo, poor man had his hands full, Pete had been celebrating."

Declan stood and pulled his t-shirt over his head.

"I know." He chuckled. "I saw him."

Taking her in his arms he gave her a long slow kiss and ran his finger down her face.

"I will see you next week, Miss Matthews. Take care of yourself."

Then he was gone. She wrapped her arms around herself, missing the warmth of his body already.

It was going to be a very long week.

CHAPTER 52.

Bernice was waiting for him at the airport in his car. She roared with laughter as he steered the cardboard Declan through the arrivals gate ahead of him and kissed it, as well as him. They talked and laughed nonstop until they walked through the door of the apartment. Kurt was sitting on the balcony, waiting.

"I think you have something for me my friend." He beamed.

"Do you want him?" Declan looked at the cutout. "Oh. I think you mean this."

Sitting opposite Kurt he reached into his bag, pulled out his trophy and handed it to his friend. Kurt turned it over in his hands and watched the light glinting on the gold surface.

"Well done." He held it aloft, mimicking the pose he had adopted so often in his own career, "It makes me feel good. Our plan worked, eh? You have deserved this."

"No," Declan said softly, watching the light reflecting off the trophy onto Kurt's pale face. "It's yours. I won it for you."

"What do you mean?" Kurt's eyes narrowed.

"The trophy. It's yours." Declan could feel himself blushing. "I didn't win that race for myself. If I had done that then I would never have won. I was too scared. I had to have a better motivation than personal glory, that wasn't enough to stop the nerves. So, I drove for you because if you had been there that trophy would have been yours anyway, we both know that. And I drove for Gerald. Tomorrow morning the constructor's trophy will be in the office, where he always wanted it."

"But what about you?" Bernice was standing in the doorway behind them, and tears were running slowly down her cheeks. "You drove the car Dec."

"I did." Declan had lowered his head so that they couldn't see his face. "I had to know I could still do it, that I hadn't lost the ability to compete. The fact that I was still a racing driver, that I still had what it took was all that mattered."

"So" Kurt looked at him. "What now?"

There was a silence, a silence filled with emotion as both men concentrated on their own thoughts. For Declan the battle with his fear was over, for Kurt, it was yet to come. Bernice looked at them both and felt her heart swelling with love for them both. She knew what the answer would be, she always had. Declan got to his feet and walked onto the balcony. Looking down at the marina he could see the yachts bobbing gently, lights twinkling. Behind them, the sea had already darkened to midnight blue. What a beautiful place to live; and what a beautiful life to live in it. He took a deep breath. Looking back over his shoulder, he spoke to the pair watching him.

"I'll see you on the grid next year Braun." There was a catch in Declan's voice. "And you had better watch your tail because I am coming to get you."

THE END

AFTERWORD

I hope you have enjoyed this journey into the world of Formula One.

If you have then please leave a review and tell your F1 mad friends.

You can follow me and find out about future projects on social media.

Facebook- A J Morris Author

Instagram - ajmorris_storyteller

ACKNOWLEDGEME NT

I would like to thank the following for their help and support in creating this book.

Phillip Jones- My talented articulate son whose skill far exceeds mine but who has always watched and encouraged me to write.

Kayleigh Evans- For the video calls, the Whats App chats and the constant support through the author journey.

Dan Parsons - For being the walking encyclopaedia of publishing that he is.

Jake Graham-Dobrowolny- For his incredible artist skills and creating the cover.

All at the YHLP Writing Group for being the most welcoming and warm group of people I have ever met.

Pamela and Geoffrey Iveson for their lifelong friendship and never ending support.

My dogs Covi and Romany for being company during the endless lonely hours that producing a book entails.

ABOUT THE AUTHOR

A J Morris

Alison Morris lives in the Welsh Valleys with her two Romanian Rescue dogs and a retired racehorse. Alongside Formula One she loves all Equestrian Sports, Tennis, Art, Literature, Travel and of course writing.

BOOKS BY THIS AUTHOR

Winners

In 1934 a horse called Golden Miller achieved what has since seemed impossible; winning the Cheltenham Gold Cup and the Grand National in the same year. Since then many have tried to achieve the double and, so far, all have failed.

But when Tom Chichester comes across a horse called Olympic Run a dream takes shape that could change history. Struggling to keep afloat in a fiercely competitive world Tom is looking for the one horse that can make or break his career. Aided by his Kiwi jockey Rick and his team of hardworking staff Tom fights to not only succeed in his sport but overcome the threat of his jealous and embittered brother. Failed relationships, an unconventional love affair, disheartened owners and his own family set hurdles in his path at every turn.

Set in the often hard and heartbreaking world of jump racing Winners follows the fortunes and failures of Tom and his team through a season of racing as they aim to make history with their great hope Olympic Run

Travels With A Rescue Dog

One woman. One Dog. A holiday. What can possibly go wrong? Travels with a Rescue Dog is the true story of my first venture at taking my canine friend on holiday. Join us on our day by day travels around the beautiful county of Cornwall.Illustrated with original drawing and photographs Travels with a Rescue Dog is a not for profit book. All proceeds will go to Dogs Trust to support them in their quest for saving more lives.

Printed in Great Britain
by Amazon